LICENSE
to Thrill

LORI WILDE

WARNER BOOKS

An AOL Time Warner Company

WARNER BOOKS EDITION

Copyright © 2003 by Laurie Vanzura
Excerpt from *Charmed and Dangerous* © 2003 by Laurie Vanzura

Cover art and design by Shasti O'Leary Soudant
Book design by Giorgetta Bell McRee

Warner Books, Inc.
1271 Avenue of the Americas
New York, NY 10020

Visit our Web site at www.twbookmark.com

An AOL Time Warner Company

Printed in the United States of America

First Paperback Printing: December 2003

10 9 8 7 6 5 4 3 2 1

To Beth de Guzman—for giving me
the opportunity to shine. Your belief in me means
more than words can say.

Acknowledgments

To the people who made this book possible: Thank you to my savvy agent Karen Solem, your knowledge of the publishing industry constantly amazes me. To my editor Michele Bidelspach, your guidance and insight were invaluable in shaping this book. And most of all, to my dearest friend Hebby Roman whose expertise on all things financial brought the whole plot together. You are appreciated.

LICENSE
to Thrill

CHAPTER

1

*N*othing but nothing scared Charlee Champagne except black widow spiders and wealthy, long-legged, brown-eyed, handsome men with matinee-idol smiles and a day's growth of beard stubble.

In her five years as a Las Vegas private investigator, Charlee had never once lost her cool. Being alley-cornered at midnight by a stiletto-wielding transvestite produced nary a wobbly knee. Getting dragged ten feet behind a robbery suspect's Nissan Pathfinder had created not a single spike in her pulse rate.

And just last week she'd averted disaster when she'd calmly faced down a half-dozen gangbangers and convinced them the banana in her jacket pocket was actually a forty-five-caliber Grizzly Magnum.

Cucumbers had nothing on Charlee.

But something about mean mama black widows and rich, long-legged, brown-eyed, handsome, matinee-idol-smiling, beard-stubble-sporting men slid right under her skin and wreaked havoc with her bravado.

She had earned both phobias legitimately. The spider

heebie-jeebies dated back to an ugly outhouse incident in rural Wisconsin when she was twelve. She had never looked at a roll of toilet paper in quite the same way since.

Her second fear, however, was a bit more convoluted. At the same time George Clooneyesque men terrified her, she was wildly, madly, impossibly attracted to them.

And the scars from those mistakes, while less noticeable than the half-dollar-sized hole in her left butt cheek, were a sight more painful than any spider bite.

As a self-defense technique, she'd developed a highly honed sense of respect for her phobias. So when the hairs at the nape of her neck spiked that Wednesday afternoon in late March, she snapped to full alert.

She sat cocked back in front of the computer in her two-woman detective agency located in a downtown strip mall, her size ten, neon blue, Tony Lama boots propped up on one corner of the desk and her keyboard nestled in her lap. She was completing the final paperwork on a missing person's case where she had successfully located a six-year-old girl snatched by her father after a custody dispute didn't go in his favor.

Immediately, her gaze flew to the corners of the room. No sign of a black widow's unmistakably messy cobweb. Slowly, she released her drawn breath, but the prickly uproar on the back of her neck persisted.

From the corner of her eye she spied movement on the window ledge. Something small and black and spindly-legged scurried.

Her boots hit the cement floor and her hand grabbed for a makeshift weapon, coming up with a well-thumbed, trade paperback copy of *Find Out Anything About Anyone*.

Pulse pounding in her throat, she advanced upon the window.

The cool cobalt taste of fear spilled into her mouth. Her legs quivered like she had a neurological disorder. Instant sweat pearled into the delicate indentation between her nose and her upper lip.

She had to force each step, but finally she hovered within killing range. She raised the book over her head, sucked in her breath for added courage, and stared down at the intimidating creature.

No telltale red hourglass.

Hmm. Charlee narrowed her eyes.

Not a black widow after all. Closer scrutiny revealed the creature wasn't even black.

Just a fuzzy wolf spider.

Oh, thank heavens.

Relieved, she sank her forehead against the windowpane and let the book fall from her relaxed grasp.

And that's when she spotted him.

Zigzagging his way through the parking lot—looking utterly out of place in the Las Vegas desert in his rumpled Armani suit, dusty Gucci loafers, and a red silk tie that appeared to cost more than Charlee's last tax refund check—meandered a fear far greater than a whole pack of poisonous arachnids.

Like a battalion of marines at roll call, her neck hairs marshaled to five-alarm status. She stumbled back to her desk, jerked open the bottom drawer, retrieved a pair of Nighthawk binoculars, fixed the scopes on him, and fiddled with the focus.

Gotcha.

Hair the color of coal. Chocolate brown eyes. A five-o'clock shadow ringing his craggy jawline. Handsome as the day was long.

Her heart tommy-gunned. Ratta-tatta-tat.

Charlee gulped. Please let him go to the Quickee-Lube-Express next door. Or better yet, the massage parlor on the corner.

No such luck. He headed straight for the Sikes Detective Agency, a determined look on his face. The one thing she still had going for her—he wasn't smiling. Charlee's hand trembled so hard that she fumbled with the binoculars.

Yipes.

She had to do something. Quick.

For some unfathomable reason, guys like him were often attracted to her and she never failed to fall for their smiles and swagger. Call it a genetic deficiency. Her mother, Bubbles, God rest her soul, had been the same way.

When Charlee was seven, Tommy Ledbetter, the devastatingly cute son of the man who owned the used car dealership where her grandmother Maybelline worked as a mechanic, had lured Charlee behind the garage for a rousing game of I'll-show-you-mine-if-you-show-me-yours.

She had obliged when he threw in a pack of Twizzlers as an added bribe, only to be caught red-hineyed by Mr. Ledbetter. Tommy, the wimp, had declared the whole thing Charlee's idea. Maybelline had gotten fired over that embarrassing incident.

Then when she was fourteen and Maybelline was tending bar at an exclusive country club in Estes Park, Colorado, Vincent Keneer, whose father owned part interest in the Denver Broncos, stole a kiss from her on the ninth green. She was in seventh heaven for a few hours only to later overhear him laughing with his friends. "Getting Charlee to kiss me was easier than turning on a light switch," he had bragged.

Charlee's temper had gotten the better of her and she'd shoved Vincent into the deep end of the pool with his cashmere vest on. Maybelline lost that job too for refusing to make Charlee apologize.

And then when she was nineteen . . .

She closed her eyes and swallowed hard. No, she refused to relive *that* excruciating memory. Some cuts sliced so deep they never healed.

What was it about her? She must secrete some kind of take-advantage-of-me-then-break-my-heart pheromone. Or maybe it was like how cats seemed to know when you were allergic to them and they singled you out in a crowd and insisted on crawling into your lap.

Why buck the odds? She needed all the help she could muster. Charlee snatched open the desk drawers in a desperate search for any kind of a disguise. Nabbing a pencil from the cup beside her printer, she harvested her hair off her shoulders, wound the thick mass into a twist, and anchored it to the top of her head.

Frumpy. Think frumpy.

If he so much as cracked a grin, even a little one, she was a goner.

Okay, librarian hair wasn't enough. She needed more. Charlee scuttled over to Maybelline's desk and rummaged through the contents.

Ah-ha! Her granny's spare pair of thick, black bifocals oughtta do the trick.

Charlee jammed the glasses on her face, grateful for the twofold shield. Now, not only would she look unflirtworthy in the heavy frames, but also while peering through the blurry lenses she would be unable to fully ascertain his level of cuteness. She hazarded another quick peek out the window, but had to peer over the top of Maybelline's glasses in order to see him without getting dizzy.

Who was this guy?

He stopped when he passed her cherry red 1964 Corvette convertible in the parking lot and ran a lingering hand over the fender like he was caressing a woman's inner thigh. Charlee's stomach fluttered as if he'd stroked *her* and her muscles tightened a couple of notches below her turquoise belt buckle.

Repo man?

Nah. She was ninety-nine percent sure she'd mailed her car payment, even though she did have a tendency to get so wrapped up in a case she sometimes forgot to eat or sleep or post her bills. Besides, the dude looked nothing like a repo man. Actually, he resembled a refugee from an investment banker caucus.

Or an escapee from a corporate law office.

A lawyer?

Oh, no. Was Elwood in the pokey again and looking to her for bail money? Charlee shook her head. As if her no-account daddy could afford the services of a guy who dressed like a *GQ* cover model.

A lawsuit?

Her accountant Wilkie had warned her that being sued was an eventuality in her line of work and he'd encouraged her to take out more insurance. But between keeping the business afloat and bailing out her old man when he was in between his Elvis impersonating gigs and had succumbed to the lure of another get-rich-quick scheme, she didn't have a lot of spare cash left over for frivolous things like insurance.

The guy had almost reached her door and Charlee, roosting on the verge of hyperventilation, did not know which way to jump. She stepped right, then left, ended up doing a strange little mambo, and finally jammed the binoculars under a chair cushion. She even considered ducking into the closet until he went away.

But what if he wanted to hire her? Business was business. She'd just completed her only pending case and she needed the money.

Yeah? So tell that to her stomach spinning like a whirligig in gale force winds. In the end, she leaped behind Maybelline's desk and feigned grave interest in her blank computer screen.

The silver cowbell over the door tinkled.

Be strong. Be brave. Be badass.

"Hello?"

Ah, damn. He possessed the deep, smoky voice of a late-night radio announcer. Charlee lifted her head and forced herself to look at the man standing in the doorway.

"Good afternoon," she replied, her tone a couple of degrees above frosty. No sense making the guy welcome. If she was rude enough, maybe he would take a hike.

The top of his head grazed the cowbell, causing it to peal again.

Dear God, he was at least six feet three, maybe even taller. And no wedding band graced the third finger of his left hand. Charlee tumbled as if she were on an Alpine ski run, a beginner who had taken a wrong turn and ended up on the black diamond expert slope with nowhere to go but down, down, down.

"Is there something you need?" she asked, making sure she sounded extra snippy and squinting disapprovingly at him through Maybelline's bifocals.

"Yes, ma'am," the paragon drawled in a smooth Texas accent.

In spite of his slightly blurry appearance, he was outrageously good-looking, right down to his straight white teeth. They had to be bonded. Nobody's natural teeth looked that perfect. His suit—while slightly wrinkled— fit like a dream, accentuating his broad shoulders and narrow hips.

He smelled like the wickedly wonderful blend of expensive cologne and the faint but manly musk of perspiration. His beautiful black hair was clipped short, making one statement while the dark stubble on his jaw made another.

Charlee wanted to rip off the borrowed glasses and feast on him like Thanksgiving turkey. The desire scared her to the very marrow of her bones.

Something sparked in his deep brown bedroom eyes and she caught a glimmer of sudden heat when their gazes met—or maybe it was just that Maybelline's glasses needed cleaning.

He sauntered toward her, oozing charisma from every pore.

Charlee forgot to breathe.

And then he committed the gravest sin of all, knocking her world helter-skelter.

The scoundrel smiled.

              *   *   *

Mason Gentry gave the woman behind the desk his best public-relations grin. The grin—and the Gentry name—opened doors. Accustomed to getting what he wanted, Mason wanted one thing and one thing only.

To track down the floozy who'd lured his grandfather Nolan—along with a half-million dollars in family company funds—to sin city.

Mason's primary aim? Locate Gramps, drag him home to Houston (hopefully with the money still intact), and get back to the investment deal he'd been in the process of bringing in before his older brother, Hunter, had taken over and sent him after their grandfather. He was still seething about the injustice. Why did Hunter earn the plum jobs while he got scut work?

Oh, yes. One other thing. Nolan's unexpected and larcenous departure had forced Mason to postpone his engagement party.

He'd planned to ask his girlfriend of three years, Daphne Maxwell, to marry him this weekend in exactly the same fashion his father had proposed to his mother. Over veal parmigiana at Delveccio's, with fifty of their closest friends joining the festivity.

At the thought of Daphne, Mason's spirits lifted. For once in his life, he would have one up on his brother. He would be married to the perfect high-society wife.

Everyone in his family loved Daphne. She was refined, cultured, and sophisticated, with a myriad of business contacts and a pedigree she could trace back to the *Mayflower*.

Daphne was everything he'd ever looked for in a wife. They had the same values, the same friends, and they wanted the same things from life. So what if there wasn't much sexual chemistry. A good marriage consisted of so much more than fireworks.

Right?

"What do you want?" the woman demanded, squinting up at him from behind an ugly pair of glasses, her long black hair spilling haphazardly from an awkward bun secured to her head with a pencil.

Could she be the woman he was searching for?

He remembered the paper in his pocket. He'd found Maybelline Sikes's name and this address scrawled on a notepad in Gramps's bedroom. The nameplate on the desk said Maybelline Sikes, but she didn't look like a Maybelline.

She looked like nothing but trouble with her determined little chin set and her smoldering emerald eyes flashing a challenge. Unlucky for her, Mason adored a challenge.

She wore an unflattering western-style shirt, faded jeans with a rip at the knee, and the most gawd-awful neon blue cowboy boots he had ever laid eyes upon. Not a shred of makeup graced her face. Granted, with her long, dark lashes and full raspberry-colored lips she didn't need cosmetics to look good, but she did not fit the image of the busty, brash, blond femme fatale in stilettos and pearls he'd concocted in his head.

Nor had he expected her to be a private detective. Really, she was way too young for Gramps. But then again, gold diggers came in all shapes, ages, and professions.

"I'm waiting." She arched an eyebrow and he noticed she clutched a pen so tight her knuckles were actually white. The lady was not nearly as composed as she appeared.

Mason draped one leg over the corner of her desk and leaned in close until they were almost nose-to-nose, his intent to intimidate.

"I want to know where my grandfather is," he said, continuing to smile but narrowing his eyes so she would understand he meant business. "And I want to know now."

She sank her top teeth into her bottom lip and unflinchingly returned his stare, but despite her bluster he could tell from the brief flicker of uneasiness flitting across her face she wanted to back away.

"You're gonna have to be more specific. I have no idea what you're talking about."

He shouldn't have noticed the long, smooth curve of her neck, but he found his gaze lingering on the pulse point jumping at her throat. She was nervous. Oh, yeah. But very adept at cloaking her uneasiness. He couldn't help but admire her grace under pressure. He had reduced many an inefficient employee to tongue-tied stammers with his silent stares. But she wasn't buying his bluster.

"Nolan Gentry. Where is he?"

She laid the pen down, steepled her fingertips, and blinked owlishly at him from behind those hideous glasses. "Let me get this straight. Do you want to hire me to find your missing grandfather?"

"He came here to meet you. Are you telling me you haven't seen him?"

"I'm sorry, mister, I don't even know who he is. Or who you are for that matter."

"My name's Mason Gentry. I'm an investment banker from Houston and I've come to retrieve my grandfather."

"What does that have to do with me?"

She met his eyes. Their glares slammed into each other.

Hot, hard, defiant.

She was a tough one all right, but he didn't miss her telltale gulp and the determined way she clenched her jaw. No matter how composed she might appear, the woman was afraid of him.

"Aren't you Maybelline Sikes?" He tapped the nameplate.

"No. I'm not. I'm her granddaughter."

Instant relief rolled over him. His grandfather had hightailed himself across the desert to see the woman's grandmother, not her. Why the knowledge lifted his spirits, he had no clue. What did it matter whether it was the granddaughter or the grandmother who was after Nolan's fortune? The results were the same.

"So what's your name?"

"Charlee Champagne."

"Beg your pardon?" he asked, not sure he'd heard correctly.

"Charlee Champagne," she repeated.

"Oh."

For no particular reason the phrase *Good Time Charlee* popped into his mind's eye along with a very provocative image of a tipsy Charlee boogieing with a lampshade on her head and wearing a very naughty black silk nightie. He could see the picture all too clearly. Perturbed, Mason shook his head to dispel the unwanted mental photograph.

Charlee sighed and then spoke as if she'd recited the details many times before. "My mother was a dancer at the Folies Bergère and had her name legally changed to

Bubbles Champagne. She and my father were never married. What can I say? She was a bit frivolous. Any more questions?"

"Do you know where I can find Ms. Sikes?"

"She's incommunicado."

"Meaning?"

"She's gone on her annual fishing retreat and she can't be reached, but let me assure you she most certainly is not with your grandfather."

"How can you be so sure?"

"Maybelline hates men. Especially rich ones."

"Who said my grandfather is rich?" Mason didn't believe her for a second. No doubt she was covering for her grandmother.

Charlee waved a hand at his Rolex. "Like grandfather like grandson."

"So, you're claiming your grandmother can't be reached?"

"No claiming to it. It's the truth."

"No cell phone?"

"She can't stand 'em. Says they give you brain cancer."

"No beeper?"

"Nope. That's the whole point of the trip. Uninterrupted peace and quiet."

"I think you're lying."

Charlee shrugged. "Believe what you want."

"It's imperative I speak with Ms. Sikes," Mason said in a controlled, measured manner. He was through fooling around with Miss I'm-Going-To-Be-No-Help-Whatsoever Champagne. He wanted his grandfather found. "If Ms. Sikes can't be reached by electronic means then I will go to her fishing cabin. Give me directions."

"No."

"What?" His glare intensified. Sweat pooled around his collar. In his mad, twenty-four-hour sprint from Houston to Vegas, he hadn't even bothered to change from his business suit and he was broiling like filet mignon at a backyard barbeque.

That's what happened when you allowed single-minded focus to overcome common sense. Stubborn persistence was his biggest flaw and his greatest strength. His father often joked Mason was like an obstinate snapping turtle, never knowing when to turn loose.

"You heard me." She raised her chin, daring him to call her bluff.

He stared openmouthed. He wasn't accustomed to being refused anything. Testiness was his first instinct but something told him venting his frustration would be the wrong tactic to take. She'd most likely dig into her view. He could see she had a bit of snapping turtle in her too.

Forcing a smile, he slipped an amiable tone into his voice. "I think maybe we got off on the wrong foot. Why don't we start over?"

"Okay."

"My grandfather Nolan disappeared out of the blue with a substantial amount of money. We found a note in his room indicating he was on his way to meet your grandmother here in Vegas. We're really concerned about him. He's been behaving a bit out of character lately. I need to speak with your grandmother to find out if she has heard from him."

"Sorry," she said. "Maybelline left strict orders not to be disturbed. I can't help you."

"Can't? Or won't?"

"Take your pick."

"So that's the way it's going to be."

"Maybelline will be home in a couple of days. You can speak to her then. In the meantime, relax. Have fun. See Vegas. Enjoy a holiday." Under her breath she muttered, "With that stick-up-your-butt attitude you certainly look as if you could use one."

Like hell.

No way was he waiting a couple of days. In a couple of days Nolan and Maybelline could run through the half million at the craps table. Besides, in a couple more days Hunter would have the Birkweilder deal—*his* deal—sewn up, and would be busily collecting accolades from their father without giving Mason credit.

He gritted his teeth and fell back on his third line of offense. When authority and charm fail, there's always money. He removed his wallet from his jacket pocket, unfolded the expensive leather case, and pulled out a crisp new Benjamin Franklin.

"How much is the information going to cost me?" He slapped a second hundred on the desk.

Charlee gasped. He could practically feel the anger emanating off of her.

What? Two C notes weren't enough. Obviously, she was as greedy as her grandmother.

"Three hundred?" Mason added another bill to the stack.

"Are you trying to buy me off?"

"Let's make it an even five."

"Buddy, you can just keep peeling until your wallet is empty, because I'll never tell you where Maybelline is. There isn't enough money in the world."

CHAPTER 2

*O*kay, he had handled the situation badly. He'd grossly misread Charlee Champagne and he'd acted like an unmitigated jackass. Mason wasn't afraid to admit when he'd made a mistake. Unfortunately, not only had she refused to listen to his apology, she had unceremoniously tossed him and his money out of her office.

He'd blown his chance with her. Charlee would never help him now.

A short nap and a hot shower later, he prowled the suite he'd taken at the Bellagio in a thick white terry-cloth bathrobe and plowed his hands through his freshly washed hair.

He was back at square one. Gramps, along with his girlfriend Maybelline and the half-million dollars, was out roaming the streets and he had no idea where to start looking.

What if they had eloped?

Mason sank onto the bed. His father would have a conniption fit. At the thought of failing and letting his family down, he groaned, lay back against the mattress, and stared up at the painted ceiling depicting fifteenth-century Italian nudes.

"Thanks a lot, Gramps. I needed this like a hole in the head."

A twinge of guilt flicked in his stomach. This wasn't about him. This was about his grandfather and what had made Gramps unhappy enough to embezzle five hundred thousand dollars and tear off in the middle of the night without a word to anyone.

He was also a little hurt. He'd believed he and Nolan were pretty close. They were both second sons in the Gentry family and understood the meaning of taking a backseat to the favored eldest. They shot a round of golf together every Sunday afternoon. They played poker with Nolan's cronies once a month. Why hadn't Gramps confided in him?

Mason's eyes traced the lines of the ceiling painting. A woman, her bare back exposed, lay on a gilded chaise lounge. He tracked the curve of her form, noticing the woman's complexion matched the exact same spiced peaches color of Charlee's skin.

What would Charlee look like naked?

Mesmerized by the concept, his imagination ran rampant as he envisioned pert firm breasts, a taut flat belly, and yards of her long coltish legs wrapped around his naked waist while still wearing her gruesome, but oddly compelling, neon blue cowgirl boots.

Startled, Mason bolted upright. Good God! He was almost an engaged man. Why in the hell was he fantasizing about another woman?

Why indeed?

A wave of embarrassment, followed by a virtual monsoon of guilt, flustered him.

"It's just because she pissed you off," Mason grumbled. "She's a challenge and you find challenges stimulating. It's nothing sexual."

Oh, yeah?

"Stop thinking about her," he commanded, annoyed with himself, and grabbed his cell phone.

He dialed Daphne's number. The minute she spoke, he started talking and it took a second for him to realize he'd gotten her voice mail.

"Daphne," he said after the beep. "It's Mason. I just arrived in Vegas. I'm thinking of you."

Even to his own ears the words sounded unconvincing. He left her his number at the hotel and then hung up, feeling worse than he had before he'd called. He wished Daphne were here so he could remember exactly what she looked like. He hated that he couldn't fill his mind with her instead of Charlee.

"Concentrate on locating Gramps."

All right. He could keep his mind on the task at hand. Think.

Maybelline probably lived right here in Vegas. And maybe Charlee had lied through those luscious lips of hers.

What if, instead of holing up in some fishing retreat as her granddaughter claimed, Maybelline was actually cozied up in a love nest with Gramps? Why hadn't he considered that before?

Rummaging around in the nightstand, Mason located the phone book and flipped to the S's. Ten seconds later he copied down Maybelline's home address. Ten minutes after that, dressed in chinos, a starched white shirt, and loafers, he took the elevator to the lobby.

Maybelline Sikes took a deep breath, smoothed nonexistent wrinkles from her navy blue slacks, and double-checked her lipstick in the rearview mirror. She patted her short, stylish hair she kept dyed the same flame red color it had been in childhood and climbed out of her ebony Toyota Tundra pickup truck.

Her heart gave an erratic little skip as she made her way up the sidewalk to Kelly's tavern. If she hadn't just undergone a complete physical and been pronounced as healthy as a woman half her age, Maybelline might have been worried. But turning sixty-three had nothing to do with her irregular pulse.

Outside the bar, Maybelline hesitated, her courage gone. She was nervous. Damned nervous. Not just about seeing Nolan Gentry again, but also because of the bad news she had to deliver. The past had caught up with them both.

"Go on," she urged herself. "Do it. You've got no choice."

Straightening her shoulders, she shoved open the door and stepped inside. She blinked against the contrast of bright desert sunlight and dim, smoky bar. The door creaked shut behind her. At four o'clock in the afternoon, the place was deserted.

Kelly, all muscles and tight black T-shirt, stood behind the bar buffing the counter. Barfly Bob, a perpetual regular with heavy red jowls and a bleary-eyed grin, sat on a bar stool nursing an Old Milwaukee.

But it was the man at the corner table who drew Maybelline's immediate interest.

"Hey, Maybelline," Kelly and Barfly Bob greeted her simultaneously.

Seven years ago, she'd worked for Kelly, before she and Charlee had started the detective agency. Maybelline waved a hand, but her gaze riveted on the man she hadn't seen for forty-seven years.

The man who had once saved her life.

She approached cautiously. He rose to his feet. The rolled-up sleeves of his blue dress shirt revealed still nicely muscled forearms for a man in his mid-sixties. He looked every inch the blueblood ex-actor with his perfect posture, commanding aura, and smart fashion sense.

Looking at him now, no one would suspect that over four decades ago Nolan had worked as a wildcatter on an oil derrick side by side with Maybelline's father. Only honed muscles and tanned skin gave even the faintest hint to his working-class past.

Immediately, Maybelline regretted asking him to meet her at Kelly's. From Nolan's point of view, the place was beyond seedy. But she had needed somewhere neutral for the meeting and Kelly's was safe.

Their gazes met and Maybelline's heart did the same swoony waltz it had done more than four decades ago when she'd walked out into the oil field with the brown paper bag lunch her daddy had forgotten and she'd made eye contact with the boss's handsome son.

She'd been thirteen. Nolan seventeen. He'd said "hi" to her and she'd been smitten, even though she'd known he was so far out of her league even a fairy godmother with a magic wand couldn't grant her most fervent wish.

Two years later, when he'd spotted her in town at the soda fountain and came over to buy her a Coke float, she'd just about died. Giggling, her friends had scattered, leaving them alone in the red vinyl booth.

Searching for something to say to the rich handsome man seated across from her, Maybelline told him Lana Turner had been discovered in a soda fountain. Once she got started, her passion for the movies took over and she'd gone on to tell him her greatest dream was to become a Hollywood makeup artist. Nolan had confessed he wanted to be an actor.

They'd talked for hours, until Nolan's father had come into the diner, found them sitting together, and caused an ugly scene. He'd called her trailer trash and forbade Nolan from ever speaking to her again.

"Maybelline," Nolan said, bringing her back to the present, his voice husky.

"Nolan," she murmured.

He smiled and his brown eyes crinkled with such joy, she caught her breath.

"You're prettier than ever."

In one precious minute Maybelline had the ridiculous whim everything was going to turn out all right. There she went again, dreaming of a fairy godmother.

"And you're full of horseshit."

Nolan's grin widened. "You haven't changed a bit. Still the same fiery, outspoken woman I remember."

With a flourish, he pulled out a chair for her and Maybelline sat. He hadn't ordered a drink, she noticed and wondered how long he'd been there.

He eased down across from her and she studied his face. The years had been kind to him and it occurred to her he'd probably had a few nips and tucks. Hey, if you could afford plastic surgery, more power to you.

Nolan wore glasses now, but then again so did she.

He wasn't paunchy like many men his age and while
he'd had some balding at the temples he still possessed
a fine shock of silver hair. She remembered when his
hair grew thick as underbrush and black as midnight. A
strange aching tugged her stomach at the memory.

All those years gone like fallen leaves.

His gaze imprinted her face, sizing her up too. Self-
consciously, she raised a hand to her cheek.

Why hadn't she worn a dress and jewelry and perfume? She hadn't worried about her looks for almost
two decades. She had believed she was long past the
point of wanting to appear desirable for a man.

There's no fool like an old fool.

"Thank you," she said. "For coming to Vegas to see
me. I couldn't handle this over the phone or through the
mail."

"It's my pleasure."

Kelly appeared at the table. Maybelline was so
wrapped up in staring at Nolan she didn't notice the bartender approach and she jumped when he touched her
shoulder. "What'll you have, Maybell?"

She looked at Nolan, and arched an eyebrow.

"Pretty early in the day for me." He raised a palm.

"You might want something to help the bad news
slide down easier."

Nolan grimaced. "Is it that gruesome?"

Grimly, she nodded.

"Bourbon," Nolan said. "Two glasses."

After Kelly walked away, Nolan laid his hand, warm
and rough and comforting, over hers. Something in her
chest caught and hung.

"It's going to be okay, kiddo." He winked. "We've
survived worse."

Maybelline took a deep breath. "Better hold your judgment until after you've seen what's in here."

She reached into her purse, took out a manila envelope, and handed her old friend a copy of the damning document that possessed the potential to destroy his entire family.

Dimples.

Charlee hadn't bargained on dimples. A man that long-legged, that brown-eyed, that darned handsome simply had no business possessing dimples as deep as Lake Mead and in both cheeks too! The good looks fairy had been far too generous with Mason Gentry.

Her knees were still weak. Damn him.

She couldn't stop dwelling on what had happened. How dare the arrogant, egotistic, rich, dimpled son of a bitch try to bribe her into ratting out the site of her grandmother's cabin?

The cheek. The gall. The sheer audacity!

Jerk. Pinhead. Dillhole.

She fumed around the office, working up a good head of steam.

And then she started to worry.

What if Mason was right? What if Maybelline and his grandfather had run off together? How ludicrous. Then again Maybelline *had* been acting rather odd lately herself. Plus, she'd taken off on her retreat almost a month earlier than usual.

Charlee massaged her temple, which had been throbbing ever since she'd worn Maybelline's glasses. She would love to pin all the blame on the bifocals, but Mason and his missing grandfather were as much the cause of her headache as the glasses.

Ah, crud. She couldn't calm down until she drove up to the cabin and made sure Maybelline was all right.

She locked up the office, stopped at the Swiftie Mart around the corner for a fistful of Ibuprofen and a cherry coke. With the evening sun shining in her eyes, worsening her headache, she flipped down the visor and headed over to Maybelline's place. She wanted to make sure her grandmother hadn't slipped back into town without telling her before she made the trek up to the fishing cabin at Lake Mead.

Seven years ago, when Charlee had moved into her own apartment, Maybelline sold the motor coach they'd called home ever since Charlee was five and had come to live with her. Her grandmother purchased a small lot in a retirement community, put up a nice prefabricated house on a slab, and settled down for the first time in nearly fifty years.

It was almost six o'clock when Charlee turned onto the friendly little cul-de-sac and had to swerve to avoid a white four-door Chevy Malibu intent on hogging the narrow lane.

The manufactured houses were inexpensive, but well maintained. Flowers flourished in window boxes, wind socks flew from weather vanes, white picket fences delineated property lines, pink flamingoes and kitschy plywood cutouts of ladies bending over to show their bloomers decorated freshly mowed lawns. A quiet, cozy place to enjoy one's golden years.

She knew something was very wrong the minute she spotted the door to Maybelline's trailer hanging open a couple of inches. Instantly on alert, Charlee did not pull into the driveway, but instead kept driving and parked a few houses down. She leaped from the car, tugged a small thirty-eight automatic from the leg holster inside her boot, and cautiously approached Maybelline's house.

With both hands, she raised the thirty-eight over her head and slid her back flat against the outside wall of the trailer until she came to the door. Softly, she toed it open farther.

She paused, listening.

Rummaging noises came from somewhere in the back of the house. Much louder than any four-legged rat.

Someone was definitely in there.

And she seriously doubted it was Maybelline since the Tundra wasn't in the driveway. Not knowing what she would find, Charlee extended the gun in front of her and bravely stepped over the threshold.

The damage meeting her eyes jolted her. She eased the safety off the gun. Couch cushions were slit open, knick-knacks broken, furniture overturned, pictures knocked askew on the walls.

Swiftly she navigated the mess and moved into the kitchen. Upended flour and sugar canisters dusted the floor, and dishes lay shattered in jagged shards. The refrigerator hung open and condiments had been knocked from the door. Ketchup, mustard, mayonnaise, and grape marmalade splattered out in a colorful Rorschach.

Anxiety settled like a cast-iron submarine deep inside her belly.

Whoever trashed the place was deadly serious. And from the sound of it, they were still in Maybelline's bedroom.

Tiptoeing through the silt of spilled baking products, Charlee eased down the hallway, careful not to trip over any scattered debris. The door to Maybelline's bedroom stood wide open and the rummaging noises continued. Inch by inch she crept forward until she could peer into the room.

She spotted a man delving through the closet, his back to her. He was very tall. Broad-shouldered and long-legged. For the first time since entering the house, her knees trembled.

He wore crisply ironed chinos and a pristine white shirt. How in the hell had he managed to wreak such havoc and stay so clean? He was concentrating on Maybelline's shoe boxes and he hadn't heard her creep into the room.

Striking cobra-quick, Charlee zipped across the floor and pressed the nose of her gun into his spine.

"Hands on the wall over your head. Now!" She barked out the order, trying her best not to notice how he smelled of sandalwood soap and fancy cologne.

He dropped the shoe box and a shower of old bills cascaded to the closet floor. Tentatively, he raised his arms.

"Palms splayed on the wall."

Leaning forward, he obeyed.

"Now spread your legs."

"What?"

She nudged him with the gun. "This isn't a toy pistol I've got leveled at your heart, buster. Spread your legs."

"Listen . . ." The intruder started to turn his head.

"Face forward."

"There's been a huge mistake."

"Yeah, like you trashing an old lady's house."

She wrapped her free arm around his chest and patted down his lean hard muscles. Her hand traveled to his waistband.

No weapon there.

She skated her shaking fingers down one long leg of his pants to his socks and back up the other leg. Her breathing rasped.

"Charlee?" he said. "Is that you?"

She should have been relieved to discover the fanny she'd just frisked belonged to Mason Gentry and not a hardened criminal. But on the contrary, her knees almost gave way.

"Gentry?" she squeaked.

"Do you mind taking your gun out of my rib cage? It's rather uncomfortable."

"Why did you ransack Maybelline's place?"

"I didn't."

"Why should I believe you?"

"Look, I'm afraid you'll just have to trust me. I did not vandalize your granny's house."

She eyed his tidy clothes again and realized he spoke the truth. Switching the safety back on, she then tucked her gun into her boot and stepped back.

Slowly, Mason turned.

He had shaved, she noticed, but instead of making him less attractive to her, she had the wildest desire to stroke his clean-shaven face, and then hold her fingers under her nose and inhale the scent of his shaving cream.

God, the man was gorgeous and he scared the living hell out of her.

Charlee bit her bottom lip to keep the terror from her expression. When she had finished her perusal and bravely lifted her gaze, she found him studying her as intently as she'd been scrutinizing him. He pinned her with deep chocolate brown eyes dangerous as quick-sand.

Watch out. Watch out.

Help!

Her face heated. She couldn't be blushing. She never blushed.

Oh, yeah? Then how come you could melt a Popsicle on your cheeks?

Hating her weakness to the man, she hardened her jaw and bolstered her resolve not to let him know how much he turned her on.

"Why are you here?" she demanded. She knew she sounded unnecessarily harsh, but hey, a girl had to do what a girl had to do to protect herself.

"I came to see your grandmother."

"I told you she was at her cabin."

"Then why are you here?"

"I thought she might have come home early. Your turn."

He shrugged, grinned wryly. "What can I say? You're not the only one with a suspicious nature."

Dazed, Charlee sank down on the mattress the vandal had stripped bare of its covers.

"Listen," he said. "I'm sorry if I frightened you."

"You didn't scare me," she scoffed, more to convince herself than him. Her heart rate thumped at a good two hundred beats per minute.

"Then why is your face as white as that mattress?"

"How did you break in?" she demanded, refusing to focus on her weakness.

"When I got here I found the door open and the place looking like it looks now. I simply walked in."

"Well, if you didn't trash the house, who did?"

They stared at each other.

"I have no idea. You?"

Charlee shrugged. "Could be connected with some case Maybelline was working on."

Mason waved a hand at the mess. "Stuff like this happens to you ladies often?"

"Not too often, but once in a while. Comes with the territory."

"Tough job."

"I didn't see a car in the driveway," Charlee said, changing the subject. "How did you get over here?"

"I took a taxi. The concierge at the hotel suggested Whiskey Flats wasn't the best part of town in which to drive my vintage Bentley."

"You drove a vintage Bentley to Vegas?"

He lifted one shoulder. "What can I say? I don't care for flying."

"But a Bentley? Through the desert? From Houston?"

"Hey, I love my car. She's my refuge from the rat race."

"She?"

"Her name's Matilda and since I had to drive to Vegas, I figured I might as well travel in style."

"You named your car?"

"What's wrong with that?" he asked, his tone a tad cranky.

"Excuse me for asking."

"Sorry. I didn't mean to snap. My brother harasses me about the Bentley. Says Matilda is butt ugly, an old man's car."

"No need to explain. I've got a '64 'Vette."

His smile returned and packed the added punch of respect for her taste in vehicles. "That was your car in the parking lot at your detective agency?"

"Guilty." She couldn't help smiling back. Oh, she was sinking deep.

"Isn't a classic Corvette a rather conspicuous vehicle for a private detective?"

"Not as conspicuous as a Bentley. Besides, I borrow Maybelline's black Toyota pickup for stakeouts."

"Gramps gave me the Bentley for my eighteenth birthday. A 1955 model. He bought Matilda the same year he was up for an Oscar."

"Your grandfather was an actor?"

"Only for a year. He bought the Bentley as a reminder of the time. Sentimental value I guess. And when he found out how much I loved her, he gave the car to me."

"No kidding? Maybelline used to be an assistant makeup artist for Twilight Studios back in the mid-fifties."

"Gramps made movies for Twilight."

Their gazes caught again.

"That's where they must have met each other," Charlee mused. "Do you suppose they were once lovers?"

"My grandfather and your grandmother?" He snorted.

"Why did you say it like that?"

"Like what?"

"As if it were completely impossible for a rich man like your granddaddy to fall in love with my grandmother."

"Oh, so now they were in love?"

"It could happen." She crossed her arms over her chest and glared at him. "Why not?"

A soured love affair would explain why Maybelline had always warned her against getting involved with rich, long-legged, brown-eyed, handsome men. Obviously, she'd been burned. Had Mason's grandfather been the one doing the burning?

"You're carrying a chip on your shoulder about money," Mason said.

"Well, filthy lucre *is* the root of all evil," she said teasingly, but some part of her did believe money caused more problems than it solved. Her father Elwood was a case in point.

"No. Love of money is the root of all evil. Money itself is nothing but a tool."

"To use to buy off anybody you want."

He raised a palm. "Listen, I want to apologize for trying to bribe you. I was wrong."

Charlee analyzed him. He seemed genuine, but his attempt to buy her off had been instinctual. He was accustomed to using money to do his dirty work.

"What were you looking for in the closet?" she asked, diverting her thoughts. Once she clambered on her soapbox about the self-indulgent lifestyles of the rich and famous, she had trouble curbing her tongue and now was not the time or place to declare war on the upper crust.

"I was searching for correspondence between your grandmother and my grandfather."

"You came up empty-handed?"

"No yellowed love letters if that's what you're asking, but I did find a clue."

He took three long-legged steps over to Maybelline's ravaged desk sitting in front of a window and picked up a pocket date book. He tossed the calendar to Charlee.

"Check out today's date."

Inscribed in red ink with Maybelline's scratchy handwriting read the message: Meet N @ K's 4 P.M.

"I'm thinking N is for Nolan."

Charlee blew out her breath. "Maybelline isn't due home until the day after tomorrow."

"Guess she had a date she didn't share with you."

"Looks like you might be right." Poking her tongue against the inside of her cheek, she stared around Mason's shoulder and out the window. Anything to keep from peering into his mesmerizing brown eyes again.

"Any idea where K's might be?"

"I have an idea."

From the corner of her eye, she caught a glimpse of something outside the window. A shadow silhouetted against the curtain.

"So where is K's?" he asked.

Charlee frowned and came up off the bed. "Mason," she said calmly. "Move."

"What?" He blinked at her.

The shadow shifted. Someone was lurking outside the window.

"I said move," she commanded and grappled for the pistol in her boot.

"What's going on?"

She waved a hand at him. "Hit the deck."

"I don't . . ."

Lordy but the man was stubborn.

"Just do what I say," she hissed. "Get down now!"

"See here, Charlee, you can't just order me around," he lectured, but then all hell broke loose.

A thick-necked man in mirrored sunglasses popped up in front of the window, a gun in his hand. Instantly, Charlee sprang forward, knocking Mason off his feet at precisely the same moment the gunman fired.

CHAPTER
3

*S*he stole his breath away.

Literally.

Mason lay sprawled on the floor, struggling to suck in air. Charlee's lean, hard body flung atop his, her firm round breasts squashed flat against his shoulder blades, her warm, sweet breath fanned his cheek.

His ears rang and the silky strands of her long, jet-black hair, combined with the pungent odor of gunpowder, tickled his nose. Disoriented both by lack of oxygen and her compelling feminine scent, he simply gasped.

What in the hell had just happened?

Charlee had slammed into him like a defensive lineman sacking a quarterback at the very same instant he'd heard a car backfiring. Why in the hell had she head-butted him into next week?

The muffled sound of a car engine—was it the same one that had backfired?—revved, followed by the high-pitched squeal of tires peeling out.

"Mason? Are you all right?" Charlee sounded distant

and far away, even though her head hovered just above his.

He pried open the eye that wasn't shoved into the carpet and blinked at the gentle slope of her nose.

"Are you hit?"

"Hee, hee, hee," he wheezed.

"You've just had the wind knocked out of you," she diagnosed and scrambled off his back. She stood over him, one hand on her gun, the other on her hip. "You'll be all right."

Mason finally caught his breath and looked up. Broken glass clung to her hair and clothes. He frowned, still trying to piece together what had just occurred.

She held out a hand and hauled him to his feet, power-gripping like a captain of industry. His gaze shifted from the shattered window and the glass shards spilt across Maybelline's desk, to the opposite wall where a bullet hole dug into the Sheetrock.

The truth hit him like an anvil.

That was no backfiring car.

"Someone shot at me."

"'Fraid so."

She bent at the waist and flipped her hair to shake out the glass. The slow toss shouldn't have been sensual, but the manner in which she raked her fingers through the glossy strands, tousling it first one way and then the next, captured his caveman instincts.

And the way her shirt inched up, exposing a narrow expanse of her bare back and a glimpse of purple thong panties peeking just above the waistband of her jeans sent a sharp spike of pure physical longing straight through him.

Mason blinked and shook his head. What in the hell was the matter with him?

"That's why you were hollering at me to move," he said, turning to eye the window to keep his gaze off the provocative Charlee. "You spotted the gunman."

"Ding, ding, ding. Very good, Sherlock."

"I could have been killed."

"You weren't."

"You saved my life." Rattled and yet desperate to hide his creeping apprehension in the face of Charlee's composure, Mason shoved a hand through his hair and determinedly ignored the nervous sweat plastering his shirt to his shoulder blades.

"Don't go all Hallmark greeting card on me, Gentry. I acted out of pure reflex. Besides, I don't think he intended to kill you. If he had, we'd both be dead."

"So why shoot at all?"

"Warning."

"What for?" Mason couldn't believe they had just dodged a bullet and here was Charlee, cool as a summer salad, acting as if nothing out of the ordinary had occurred.

"I dunno. Encourage us to lay off the case?"

"What case?"

"I'm not sure."

"Do you think the shot has anything to do with our missing grandparents?"

"Maybe."

"Wow, you're a fount of information."

"Hey, I don't know, okay? I'm a detective, not a psychic."

"But why would someone shoot at me?"

"Don't take it personally."

How else was he supposed to regard a bullet aimed at his head? She expected him to simply shrug off a murder attempt?

"Probably has nothing to do with you at all." Charlee stuck the pistol in her waistband.

His eyes tracked her. He spied a tantalizing flash of flat, hard belly when she lifted her shirt. He licked his lips, dry from the arid desert air. "Who could have pulled the trigger?"

"Maybe the same creep who ransacked the place. Maybe not." She headed for the door. "You coming?"

"Where are we going?"

"To Kelly's tavern."

"K's?"

"You got it."

"Aren't we calling the police?"

"If we do, we'll be tied up with red tape for hours. You're welcome to stay here and file a report if you wish, but daylight's burning and I'm getting worried about my grandmother."

He looked from Charlee to the ruins around him and back again. She arched an eyebrow and shot him an are-you-coming-or-not look. His upbringing screamed at him to call the police. Someone had shot at them, for crying out loud, and he wanted an accounting.

But she was right. His house had been burgled before. He knew the routine. Filing a police report involved hours of paperwork and in the meantime Maybelline Sikes and his grandfather were off doing who knew what with a half-million dollars and possibly being shadowed by some two-bit thug who thought nothing of ransacking an old lady's trailer and then shooting at people through a bedroom window.

The mental picture convinced him.

"Let's roll," he said.

Mason sat in the passenger seat. The hotels and casinos slipped past them in the gathering dusk as they drove down the Vegas Strip. The Luxor, Excalibur, MGM Grand, The Flamingo, Caesar's Palace. Tourists packed the streets, many on spring break. But Mason didn't watch the eclectic crowd or take in the bright lights. His attention was centered solely on Charlee.

She drove as she did everything. With a gritty sense of purpose. She stared straight ahead, her eyes glued to the road as she zipped around slow-moving vehicles, frequently changing lanes. Her speed continually edged over the posted limits and she often did not come to a complete halt at stop signs.

He bit down on the inside of his cheek to keep from telling her how to drive. It was her car. If she didn't mind getting it whacked, what business of his was it? He was just glad he was wearing his seat belt and paid extravagant health insurance premiums.

Ten minutes later, Charlee parked her Corvette outside a small neighborhood bar flanked on one side by a twenty-four-hour wedding chapel and a tanning salon on the other. She removed her gun from her waistband, leaned across his knees, stuffed her weapon in the glove compartment, and locked it.

Her breasts brushed lightly against his thigh in the process. Panting like a 1-900-Phone-Sex regular, Mason fumbled for the door handle and struggled to control his out-of-whack libido.

Charlee exited the car, just as she'd slid in, by hoisting her delectable fanny over the door frame Magnum,

P.I., style. He tried to imagine Daphne alighting from an open-topped vehicle in such a blasé manner and he laughed out loud.

"What's so funny?" She whirled around and stabbed him with her stare.

"Nothing."

"I know what you're thinking."

"You do?"

"Typical white trash bar."

"I never said that."

"You didn't have to. I can read you like a mail-order catalogue."

"Hey." He raised his palms. "Don't assign your prejudices to me."

"What's that supposed to mean?"

"You have a problem with where you've come from."

She shrugged and turned away, but not before he caught the uncertain expression on her face. He'd nailed her insecurities. He hurried to open the door for her and she blasted him with a quelling glare.

"After you." He bowed with an exaggerated flourish.

She snorted, tossed her head sassily, and trod over the threshold into the crowded, smoky tavern. The run-down bar was a far cry from his usual watering hole, the exclusive Hidden Hills Country Club in River Oaks.

The jukebox blared a Garth Brooks classic about friends in low places. The smell of beer, menthol cigarettes, and stale popcorn filled the air. A leather-clad, tattooed crowd packed the room. They sized Mason up with suspicious glances as he and Charlee made their way toward the bar.

A few people called out greetings to her. She smiled and nodded but didn't stop to chat. She was a woman on

a mission and being with her made him feel more resolute. His growing respect for her shot up a notch.

Two men on bar stools scooted over for Charlee as
she bellied up to the bar but they closed ranks around
her, leaving Mason standing awkwardly to one side and
fending off their glares. She spoke to the bartender, but
between the loud music, laughter, and hum of voices, he
couldn't hear what she said.

He tried to lean in closer, but one of the men on the
bar stool jostled him with his elbow, sloshing beer over
Mason's arm. He frowned and started to say something
but the guy was skunk-drunk. He wrote off the shove as
an accident.

"Excuse me," Mason said. "Could I please step up to
the bar?"

"Can you?" the guy, who wore a black leather vest,
chains, and a gold spike through his chin, challenged.

How tedious. Obviously the beer slosh hadn't been
an accident. Mason sighed inwardly. He didn't have
time for this crap. "Come on, mister. I don't want any
trouble."

"Oh, yeah? Then how come you dragged your preppy
ass in here?"

"Since you've been imbibing heavily I'm choosing to
ignore that remark."

The guy looked over at his buddy. "Did he just insult
me, Leroy?"

"Yup," Leroy, who had a cobra tattooed on his forearm, agreed. "I didn't go to *coll-ege,* but I do believe he
just insulted you, Thurgood."

"I'm with her." Mason nodded at Charlee. "We'll be
gone in a couple of minutes. No need to start something."

"Hidin' behind the skirt, are you?" Thurgood mocked Mason.

"Just move aside, please," Mason said calmly.

"Whatcha gonna do if I do this?" Thurgood plastered a hammy palm on Charlee's fanny.

"Hand off my ass, Thurgood," Charlee said over her shoulder.

Not only did Thurgood not remove his hand from Charlee's backside, but he looked at Mason and wagged his lascivious tongue.

Anger, hot and quick, shot through Mason. He slapped a hand around Thurgood's wrist and jerked him off the bar stool.

Two seconds later, Thurgood lay flat on his back on the floor, Mason's Italian leather loafer pressing against his windpipe.

"Hey, Thurgood, looks like the preppie's kicking your ass." Leroy laughed and slapped his thigh.

Charlee turned away from the bar to watch Mason with a bemused smile.

"I think you owe the lady an apology."

"Yeooow."

"Apologize," Mason said, increasing the pressure on Thurgood's Adam's apple.

"I tworry, Charlee," Thurgood rasped.

Charlee peered down at the man. "Maybe next time you'll keep your hands to yourself."

He nodded, or as much as he could manage with a shoe at his throat.

"Let's get out of here," Charlee said to Mason. "I got what we came for."

"Catch you later, Thurgood." He lifted his foot from

the man's neck and followed Charlee's provocative fanny straight out the door.

"You've been holding out on me, Gentry," she said once they were on the sidewalk. "Not quite as blue-blooded as you appear. Where'd you learn those moves?"

"Fourth-degree black belt, tae kwon do."

"No shit." She shot him a pensive look and then smiled.

"No shit."

"Oooh, now I'm really titillated. Cursing and everything. What would your mama say?"

"Are you making fun of me?"

"Who me?" Charlee started to slide over the door frame and into the driver's seat.

"Wait."

"What?"

Mason hurried over to the driver's side and opened the door. "A lady should allow the gentleman to open the car door for her."

Charlee shook her head. "For one thing, no one has ever accused me of being a lady, and for another, you just blew it."

"Blew what?"

"I was actually beginning to like you and then you had to go and remind me what a pompous jackass you are."

"What? What'd I do wrong?"

She slammed the car door shut and then climbed over the door frame with a glower. "Get in."

Women. Who could figure them? Try to do something nice and you ended up making them mad.

"So what did you find out about our grandparents?" he asked after she started the engine.

"Maybelline did indeed meet some guy, who sounds like he could be your grandfather, at four o'clock this afternoon."

Mason exhaled sharply. Okay. Now they were getting somewhere.

"According to the bartender, the man left with her."

"Anything else?"

Charlee swiveled her head to look him squarely in the eyes. "I've never seen Maybelline cry. I mean not ever. Not at weddings, not at funerals. Not when I graduated high school. Never."

"So?"

"Kelly claims when they left the bar, not only was your grandfather looking pretty grim but my grandmother was bawling her eyes out."

Nolan Gentry sat beside Maybelline in the Las Vegas airport waiting for their flight to L.A. Absentmindedly he drummed the manila folder she'd given him against the metal armrest.

The contents of the file confirmed the awful news Maybelline had broken to him over the phone two days earlier. If he didn't intervene, the financial empire his father had started and he and his older brother Harry had built into a Fortune 500 dynasty would be utterly destroyed, ruining not only Nolan but his son and grandsons as well.

And the damnable thing was he couldn't say anything to anyone. Not yet. The necessity for silence was the reason he'd taken the five hundred thousand dollars from company funds. And because he hadn't known what other expenses he might incur. Such as paying off a blackmailer.

What he hoped—no, what he prayed—was that the family would send Mason to find him. It had to be Mason. Only his second-born grandson would truly understand the moral dilemma facing them.

And if they didn't send Mason?

Nolan shook his head. They would send Mason. Poor boy always shouldered the dirty work.

He peered over at Maybelline. She too had a lot invested in the outcome. If things turned out badly, her only son might end up dead.

Giving her a comforting smile, he squeezed her hand. "Everything is going to be okay."

She nodded, but he could tell from the skepticism in her eyes she wasn't buying his empty promise, not for a minute.

Her tears had damned near killed him back there in the bar. He'd only seen her cry one other time. The despair over discovering she was pregnant with a married man's baby had been so strong it sent her to the top of the HOLLYWOOD sign with the aim of ending her life.

Thank God, he'd been there to talk her down. He'd saved her life that night and now, almost fifty years later, she was saving his.

She smiled back at him and Nolan couldn't help wondering, What if?

What if he'd won the Oscar in 1955?

What if his father hadn't had a heart attack when he did?

What if he had refused his dying father's edict to come home, marry Elispeth Hunt, and mingle the nouveau riche Gentry oil-field blood with respectable old money breeding?

What if he'd stayed with Maybelline?

His old heart took an unexpected dip at the prospect. What indeed?

He gazed over at her. She was still damned beautiful in his eyes, slim and sexy despite the passing years. Headstrong and feisty. That's why her tears had frightened him so. Maybelline had never been a softie. Damn, but there were so many things he wanted to say to her. So many things he wanted to undo.

It was a useless endeavor, trying to recast the past. He'd made his choices, both good and bad. But now, the chickens had come home to roost.

She raised a hand to hide a yawn. "Long past my bedtime."

"You always were a morning lark."

"And you were the night owl. Remember when we shared the cottage in Venice Beach? You were usually coming to bed when I was leaving for work."

"I remember," he said softly. "You were three months pregnant with Elwood."

"And you'd bring me 7UP and saltines to help with the morning sickness."

Nolan patted her shoulder. "You can lean on me, May," he said. "Take a nap. I'll wake you when they start boarding the plane."

She hesitated, and then she took off her glasses, slid them into her purse, and gingerly rested her head on his shoulder.

Nolan inhaled sharply. He hadn't expected the weight of her against him to feel so good. Her hair smelled like ripe peaches and he remembered the day in his daddy's oil field when he'd seen her for the very first time.

She had worn a satiny green dress with a flared skirt that twirled when she walked and black and white saddle shoes. He recalled the dress was green because it contrasted dramatically with her fiery red hair. His fingers had itched to stroke her glossy locks.

Slowly, he reached out and traced a finger over her hair. Still soft as silk. His gut clutched.

You're too old to be feeling this way. Much too old by far.

She'd already fallen asleep, the gentle rise and fall of her chest luring him more surely than a siren's song. She'd always possessed the knack to fall asleep as easily as a child and nothing short of a major earthquake roused her from a sound slumber. Using his free hand, he reached for the jacket he'd draped across the seat beside him and gently spread it over her shoulders.

A tenderness so strong the feeling threatened to overrun his eyes with tears had Nolan clenching his teeth. Not once in his forty-three-year marriage to Elispeth had he felt one-tenth of the tenderness he felt right now for Maybelline. Not even when Elispeth had given birth to their son, Reed.

Maybelline was everything Elispeth was not.

She was bold and brave. When he realized Maybelline had run off to Hollywood both to escape her physically abusive father and to pursue her dream of becoming a makeup artist, her burst for freedom had given him the courage to defy his own father and go into acting. Elispeth, on the other hand, had been so timid and mousy she'd never even raised her voice. No fire. No vim. No vigor.

Maybelline did things her own way, blazed her own path. She didn't care if people gossiped about her. Elispeth followed the herd, decorating her house right down to the knickknacks exactly as they were depicted in some New York interior-decorating magazine. Elispeth had never stepped out of line. Had always done what was expected of her.

Maybelline was whip-smart and had more common sense in her pinkie than most people had in their entire bodies even though she had never finished high school. Elispeth had a masters degree from Sarah Lawrence but didn't have the good sense to call a doctor if Reed was running a fever.

And most of all, whenever he was with Maybelline, *he* was different. She made him laugh and take risks. She had once teased him into shaking off his stuffy exterior and going skinny-dipping in a pond. She'd dared him to stretch his acting talents and try for a part he never believed he could win. She had challenged him in a hundred wonderful ways. Around her, he was more alive. More of a man.

No, that wasn't fair. Elispeth had been a good woman. She'd done her best. He had no call comparing her to Maybelline. It wasn't his dead wife's fault he'd been in love with another woman when he married her.

Nolan shook his head. The scary thing was that his grandson Mason was about to stumble into the same trap he'd tripped over as a young man: marrying the wrong woman simply to appease family demands. Daphne Maxwell was a lovely girl but she was Elispeth all over again. What the boy needed was a Maybelline of his own.

To lure his mind away from thoughts he shouldn't be having, Nolan looked up at the departure board. Their flight was delayed. Sighing, he debated what to do when they arrived in L.A. Obviously, it would be too late to go to the accounting firm straightaway. They'd have to obtain a room for the night. Make that two rooms.

He closed his eyes and had just dozed off when a hand clamped down on his shoulder.

"Mr. Nolan Gentry?"

Startled, Nolan's eyes flew open. There, standing in front of him, was Elvis. Pudgy Elvis in his famous white rhinestone-studded jumpsuit.

He blinked. Was he dreaming? He half expected Elvis to launch into a rousing, hip-swinging rendition of "Viva Las Vegas."

"Mr. Gentry?" Elvis repeated.

No, not *the* Elvis, but an Elvis look-alike. The town was chock-full of Elvis impersonators.

"Yes, I'm Nolan Gentry."

"Mr. Gentry, I have a gun in my pocket. I want you to wake your companion and follow me."

"What?"

"Do you need me to repeat what I just said?"

"You've got a gun? But how did you get a gun past airport security?"

Elvis snorted. "Don't you watch nighttime news shows like *20/20* where they smuggle all kinds of weapons past the metal detectors?"

"I don't believe you have a gun. Show me."

"You think I'm gonna whip it out in public?"

Defiantly, Nolan crossed his arms over his chest. "I'm not going anywhere with you."

Elvis sighed. "Okay, let's try this another way. If you want to see the Oscar files, then you're going to have to come with me."

Nolan's gut squeezed. How did Elvis know about the stolen files? "What?"

"Yep. Believe me when I say I can make or break you, pal. Now move."

Nolan shook his head. Nothing made any sense. He had to be dreaming. Otherwise, all proof pointed to the fact that he and Maybelline were being kidnapped by the King of Rock and Roll.

CHAPTER 4

"Where to now?"

Charlee slid a glance over at Mason, amazed he'd asked her opinion.

He sat ramrod-straight, his seat belt snugly fastened around his trim waist, his eyes locked on the unruly Vegas Strip traffic. After his lady and gentleman crack about the way she climbed into her car, she'd pegged him as a control freak who preferred his women submissive and relegated to a pedestal.

She grinned to herself, amused at how uptight he was. She'd bet anything he rolled his toothpaste tube up from the bottom instead of squeezing it in the middle like she did. No, wait. He was probably so regimented he used a toothpaste dispenser and carefully measured out each drop. She'd wager a month's pay that he labeled his possessions, hated for the food on his plate to touch, and always counted his change to make sure he'd gotten back the correct amount.

Good thing they wouldn't be together long. She would drive him crazy with the way she stuffed underwear in the same drawer with socks, ate standing over the kitchen sink, and tossed her change in the bottom of her purse without ever looking at it.

"You're asking my opinion?"

"You are the private investigator."

"Somehow I got the impression you have a hard time letting other people take charge."

His smile was forced. "Not when the other person has more information. Vegas is your home turf. You're more than welcome to step up to the plate."

"Thank you. I will. We're going to see someone who might have an idea where our grandparents are," she said.

"Oh?" Mason leaned closer and she caught a whiff of his sandalwood soap. She wondered if he tasted as clean as he smelled. "Who?"

Charlee's mistrustful nature had her biting her bottom lip and hesitating before revealing any more information than absolutely necessary. After all, what did she know about the guy other than the fact he dazzled her like dynamite and kicked-ass at tae kwon do?

In and of itself, that fact was suspicious. How many spoiled, rich pretty boys possessed the discipline for advanced martial arts?

Once she thought about it, Charlee realized everything had been hunky-dory in her life until he'd shown up. Now Maybelline was missing, her place had been ransacked, and someone had shot at them.

What if he had lied about his identity? He could be anyone. A hit man or an undercover cop or even, heaven forbid, an IRS agent. Plenty of people would gladly line up to take pot shots at IRS agents.

"Charlee?" he prodded, more irritating than a pebble in her boot. "Who are we going to see?"

Don't tell him a damned thing.

She pretended to concentrate on navigating the Corvette around a slow-moving eighteen-wheeler, but he didn't buy her stall tactics.

"If the matter concerns my grandfather, I have a right to know."

As much as she wanted to, she couldn't disagree. After all, she had no real reason to believe Mason was anything other than what he claimed. Charlee reluctantly relented.

"We're going to see my father."

"From the tightness in your voice I'm guessing you two don't get along so well."

"You might say that." Charlee gripped the steering wheel far tighter than necessary. "Let's just hope my old man isn't involved in what's going on between our grandparents."

"Care to elaborate?"

Charlee took a deep breath. "No."

To her surprise, he nodded and said, "Fair enough."

Mason certainly didn't seem like the sort of guy to let things pass easily and Charlee shot him a pensive glance. Maybe something in her body language warned him off.

Whenever Elwood popped into her brain, she couldn't help tensing up. She understood even without the help of a Freudian psychologist that the roots of her prejudice against wealthy, long-legged, matinee-idol-smiling, beard-stubble-sporting men started with her father.

Mason's decision not to pressure her had a tongue-loosening effect. Charlee had no idea what possessed her but she found herself saying, "Don't get me wrong. I love my father. I mean he *is* my father after all, but a stand-up guy he ain't."

"We all have family issues."

Charlee laughed. "Yeah. Well, some of us have issues and then some of us have *issues*."

"Rotten childhood?"

"Rotten isn't the word for it."

Why was she yammering like an Oprah guest? She wasn't a poor-me-I-never-got-over-being-mistreated-by-my-parent type. And she most certainly wasn't a whiner.

She pressed the tip of her tongue against the roof of her mouth to keep from speaking, but then Mason reached over, flicked off the radio, and casually let his fingers trail over the back of her hand. She didn't know if he'd touched her on purpose or not, but a hint of sympathy was all it took. How truly pathetic was she? Words erupted from her in a mindless purge of verbiage.

"Once upon a time, my father, Elwood Sikes, was the best Elvis impersonator in Vegas." Charlee left the Strip and downshifted as she slowed for a yield sign. "This wasn't long after the real Elvis died and Elwood's career blazed hot, hot, hot."

"Hmmm."

"Oh, he was a charming bastard. Had tons of women flocking after him, which was the main reason my mother didn't marry him even though she was pregnant with me. She might have been a naive Louisiana Cajun in over her head in sin city, but she wasn't dumb."

Charlee waved a hand. Had she ever told her story to anyone? She couldn't remember. She wanted to shut up, to keep her private life private, but spewing out her anger felt so good, she just kept blabbing.

"Anyway, my father fell for his own publicity hype. He believed the money he raked in would last forever. He bought a pink Cadillac and a fancy house with an Olympic-sized swimming pool and he wore diamond rings on every finger. The typical cliché. I'm told he bought me tons of toys but I don't remember."

"It must have been a very exciting time for him," Mason said.

"Too exciting. He started gambling. Caught the fever and lost every penny. After that he became real friendly with the whiskey bottle and they canned him from the Elvis gig for showing up drunk. Everything was repossessed. He lost it all. The money, the house, the women. He simply couldn't deal with the failure. He's spent the rest of his life trying to get it back by chasing get-rich-quick schemes and getting thrown in jail on a semiregular basis." Charlee sighed. "And I've spent a small mint bailing him out."

Mason ticked his tongue in sympathy.

"He littered my childhood with a string of broken promises. One time he swore he'd take me to McDonald's for my fifth birthday. My mother dressed me up in a pink satin dress and black patent leather Mary Janes. I can still remember the dress had a white sash with blue flowers. I waited and I waited and I waited, but Elwood never came."

"Must have been pretty difficult for you."

Charlee shook her head in denial. "Hell, I was used to him standing me up. But his reappearing acts were even worse. He'd show up, usually drunk, with some big-haired, big-chested bimbo who he expected me to call Mama on his arm and a wad of ill-gotten cash in his pocket."

"I can't even imagine."

"Worst thing, after my mother died, Elwood just dumped me on Maybelline. Not that I regret being raised by my grandmother," she added swiftly. "It's just I'd always hoped . . ." she trailed off.

A fire-engine siren shrieked nearby. Thank God for the interruption, otherwise she might have told him every sordid detail of her painful past.

"Better pull over," Mason advised. "I think they're coming this way."

She looked in the rearview mirror at the same time the fire truck rounded the corner. Startled, she jerked to a stop at the curb and realized her hands were shaking. Not from the unexpected arrival of the emergency vehicle but from the sheer volume of her verbal diarrhea. She could not have shocked herself more if she'd stripped off her shirt and flashed him her boobies.

The car idled softly, accentuating the quietness between them.

"Are you okay?" Mason asked, his voice heavy with concern. He touched her again and there was no mistaking the intent this time—firmer, lingering, his thumb gently rubbing her knuckles.

Charlee jerked her hand away and looked into his face. She stared at his wide, generous mouth and found herself wondering if he was a good kisser. Startled, she focused her gaze on the road.

An odd twinge twisted through her. A strange mix of anxiety, gratitude, and uncertainty.

What in the hell was going on here?

You're just worried about Maybelline. Remember,

*you're highly susceptible to brown-eyed, handsome
men. Nail your guard back up, pronto.*

A second fire truck zoomed by and then a third.

Struggling to appear nonchalant, Charlee tugged her
hand out from under Mason's and slowly pulled the
Corvette back into traffic. She smelled smoke in the air
and the odor thickened the closer they came to the run-
down apartment complex where her father lived.

By the time they turned onto her father's block,
Charlee's heart hammered hard even before she spotted
the flames licking brightly against the night sky. Dread
weighed her down at the sight of firemen scurrying
across the lawn with fire hoses and axes.

Apartment residents stood to one side staring owl-
eyed as their homes flashed in a crescendo of sparks.
Gawkers stopped to rubberneck.

From the corner of her eye, Charlee spied a white,
four-door Chevy Malibu easing slowly down the street.
She parked in the lot of a nearby dry cleaners and, without even thinking about Mason, climbed out of the car
and beelined over to the small apartment complex.

Please let Elwood be okay, she prayed.

She tried to approach one of the firemen, but he
brusquely waved her off. A ruddy-faced police officer
with a Boston accent came over to escort her across the
street with the other bystanders.

"This way, miss."

"My father," she said. "He lives in apartment 16c."

"Everyone's been evacuated. There've been no casual-
ties. If your father is here, he'll be in the crowd. Now step
aside."

"What happened?" Charlee fisted her hands. "I have
a right to know."

"Step aside," the policeman repeated with a stern frown.

The smoke, the fire, the heat, the noise, and the chaos overwhelmed her.

Dammit, Elwood, where are you?

She wanted to argue with the cop, to demand he tell her something more, but she couldn't find her tongue. She simply stared at the dramatic flames scampering across the roof of the apartment building and she felt all the courage drain from her body.

"Excuse me, officer," Mason interrupted. He moved closer to the man, lowered his head, and spoke so low Charlee couldn't hear what he said.

What magic he wrought, she did not know, but a few minutes later he walked over and took her elbow. "Let's go back to the car."

"Why? I want to know what's happening."

"Just do as I say."

"Listen here, Gentry . . ." Charlee balked, grateful to have someone to take her anxiety out on.

"Now is not the time to straddle your high horse. I've got unfortunate news."

"What?" Her contrariness vanished. She gripped Mason's forearm and imagined the worst.

"The fire originated in your father's apartment."

Charlee blinked. "Is he . . . hurt?"

Mason shook his head. "The apartment was empty when the firemen arrived."

"Thank God."

"They believe the fire was arson."

"Arson?"

"I hate to tell you, but the police suspect your father intentionally started the blaze."

* * *

Charlee sank into the chair in her office and forced herself not to bite her fingernails. She balled her hands into fists and dropped them into her lap. She absolutely refused to jump to conclusions about Elwood. Just because his apartment caught fire didn't mean he was up to his old tricks.

Believe that and there's a bridge in Brooklyn someone is dying to sell you.

Sighing, she flicked on Maybelline's computer and leaned back in the chair as she waited for the hard drive to boot up.

After leaving the scene of the fire, Mason had insisted on going back to her grandmother's trailer to help her clean up the mess and repair the broken bedroom windowpane. She'd been touched by his offer and then angry with herself for going all soft and gushy inside just because some guy did a decent thing.

Plus, she couldn't stop thinking about the way his hard, lean back—all sinewy and masculine—had felt beneath her when she'd knocked him to the floor and saved him from the gunman's bullet. Even now, hours later, the memory of his body caused the moisture to evaporate from her mouth and her pulse to speed up.

She wasn't falling for his charms. No how. No way. She understood that old song and dance. Guys were oh-so-delightful at first, at least until they landed you in their beds. After they got what they wanted, it was so long, Charlee, been nice knowing you, don't let the door hit you in the ass on your way out.

It was closing in on two A.M. but she was too wired to sleep. After dropping Mason off at the Bellagio, she schlepped down to the office to hunt through May-belline's files in search of clues.

But instead of probing the database on the hard drive, she found herself logging onto the Internet. She never consciously decided to Google him, but the next thing she knew, there she was, typing Mason's name into the search engine.

And up popped a string of references.

Links to newspaper articles and magazine interviews and high-society pages. She discovered his family held a seat on the New York Stock Exchange.

When she stumbled across a detailed listing of the numerous companies they owned—including a silver mine in New Mexico, a flagship hotel in the Bahamas, and a top accounting firm in Hollywood—Charlee realized his family was richer than God and she was in far deeper trouble than she ever imagined.

Damn her and her illogical Prince Charming complex.

She found a photograph of Mason escorting a gloss-ily beautiful blonde to some debutante shindig and the pinch of jealousy biting into her stomach scared her.

Good gravy. What did she have to be jealous of? She could never compete with such a woman. Nor did she want to. She'd had her fill of rich men.

Briefly, she thought of Gregory Blankensonship, the first man she'd ever loved, and winced. Would she ever recover from his betrayal?

Oh, stop whining. You've got work to do.

Determined, she logged off the Internet, picked up the telephone, and began calling hospitals, hotels, air-lines, and bus stations. Maybelline, Nolan, and Elwood simply couldn't have disappeared into thin air.

She might not be lucky in love, but she was a damned fine private investigator. And one way or another, she would find them.

Mason had come to Vegas to find his grandfather and drag him back home in time to prevent his brother from taking sole credit for closing the biggest deal in the history of Gentry Enterprises. Retrieving Gramps should have been quick, clean, and simple.

But instead of achieving his clear-cut goal, a little more than twelve hours after arriving in town, Mason found himself embroiled in a royal mess featuring one testy lady P.I., her missing granny, a ransacked trailer house, a disgruntled gunman, and a very suspicious fire. What he couldn't figure out was how Gramps fit into the chaos.

Mason had tumbled into bed, certain he would fall asleep within minutes, but slumber eluded him. Two-thirty and he lay wide awake listening to the bedside clock tick off the seconds. Dammit. Charlee had promised to come around for him at six A.M. so they could start searching for their grandparents again.

Charlee.

Now there was one hell of a woman. Tough and unflinching, she didn't coddle her fears or back away from the truth.

It was a thrill watching her mind work. He could actually see her mental cogs whirling. It was in the tilt of her jaw, the furrow of her brow, the tightening of her facial muscles. The way she focused on whatever task lay at hand was a thing of beauty.

And being with her was strangely exhilarating. As if by proxy her fervor would rub off on him. He wondered if she realized how the intensity came over her. The way her green eyes changed colors and took on a lively ferocity when she was on the hunt.

She was a woman warrior, proud and strong. He thought of the way she'd looked at Maybelline's house, gun in hand, a determined set to her chin. Suddenly his senses were as full of her as they had been at the moment the gunman fired.

The womanly aroma of her hung in his nose, the imprint of her firm body lingered against his back, the sound of her rich, smoldering voice haunted his ears. She stirred his imagination and aroused a dormant passion he never realized he possessed.

He liked her long, lean limbs and the bronzy glow of her skin. He liked the straightforward scent of her — honeysuckle soap and crisp spray starch. Not frilly or overdone. Just clean and honest and free.

And her luscious tresses. Masses of straight black hair hanging down her back in a curtain of sheer delight or bouncing provocatively when pulled back in a sleek ponytail. Too bad . . .

Too bad what, Gentry?

Too damned bad he was stewing in his hormones. Charlee Champagne was strictly off-limits for so many reasons he couldn't begin to count. Groaning, Mason stuffed a pillow over his head and willed his mind empty.

He must have finally dozed off, because he woke with a jerk when the telephone rang. Blindly, he fumbled for the receiver in the dark and brought it to his ear.

"Lo," he mumbled.

"Gentry, it's Charlee."

As if he didn't recognize her sexy, smoky voice. "What time is it?"

"Four o'clock."

"What are you doing up?"

"Couldn't sleep."

"Go away for a couple of hours, will you?"

"Can't. Got some hot news." He could tell from the thrill in her tone she was jazzed up. A cougar on the prowl.

Shaking his head to clear away the cobwebs of aborted sleep, Mason propped himself against the headboard. "I'm listening."

"I did some digging and I found out Nolan and Maybelline booked a red-eye flight to L.A. last night."

"They're in L.A.?"

"No, they never got on the plane."

"So they're still in Vegas?"

"That's what I aim to find out. I'm headed over to the airport to interview the gate agent and figured you might wanna come along."

"Sure. Sure." Mason yawned and ran a hand through his hair.

"See you there in twenty minutes," she said and hung up the phone.

Twenty minutes later, Mason parked his Bentley in the infield parking garage, then walked over to wait on the curb outside the terminal.

Charlee screeched her Corvette to a stop in a passenger loading zone and leaped from the car. She wore a straw white Stetson cocked back on her head and twin braids streamed down her back. She looked absolutely adorable; although he had the impression she was shooting for badass. Daphne would proclaim her a fashion disaster, but Mason appreciated that she dressed the way she pleased, in-vogue styles be damned.

He pointed at the NO LONG-TERM PARKING sign. "You're not going to leave your car here."

"Nobody's gonna tow me away at this time of the morning." Her fast-talking disregard for the posted sign told him she was wired on adrenaline and so eager to leap into the investigation she couldn't be bothered looking for a parking space.

"Don't count on it."

"I'm on the hunt. I need my vehicle at the ready in case I need to make a quick exit."

"Parking in a passenger loading zone and risking being towed is not the way to achieve your goal."

"Oh, hush. How are they going to know I'm not loading passengers? We won't be long. Come on."

Mason didn't budge. "Charlee, move your car," he insisted.

"Relax, Gentry. Boy, you are uptight. Love the sheet creases by the way." On her way past him, she reached up and lightly fingered his cheek.

Her touch burned electric. Mason growled, desperate to deny the tingle of awareness warming his face.

Blithely, she stalked into the concourse and he had no choice but to follow or get left behind. Fine, let her car get towed.

In spite of himself, Mason found his eyes locked on the sassy sway of her blue-jeaned behind. Good thing she wasn't his girlfriend. They would clash like cymbals over every little thing. He couldn't imagine living with someone so stubborn.

Girlfriend? What in the hell prompted that outlandish concept?

Because she's the girl of the dreams you never even dared to dream. She's wild and free and full of spirit. And she would scare the living hell out of your family.

He shook his head. Blame his crazy meandering thoughts on his poor sleep-deprived brain. He was officially losing his marbles.

Gramps, you owe me big time.

Charlee pranced through the security checkpoint, but Mason set off the buzzer. The attendant motioned him aside for a wanding. They required him to empty his pockets and remove his shoes before they were satisfied he wasn't planning on blowing the place to kingdom come.

He hurried through the terminal. His impatience escalating when two thick-necked guys in black sunshades bumped into him. If he hadn't been so intent on locating Charlee, Mason might have paid more heed to the duo, but because he was in a hurry, he blew off their rudeness. By the time he caught up with her, she was deep in conversation with a gate agent.

He walked over and touched her shoulder. When she turned away from the gate agent, he was startled to see her normally golden skin had gone pale. The look on her face sliced a chill straight through his bones. He felt confused, angry with whomever or whatever had created her obvious distress. He fisted his hands, ready to beat someone to a pulp on her behalf.

"Charlee? What's wrong?"

She quickly gained control over her emotions, smoothing out her forehead and pressing her lips firmly together.

"We're in luck. The same gate agent is still on duty.

He remembers Maybelline and Nolan. They left with some guy just before the plane arrived."

"What guy?"

Charlee didn't meet his gaze and he realized instantly she was keeping something from him.

"Charlee?" he prodded.

"I dunno, but the gate agent said he watched all three of them head over to the rental car area."

He narrowed his eyes. "Is that everything?"

She hesitated.

"What aren't you telling me?"

She studied the scuffed toe of her boots, jammed her fingertips into her front pockets. "Our grandparents were arguing with the guy. Like they were upset and didn't want to leave with him. Actually the gate agent even offered to call security, but your grandfather told him everything was all right."

"Does he remember what the guy looked like?"

Charlee took a deep breath. "Yeah. He was wearing a white, rhinestone-encrusted jumpsuit."

"That's certainly memorable. Sounds like Elvis Presley."

"Or an Elvis impersonator."

Their eyes met and he knew what she was going to say before the word left her mouth.

"Elwood."

CHAPTER
5

*F*oreboding slithered through Charlee's insides like a snake shedding its skin. Why would Maybelline and Nolan run off with Elwood? She had a bad feeling about the whole deal. Mason's grandfather had arrived in Vegas with a large sum of money in his pocket and large sums of money attracted Elwood like flies to cow patties.

Her father had been jailed for many penny-ante schemes from peddling weed to hoodwinking tourists with three-card monte to blackmailing a high-profile ex-lover. However, none of his crimes had merited a felony charge. Maybelline had washed her hands of him years ago, but Charlee couldn't admit defeat when it came to her father no matter how many times he disappointed her.

Maybelline rarely spoke to her only child. Why would she leave the airport with him when she'd planned on catching a flight to L.A.?

Unless . . .

Charlee started to gnaw on her thumbnail and realized Mason was studying her. Shamefaced, she quickly tucked her hand behind her back.

"Let's go talk to the rental car people," she said in a decisive tone and stalked toward the counter.

The woman behind the desk didn't glance up from her tabloid magazine. Charlee splayed her palms against the black Formica countertop and cleared her throat.

"Excuse me."

Unhappy at being dragged from her celebrity gossip, the woman glared at her. "Yeah?"

"A middle-aged Elvis impersonator along with an older couple rented a car from you earlier this morning. I'd like to know where they were headed, please."

The woman frowned. "I can't release that kind of information."

"I'm a private detective," Charlee said in her most professional tone and flashed the woman her ID. "And I'm investigating a possible crime. If you could do a little finger-tapping on your computer keyboard I'd really appreciate it."

"Sorry, no can do."

"It's a matter of life and death. I must know where they're headed."

"You're not the police. I don't have to tell you anything." She continued reading her gossip rag.

Charlee gritted her teeth and contemplated shoving Ms. Congeniality out of the way and commandeering her keyboard, but before she had time to discard the idea as a not particularly viable one, Mason placed one finger on the woman's magazine and slowly pushed it downward so she was forced to look him in the eyes.

"Hi there." He shot the woman a grin so dazzling

even an ardent man hater could not have resisted him and clearly she was no man hater.

"Oh, my!" the woman gasped breathlessly as if one of the movie stars from her magazine had sprung to life right in front of her. "Where did you come from?"

Mason leaned nonchalantly closer and studied the name tag situated just above the woman's breast. "Lila," he crooned. "What a lovely name."

"Why thank you," the woman simpered and batted her eyelashes. "I was named after my great-grandmother."

"How do you do." He offered his hand.

"I'm doing very well now that you're here." She angled a sultry glance at him and pumped his hand as vigorously as if she were pulling the handle on a slot machine.

Charlee snorted. Enough with the friggin' foreplay, Gentry, get to the point.

"Listen, Lila, I'm hoping you can do me and my"— Mason glanced over his shoulder at Charlee—"sister here a favor."

Sister? Charlee burned a hole through him with her stare. What was the big idea telling Ms. Congeniality she was his sister?

"She's your sister?" Lila asked.

Mason lowered his voice. "I know. Her manners are so atrocious you'd never suspect we were raised by the same parents."

"No indeed," Lila whispered back as if Charlee weren't standing right in front of her.

Mason murmured something else that Charlee couldn't quite hear. Lila giggled girlishly and then typed into the computer. Let some rich handsome guy smile at her and ole Lila folded like a house of cards.

"The party you're interested in rented a red and white Chevrolet camper. License number LYG-123. It's supposed to be returned to the Tucson office on Monday."

Monday? Why so much time? It didn't take but maybe eight or nine hours to drive to Tucson. Why keep the rental until Monday? Charlee nibbled on her bottom lip and tried to figure out what stunt her father was pulling.

"Thank you so much, Lila." Mason gazed deeply into the clerk's eyes and flashed her his dimples, looking like some swoonily gorgeous soap opera star. "You've been an immeasurable help."

"Hang on a minute." Lila was practically panting. She tore off a scrap of paper from the yellow legal pad on her desk, jotted something on it, and slipped the note into Mason's hand. "Call me." She winked.

Charlee rolled her eyes, wagged her head, and mocked the awestruck clerk by silently mouthing, "Call me."

See. Precisely why she didn't trust wealthy, long-legged, brown-eyed, handsome men any farther than she could toss 'em. They would do anything to get their way. Completely shameless, the lot of them.

"Bye." He wriggled his fingers at Lila, and took Charlee by the elbow. "Let's go, sis."

"What's up, Slick?" Charlee untangled herself from him the minute they were out of earshot. "The gossip rag queen gave you her phone number?"

"Not that it's any of your business, but yes."

"You gonna call her?"

Mason frowned and tossed the woman's number in a nearby trash can. "Of course not."

Charlee shook her head. "Cruel bastard. You trifled with that woman's affections."

"All for a good cause."

"And by the way, what was that remark about my being your sister?"

"Hey, it got us what we needed." He guided her through the concourse, which had grown more crowded since they'd first arrived. "Do you think she would have opened up to me if she thought you were my girlfriend?"

"I'm not your girlfriend."

"I know that and you know that, but Lila didn't know that."

"You're such a liar."

"Sounds like sour grapes to me."

"What are you talking about? Sour grapes over what? That Lila was drooling on you? *Puh-leeze,* I could care less."

"You're just testy because my method worked and yours didn't. You can catch more flies with honey, sweetheart. Remember that."

"Hmmph," Charlee mumbled under her breath while at the same time her pulse revved to realize he'd inadvertently called her sweetheart. Oh, this was completely disgusting. How could she let herself get all flustered and fluttery over some pretty boy?

Perturbed at her reaction, she searched for something rude to say. "Honey my ass. You snagged her with the matinee-idol smile and your sultry brown-eyed stare."

"Pardon?" He lowered his head to hers, those very eyes in question twinkling with a mischievous light. "I didn't quite catch that. Did you just compliment me?"

"Ahem. I said, the red and white camper is only a few

hours ahead of us. If we pick up the pace, maybe we can overtake them before they reach Tucson."

"That's what I thought you said."

"Yeah. Right."

"Really, Charlee, you've got to learn to express your opinion more often," he teased.

"Leave the sarcasm to me, Slick. It doesn't suit you. Stick with your forte."

"And what is that?"

"Conniving women."

"Ah, so that's my forte. I always wondered what it was." He ran a hand over his beard stubble. The soft, rasping sound knotted her stomach.

"Smart aleck."

"So tell me, Charlee, if tempting women is my forte, how come my charms don't work on you?"

What in the hell was wrong with him? Mason berated himself. He didn't flirt. He wasn't a hound dog. He respected women. Considered them his equal in every way. He was about to become engaged. Daphne trusted him and Mason honored that trust. He would not allow something as insignificant as sexual magnetism orchestrate his downfall. Not when he was so close to achieving everything he'd ever wanted.

Maybe the impending engagement was the problem. Maybe, somewhere deep down in his subconscious, since he was out of town, away from his normal surroundings, he was simply letting himself go one last time before settling down.

You're just flirting with Charlee, not seducing her. What's the harm? You flirted with the rental-car woman and that doesn't bother you.

Charming the rental-car clerk was business. He had needed information. He turned on the charisma. He'd gotten what he wanted from Lila.

And what about Charlee?

What did he want from her?

Stunned, Mason paused. Nothing. He wanted nothing from her. He only wanted to find his grandfather, bring him back home, and get on with his life. If things went according to plan, bright and early Monday morning, he'd walk into his father's office to close the Birkweilder account, successfully wresting his deal back from Hunter.

At the thought of the look on his brother's face when he showed up to overturn his competitive coup, Mason smiled.

And the sooner he and Charlee got on the road after that camper, the better. Even if it meant throwing himself into the nerve-wracking crucible of Charlee's hot rod Corvette and enduring her gawd-awful driving for the next several hours. Whatever it took to achieve his goal, he would do it.

What about the Bentley?

What indeed? The idea of leaving his baby in the airport parking garage gave him hives. He would insist Charlee follow him to the Bellagio to drop off the Bentley before they headed for Tucson.

He turned to her, but she'd already sprinted ahead of him, running through the automatic doors to the passenger loading zone where she'd parked.

"It's gone!" she trilled and threw her arms in the air. "They towed my Corvette. Dammit!"

Mason opened his mouth to murmur a smug, "I told

you so," but before he could get the sentence out, she whirled around and shook a finger under his nose.

"Not a word. Don't you dare say a word."

He clamped his lips together.

"And stop smirking. I know a smirk when I see one."

Mason shrugged and tried hard to stop smirking.

"Crap." She paced and smacked a palm repeatedly against her forehead. "Crap, crap, crap. I don't have the money to get it out of the police impound and both my thirty-eight and my cell phone were locked inside the glove box."

She looked so distraught that his temptation to gloat disappeared. He had the strangest desire to haul her into his arms, hold her close, and promise her that everything would be all right. He had no explanation for the urge. She wasn't the damsel in distress type and he knew she'd sooner poke him in the ribs with her elbow as thank him for his attempt to comfort her, so he sensibly kept his hands to himself.

"Calm down," he said. "I'll pay to get your car out of the impound."

"No. I can't let you do that."

"Why not?"

"I've had bad luck when it comes to borrowing money from men. It never works out. When you owe men money, they have certain expectations."

"Expectations?" He arched an eyebrow.

"Oh, come on, don't force me to spell it out for you."

Startled, he met her gaze. "Do you mean sexual favors?"

"Well, duh."

"There have been men in your life who have given you money and then expected sexual favors in return?"

The idea of someone treating her like a disposable sex object caused a ball of anger to clog his throat.

"I said men expected it from me, not that I did it. Jeeze, what do you think I am?"

"I didn't mean . . . er . . . that's not what I meant to suggest."

Oh, great. Way to stick your foot in your mouth, Gentry. You basically called her a prostitute.

"So you can understand my reluctance to accept your offer of financial assistance."

"Charlee, I am not other men. Besides, this is an emergency. We need to get on the road as quickly as possible if we have any hope of overtaking the camper before it reaches Tucson. They've got several hours on us."

Hesitating, she pursed her lips and looked as if taking his money would literally kill her. "Okay. But the minute we find Maybelline, I'll get the money from her and pay you back."

"That'll be fine."

He reached in his jacket pocket for his wallet. Hmm. He almost always placed his wallet in his front left pocket. Maybe in the haze of hurrying to the airport he'd put it in the right pocket instead.

He patted the other side.

Nothing.

A sickening feeling sank to the bottom of his belly. He checked the back pockets of his trousers.

Not there.

No wallet. No credentials. No money. No credit cards.

Grinding his teeth, he recalled the two thick-necked

men in black sunshades who'd bumped him as he'd come out of the security checkpoint.

Panic surged through him. It was an overblown corollary that didn't match the circumstances. He could cancel the credit cards and wire home for money. He could call the police and report the theft. No need for alarm.

Except time was critical if he wanted to catch up with his grandfather.

And there was the niggling little voice in the back of his mind. The same voice that had been whispering negative messages to him ever since he was a kid trying to compete with Hunter for their parents' attention.

If you're not a Gentry, who are you?

Without his ID, he wasn't a Gentry. Without his driver's license he couldn't even drive his Bentley.

How was it Charlee had so eloquently expressed herself? Crap, crap, crap.

Somehow crap just didn't seem strong enough.

"Something the matter?" Charlee asked.

"My wallet," he said. "It's been stolen."

"Give me your car keys." Charlee held out her palm.

"What?" Mason stared at her as if she'd suggested sacrificing his firstborn child to Pele the volcano goddess. What in the devil was she yapping about?

"Give me your keys," she repeated and curled her fingers in a "gimme" gesture he would have found cute if he hadn't been so upset. "We'll have to take the Bentley."

"No."

"Look, we don't have a choice. My 'Vette's been towed."

"It was towed because you recklessly disregarded the passenger loading zone sign and, I might add, my advice not to park there."

"Oh, here we go." Charlee sank her hands on her hips. "Mr. Uptight-by-the-Rules is giving me a lecture. Go ahead, let me have it, get it out of your system."

She was looking to pick a fight, but he refused to give her one. This wasn't the time or the place. "Chastising you isn't part of my agenda. I'm more concerned about the loss of my wallet. If you'll excuse me, I'm going to make a phone call to the authorities."

"Well, while you're calling the cops, I'm going after our grandparents before Elwood does something truly stupid. Hand over your car keys and I'll be on my way."

"You're out of your ever-loving mind if you think I'm letting you take off across the desert alone in my Bentley."

"You really have a problem relinquishing control, you know that?"

"Me? You're saying *I'm* a control freak?" Incensed, Mason splayed a palm over his chest.

Easy, you know she's just gigging you because she's mad at herself.

"Do they drink tea in China?" She jerked her chin up, the look in her eyes challenging him.

"I'm the control freak? You're the one who refused to move your car simply because you didn't want to take my advice." Okay, so he couldn't keep his mouth shut about the damned car.

"That's sooo not the reason I didn't move the 'Vette. And just look at you." She waved a hand at him. "Your clothes are perfectly pressed. Not a hair out of place. Your friggin' shoes are even shined. Only a control freak is that put together at six o'clock in the morning."

"Or someone who happens to take pride in the impression he creates."

"Yeah, the impression of a control freak."

A plane took off overhead, drowning out his reply, which was probably a good thing. The woman could try the pope's patience.

"You can't even let the wallet go, can you?" he heard her say after the plane had cleared the airport. "Gotta run to the police."

"My driver's license is in there. And my credit cards. My triple A card. Not to mention eight hundred dollars in cash."

"It's gone, Mason. The cops won't be able to get it back for you. Be realistic. But you can't let anything go, can you?"

He gritted his teeth hard. Calm down. Breathe deep. "You don't understand."

"Control freak."

"Woman," he ground out and sent her a don't-mess-with-me warning, "you have a talent for pushing a man to the limits of his patience."

"I'm trying to get you to quit your yammering and get on the road before something serious happens to our grandparents. We're wasting precious time." Charlee tapped the face of her wristwatch.

"I'm not so convinced a crazed trip through the desert is the most prudent move. How do we know for sure that's where they're going?"

"We don't, but do you have a better idea?" She cocked her head and spread her arms wide. "I'm open to input."

He paused, then admitted, "I don't have any better ideas."

"Okay then, Slick. Let's hit the highway."

Thirty minutes and twenty-five desert miles later,
Charlee was seriously regretting goading Mason into the
road trip. He'd been on his cell phone to his secretary,
instructing her to report his credit cards stolen and wire
money to him in Tucson.

He had also talked briefly with his father but Charlee
noticed he didn't give many details about what had happened. He just told him that he had discovered Nolan
was on his way to Tucson and he was following him. He
never mentioned either Maybelline or herself.

It was strange listening to the one-sided conversation. She had the feeling Mason tiptoed around a lot of
hot button topics with his father. Like stolen wallets and
Elvis impersonator kidnappers and sassy lady private
investigators who didn't drive to suit him.

He had hated giving her the keys to his Bentley, but
when she suggested he go ahead and take the wheel
even though he didn't have his license, he had actually
lectured her from the highway safety manual.

She could tell by the way he had painstakingly pulled
the keys from his pocket he would much rather have a
tooth extracted without Novocain than let her behind the
wheel of his vintage vehicle. But apparently his sense of
right and wrong was so deeply engrained he couldn't
conceive of driving without a license.

Too bad for him. Nice for her. She got to pilot a
Bentley.

Ah, but at what cost.

"Slow down," Mason demanded, his face the color of
a yucca in full bloom as Charlee took a bump in the road
at seventy-five miles per hour. The Bentley glided

through the dip on marshmallow shock absorbers—smooth and sweet. "What's the speed limit through here?"

"Control freak."

"If you say that one more time . . ."

"You'll what?" she dared, surprised by the quick thrill of pleasure pulsing through her at his threat. "Take me over your knee and spank me?"

"Not that you couldn't use a good spanking." He glowered. "But I don't strike women."

"Not even if I like it?" She winked, both terrified and turned on by her naughty boldness. He was so damned stuffy, she couldn't help but try and shock him. Shocking this uptight blue blood, however, was a bit like dynamiting carp in a horse trough.

She was so busy teasing him, the right front tire left the road and strummed irritatingly across those wake-up-you-desert-hypnotized-ninny strips.

"Keep your eyes on the road," he yelled.

Startled, she jerked the steering wheel, ended up overcompensating and weaved slightly into the northbound lane. Luckily, there was no oncoming traffic.

"Shit!" Mason exclaimed and lunged for the wheel.

She jabbed him in the rib cage with her elbow before he could slap his hands on the steering wheel. "Back off, I'm driving."

"Oww." He rubbed his ribs. "You're a lunatic. You know that?"

"Don't grab the wheel when someone else is driving."

"Where the hell did you get your driver's license? Britain?"

"That's a pretty good one actually. Maybe you do have a sense of humor."

"I wasn't trying to be funny. Stop the car."

"Don't get your knickers in a knot. Nobody was coming. And besides, I wouldn't have wandered into the other lane if you hadn't hollered at me."

"Stop the car."

"So what, now you're going to drive? I thought you couldn't drive without your license." Charlee peered over at him. She started to make another smart remark, but she saw the muscle in his jaw tick and realized just how angry he was.

"I do want to see my grandfather one last time before I die. I'll take my chances. Stop the car."

"Wooo. Now you're breaking the law."

"Hush, woman," he commanded.

His tone told her to back off if she didn't want to see a Texas aristocrat lose his temper. Trying hard not to grin, Charlee slowed the Bentley and pulled onto the shoulder. She cut the engine and scooted over to the passenger side when Mason got out.

She darted a look over her shoulder. He stalked purposefully around the car. A delicious little shiver, like a cat running up stair steps, scampered through her. What was it about the proud set of his shoulders, his determined ground eating stride, the way his hair tapered down the back of his neck that so tickled her fancy?

Mercy.

Knock it off, Charlee, unless you're looking to get hurt. Stop thinking about him. He's nothing but trouble with capital letters.

Fat lot of good that lecture accomplished.

Something about him—exactly what she couldn't

say—touched her in a way she'd never known. Her emotions were confused, muddled. She was sexually attracted to him, oh, yeah, but her feelings for him were more than just that. It was passion taken to a whole new level. The sensation burned inside her chest sharp and clean and bright. But she couldn't name the feeling, even if someone had offered a million tax-free bucks to do so.

The pulse at the hollow of her throat jumped and sweat popped out on her brow as a myriad of naughty fantasies flashed through her mind. She could almost feel his strong masculine hands on her body, his fingers tickling her tender flesh.

He slid behind the wheel and slammed the car door after him, breaking her from her illicit reverie. Charlee's hands shook so hard she had to sit on them.

She'd been too long without sex. That's all there was to it. She had to stop her flights of fantasy.

"You okay?" he asked gruffly. "You're looking a little weird."

"I do?"

"You're all red in the face." He arched an eyebrow. "Like someone caught watching a nudie peep show."

"Excuse me?"

Immediately, she went on the offensive. Maybelline had drilled into her head the best defense was a good offense and boy, was she ripe for defending herself before Handsome Dimples here discovered just how much power he wielded over her.

"Are you embarrassed about something?"

"This is the desert, in case you haven't noticed it's over a hundred degrees outside. That's why my face is red. No other reason. Now get the engine started and crank up the AC."

"Anything you want as long as I'm driving," he said, pulling back onto the road. He turned the air conditioner on high and then stuck a Charlotte Church CD into the CD player.

Eww. Ick.

She should have known he would have highbrow taste in music when what she wanted to hear was something loud with a strong, throbbing beat. On second thought, perhaps Charlotte was the better choice. Nobody could have sexual daydreams with that glass-shattering noise.

Sighing, Charlee forced herself not to notice what an exceptionally fine profile Mason presented and instead directed her gaze out the window at the arid roll of landscape stretching out before them.

It was going to be a very long trip.

Just then Charlee caught the reflection of a white Chevy Malibu in the side-view mirror. They were the only two cars on the road for as far as the eye could see.

Something in the back of her brain niggled.

For the third time in the last twenty-four hours she'd spotted a four-door white Chevy Malibu. The car was a common enough make and maybe she was jumping to conclusions, but the first time she'd noticed a white sedan had been outside Maybelline's trailer after it had been ransacked. The second time had been at the apartment fire. Coincidence?

She didn't think so.

While Miss Church trilled her earsplitting soprano, Charlee kept an eye on the sedan. It stayed a good ten car lengths behind them.

"Speed up," she told Mason.

"I'm already doing seventy."

"Just speed up."

"Why?"

"Do you have to be a privileged pain in the ass about everything?"

"I don't want to get pulled over. Lest you forget I have no driver's license."

Charlee sighed. "Remember when we were in Maybelline's trailer and I told you to duck and you wouldn't listen to me?"

"Yes."

"Well then, speed up."

"Are you saying there's a mad gunman after us?"

"Maybe."

Mason sped up.

Charlee squinted into the side-view mirror.

The Malibu sped up too.

"Slow down."

"What?"

"Please don't make me repeat myself."

Thankfully, he didn't argue, but slowed the Bentley.

The Malibu decelerated.

Charlee sucked in her breath. No doubt about it.

They were being followed.

♥ ♥ ♥

CHAPTER
6

I still can't believe your son kidnapped us." Nolan shook his head and for the hundredth time tested the ropes binding his hands behind his back.

He and Maybelline were locked in the back of a rented camper together and without the benefit of air-conditioning. A swelter of sweat dampened the back of his shirt and his arthritis nagged at him to shift positions.

The camper's side windows were wide open but the blast of desert air was anything but cooling. Maybelline's kid was a jerk, but considering who his daddy was Nolan wasn't too surprised.

"I should have left him on his father's doorstep when I had the chance," Maybelline grumbled.

"You were too good of a mama, you couldn't have abandoned him."

"Good mama. Ha! That's awfully sweet of you to try and make me feel better, but if I were a good mama would my son be such an asshole?"

"You raised your granddaughter and from what you tell me she's turned out great," Nolan soothed.

"I raised her because my no-account son wouldn't do his duty." Maybelline paused. "Charlee is the best thing in my life, but I worry I did her a huge disservice. Moving around like I did. We never stayed in one place longer than a year or two."

"Why's that?"

"After growing up in Red Bay, Texas, you've got to ask me that question? I didn't want any small-minded, small-town attitude painting Charlee with the same brush I got painted with. Every place was a new start, a grand new adventure. And she never complained."

"But?"

Maybelline shrugged. "She has trouble making friends. I mean she has a lot of acquaintances, people she can hang out with, but nobody she tells her secrets to. She never learned how to get close to people. I figure that's all my doing. I wanted her to be free to choose her own life, not be defined by what others thought of her. I taught her to be tough, to stand on her own two feet and not depend on anyone. Well, she's free and independent all right, but I worry she'll never be able to trust a man enough to let him love her."

"Hmm, strong, brave, independent, and knows her own mind. Charlee sounds a lot like someone else I know," Nolan said.

"I don't want her to end up like me."

"What's wrong with the way you ended up?"

Maybelline didn't meet his eyes. "It's a lonely way to live."

Her pain cut him to the quick. For the last forty-seven years, while he'd been surrounded by his loving family,

Maybelline had been out in the world struggling to raise first her son and then her granddaughter alone.

"I'm sorry about Elwood," he said, not even beginning to know how to apologize to her for the loneliness she'd suffered. He felt guilty somehow that she'd never found anyone to love. "We can't be held responsible for what our grown kids do, Maybelline."

"Try telling Elwood that. He blames me for everything gone wrong in his life."

Nolan thought of his own son and winced. Reed was bound to blame him for the mess he'd gotten the family business into and with good reason. He was to blame.

"What's with the Elvis costume?" Nolan asked, changing the subject. "You'd think Elwood would want to be as inconspicuous as possible. Seeing as how he's committing a felony."

Maybelline snorted. "Obviously you don't know my son. He craves attention. Got a big dose of his daddy's theatrical blood in him. Wears that damned white jumpsuit everywhere he goes. Sometimes I think he imagines he really *is* Elvis."

"What do you think he's planning on doing with us?"

"I don't know. I never could decipher what went on in that boy's head." Maybelline sighed.

"Don't worry, I'll get us out of this mess and without hurting your son."

She eyed him skeptically. "Nolan, you can stop being so protective. I'm not that pregnant sixteen-year-old you took under your wing."

"Even back then it took an act of Congress to get you to let me help you."

"I've been fighting my own battles for a long time and the last thing this old bird needs is for some man to start blowing smoke up her dress. I'm a realist. Elwood is not the brightest bulb in the package and the odds of something getting screwed up in his little kidnapping scheme are pretty high. In fact, I've been sitting here composing my obituary."

"Still bracing yourself for the worst." Nolan looked her squarely in the eyes.

Maybelline notched her chin up in that stubbornly defiant way of hers. Lord, she was a fighter, in spite of her silly speech about writing her obit. "I didn't get life handed to me on a silver platter. The school of hard knocks kinda takes the rosy shine off positive thinking."

"No need to snap at me because you're feeling guilty," Nolan said, reading her like a road map. "What Elwood is doing is not your fault. Everything is going to work out fine. You'll see."

"Your cockeyed optimism is treading on my last nerve," she groused.

"I know." He grinned. "And you love me for it."

"You've gotten kinda egotistical in your old age, Nolan Gentry."

"You think so?"

"Maybe not. Maybe you were always egotistical and I just forgot."

The camper hit a bump and bounced Maybelline against his shoulder. The contact was comforting. He wished his hands were free so he could wrap an arm around her.

"The boy drives like a maniac," she said, but didn't try to inch away.

Nolan liked having her next to him, even if their combined body heat raised the already miserable temperature in the camper. He wondered if she liked the closeness too.

"Where do you think he's taking us?"

"I've been racking my brain over that question for the last hundred miles trying to second-guess him and can't come up with an answer. I just hope it's not Mexico. He's got a fascination with Mexico."

"What I don't understand is why he won't give us the files, take his blackmail money, and go on his merry way."

"I think that's the rub. I think he's lying. I don't think he has all of the files. Just a few papers like the copies I gave to you. Not enough to prove anything in court."

"Sooner or later he's got to stop to let us out. We'll try to talk some sense into him then," Nolan said.

"Either that or we'll bash him over the head and take the camper," Maybelline said grimly.

"Woman, you are bloodthirsty." Nolan chuckled.

"If I'd whopped his britches when he was little maybe he wouldn't have turned out like he did."

"It's going to be all right. Have faith."

"Easy for you to say, old man. You've had lots of experience with things turning out the way you want them to turn out."

"Well, you're with me now, Maybelline, so you better get used to things turning out right for you too."

She made a derisive noise but he saw a flicker of hope in her eyes. "I'll believe it when I see it."

Mason felt edgy in a way he couldn't define. Tension knotted the muscles across his back so tight they ached. Every time he glanced in the rearview mirror and saw the Malibu, an angry testiness soured his gut.

Who were the people following them and what in the hell did they want? Out here on this lone stretch of highway he and Charlee were incredibly vulnerable. What if the white Chevy tried to run them off the road? Then what? His knowledge of tae kwon do was no match for two men with a gun. Too bad Charlee had left her weapon in the Corvette.

Whatever happened, he would fight to the death to keep her safe.

"We're going to have to ditch the Bentley in Phoenix," Charlee said.

"What?"

"We'll never be able to elude our *compadres* back there while we're driving this white elephant." She jerked a thumb over her shoulder and her braids bobbed provocatively from beneath her battered straw cowboy hat.

"Hey, no insulting Matilda."

"Hell, Gentry, we might as well be piloting a Goodyear blimp. There's no such thing as incognito in a vintage Bentley."

"We're not leaving the car."

He stubbornly clenched his jaw. His attitude might not be practical but Matilda was his prize possession and he wasn't about to abandon her. The car had been his ticket to freedom when he was sixteen, allowing him—if only briefly—to escape the high demands of his family. He would sneak off in Matilda during his parents' business parties when he was supposed to be currying political favors. But even more than that, Matilda represented the lurking wildness inside him that had all but disappeared after his best friend Kip was killed.

Matilda was the one solid thing that kept Kip alive for him. They'd shared their first beer together, sitting on Matilda's hood in his parents' garage, listening to Nirvana and talking about girls. They'd cruised the local strip, listening to Boyz II Men and trying to pick up girls. They'd parked by the lake, listening to UB40 and trying to get to second base with the girls they'd picked up.

He wondered what Kip would think of Charlee and he knew immediately they would have been rivals for her affections. Kip had always gone for the sassy ones.

At the memory of his buddy, a lump tightened his throat. It had been almost ten years since the accident but the loss still gnawed at him with a painful sting.

He would never stop feeling responsible. He had never stopped trying to make amends by staying on the straight and narrow and doing exactly what his family expected of him. It was the least he could do to pay for his gravest mistake.

Yeah, but Kip wouldn't hold you responsible and you know it. He would be mad because you've stopped doing what you loved.

Unable to handle the thoughts of how he'd failed his friend, Mason stiffened his upper lip and stared straight ahead.

"I know a woman in Phoenix. We can leave the Bentley with her and borrow her Neon," she persisted.

"Over my dead body," Mason growled. He knew it was prideful of him to be so mulish. Vain even. But he didn't care. Charlee would just have to deal with it.

"Don't tempt me." She looked completely serious with her dark eyebrows drawn into a V and her lush full lips pursed.

"I'm getting the distinct impression you're frustrated with me," he said.

"You pick up on that all by yourself?" She glared.

"I don't understand why you're so upset."

"For one thing, I'm worried about my grandmother and you're putt-putting along at sixty miles an hour. We'll never catch up to the camper at this rate."

"How serious can it be? They *are* with your father."

"Which is precisely what I'm worried about. You don't understand. My father is both unpredictable and easily influenced by others."

"All right," Mason conceded. "I'll drive faster." He sped up to sixty-five.

Charlee groaned and rolled her eyes.

"What now?"

"You drive like a little old lady on Zoloft. Hands at ten and two o'clock, eyes straight ahead. I swear, Gentry, you're old before your time."

"I drive by the rules of the road."

"You live your entire life by someone else's rules, is what you do," she mumbled.

"What?" He cocked his head. "I didn't quite catch what you said."

"Nothing."

"You muttered something. Let's hear it."

Charlee folded her arms over her chest. "I said, lest you forget, we're being followed."

"That's not what you said."

"Pretend it is."

He knew exactly what she'd said and she was right. He was a law-abiding man. Where would society be if everyone threw the rules of civilized behavior out the window? Charlee probably went for those swaggering bad boy types who broke the law and broke her heart with equal ease.

"So let them follow us."

"Need I remind you my grandmother's trailer was ransacked, we were shot at, and someone torched my father's apartment complex?"

"Your father did that."

"No he didn't."

"Whatever you say."

"What does that mean?"

"I'm tired of arguing with you." The woman could wear a professional filibuster into the ground.

"Oh, no, no, no." She shook a finger. "You don't believe me and simply saying you do doesn't change your mind. You can't just give in because you don't want to argue."

"Yes I can. See, I'm shutting up. No more arguing with you."

Gleefully, Charlee found the chink in his logic. "Good, then let's ditch the Bentley."

"No."

"Thought you weren't going to argue."

"Sit back and hush."

He wondered if he was going to have to kiss her in order to shut her up. Why was kissing her such an appealing idea?

This had to stop. He was almost engaged.

Think of Daphne.

Determined, he tried to call up Daphne's image and his mind went blank. He struggled to summon her scent but instead of the floral aroma of Daphne's expensive perfume, he could only smell Charlee's fresh soap scent. Instead of mentally seeing Daphne's sleekly coiffed

blond hair, he saw long, jet-black tresses twisted in beguiling braids. Instead of hearing Daphne's dulcet ac-
quiescence, his ears vibrated with the sound of
Charlee's deep, throaty-voiced firmly held opinions.

Something about Charlee called to that wildness inside of him he'd buried along with Kip. The wildness
that scared him because he knew what trouble it could
cause. The wildness he missed and feared with equal intensity.

Why did she stir him so? Not just physically. That
was easy. The woman was a looker with a body that
wouldn't quit. No, there was an energy about her, a
power that compelled him on a level he could not explain.

She moved him in ways far beyond his experience.
Her courage sparked a corresponding bravery inside
him. Her audacity dared him to rise to the challenge.
Her toughness engendered his strength.

Charlee was a force of nature that had blown into his
life and altered everything.

His stomach lurched but he convinced himself it was
because he hadn't eaten breakfast. They drove for several miles in dead silence. Eventually they approached
the outskirts of Phoenix. Mason struggled not to glance
over at Charlee again, but no matter how hard he tried
he could not seem to deny the unsettling awareness ra-
diating between them.

Was this what people meant by chemistry?

In spite of his best intentions to the contrary, he
found his gaze veering from the highway stripes to the
woman at his side. She was gnawing on a thumbnail and
when she realized he was watching her, she jerked her
hand from her mouth and dropped it into her lap.

"Nervous?"

"Who me? What have I got to be nervous about?"

"The Chevy Malibu."

"Oh, yeah. That." Charlee checked the rearview mirror.

"Are they still behind us?"

"I don't see them, but I know they're back there."

"Maybe we can lose them in the Phoenix traffic."

She nodded. His gaze traveled from her face, down the curve of her neck to the skin exposed beneath the opening of her collar. He moistened his lips, mesmerized by the swell of her breasts and the way they moved when she breathed.

Heaven help him, he was ogling her. Mason jerked his gaze back to the road.

"Get an eyeful?" she asked tartly.

The woman didn't miss a trick. When was he going to realize Charlee was sharp as a suture needle and twice as prickly?

"I apologize. I shouldn't have stared at you."

"Damn skippee. I'm not some amusement park ride for the slumming rich boy."

"I don't think of you in that way," he protested, flustered because he'd been caught visually undressing her like some horny fifteen-year-old.

Charlee pushed the brim of her hat up with one slender finger and peered down at her breasts as if trying to fathom the appeal. Surely the woman was aware of just how sexy she looked.

"You know," she said a few moments later. "After my mother died and Maybelline took me in, she bought us a travel trailer. She showed me the kind of life skills they don't teach you in school."

"Odd view on child rearing."

"She said she didn't want me to get in trouble the way she had when she was young. She worked odd jobs to support us. Mechanic, bartender, hotel maid, even drove a school bus. She took me with her everywhere she went." Charlee paused.

Mason contrasted her past with his childhood. His entire life spent in one place, raised by nannies and housekeepers, seeing his parents only on occasion as they flitted from party to party, from one business deal to the next, from Paris to Japan to Timbuktu.

"I remember one time, when I was, oh, about fourteen, Maybelline got hired as a housekeeper for a state senator in Utah. I developed early figure-wise and the old letch couldn't keep his paws to himself. One afternoon he cornered me in the kitchen pantry and stuck his hands up my blouse. He told me if I'd do him a few favors he'd pay me handsomely.

"I told him if he didn't get his grubby mitts off me I was going to send his balls up to visit his throat. I always wondered what made a man think he could manhandle his servants."

"Charlee," Mason said, feeling awful to the core, "I hope you don't think I'm that sort of man."

"Of course not." She grinned. "I was just pondering the power of boobs."

Disconcerted, he too pondered the power of boobs. Why did Charlee excite him in a way Daphne never had? And not just Daphne. None of his elegant, refined female counterparts had ever made him yearn to do something totally rash and reckless the way this pert private detective did.

A sense of longing swept over him, for something he'd never had. The freedom to follow his heart.

And if he married Daphne, he never would.

There was the rub.

He felt as if Charlee held the key to his freedom if only he was brave enough to reach out and take it.

Was he?

For one crazy, foolish second, he envisioned Charlee as his fiancée.

Mother would faint. Father would have a coronary. Hunter would gloat and say something like, "Way to make me look good."

If he was married to Charlee he'd be whispered about behind his back. His social contacts would dwindle, his business accounts would suffer. He had seen the phenomenon before when anyone in his circle married someone from the outside. Never mind that this was the new millennium. High society still operated on a class system.

Besides, why would he want to do something so cruel as to cage a bright, vibrant woman like Charlee in his claustrophobic, walk-on-eggshells-or-get-ostracized world? He would never be that selfish.

"So whatever happened with the senator?" he asked, changing lanes and passing a slow-moving tractor-trailer rig.

She studied him for a long while before replying. "The guy ended up paying me not to squeal on him to his wife and I gave the money to a women's shelter."

"Pretty resourceful for a fourteen-year-old."

"Told you, Maybelline was determined to give me a real life education and that she did."

"Maybe too much of an education. You grew up way too soon."

"Not soon enough. If I'd really been resourceful, I would have gone to the newspapers, created a scandal, got the sucker thrown out of office before he used his power to disgrace some other poor maid."

Mason looked at her. He thought of his own house-keepers and of the servants who had worked for his parents. He realized with a disturbing jolt he never considered them as anything more than his employees.

Sure, he paid well, did his best to treat them with compassion, but he'd never imagined what their lives were like when they weren't cleaning his house or taking care of his needs. Guilt needled him and he swore to himself when he got home he would take more of a personal interest in the people he employed.

"The Malibu's right behind us," Charlee said.

Mason swore under his breath. He'd forgotten about being followed.

"Slow down. Let them get closer."

"What for?"

"Just do it and don't give me any grief for once, okay?"

She'd been right on the previous occasions. Resisting the urge to ask for more details before embarking on her plan, Mason slowed the car.

"Get in the middle lane."

He turned on the blinker and moved over.

"Thank you," she replied tartly and stuck out her tongue at him.

"You're welcome." He fought the strange thrill darting through him at the sight of her glorious pink tongue.

Holy guacamole but her sauciness inflamed him.

"Slower." Her eyes were trained on the mirror, her body tensed, her muscles on alert.

"I'm practically crawling as it is."

"I want them right on our tails so when you radically veer off at the next exit ramp they won't have time to follow us."

"Oh." He checked the rearview mirror too and saw the Malibu was on his bumper.

"Here we go." Charlee inhaled audibly.

Up ahead Mason spotted the Los Angeles exit sign.

"Keep driving, keep driving."

"But I thought you said . . ."

"Wait, wait."

If he waited any longer it was going to be too late to make the exit ramp.

"Floor it, floor it, change lanes, go, go, go." She barked orders like a prison warden.

Dear Lord, there were a string of cars in the inside lane.

"Now!"

He couldn't do it. He couldn't drive erratically on purpose and risk their lives. What if they had a wreck? What if they hurt someone?

For one damn time in your life, don't overthink things. Just friggin' let go and do it.

Mason stomped the foot feed. Matilda leaped to the challenge. She shot forward like a torpedo. He swerved across the white line, barreling straight for the exit ramp.

Holy crap, we're going to die.

He braced himself for an impact and prayed Matilda could handle whatever came her way.

Car brakes squealed. Horns blared. The smell of

burning rubber spewed into the air. The brash flavor of raw adrenaline flooded his mouth as they sped pell-mell up the overpass, leaving the Malibu stuck below them on the other freeway.

They were free.

"Yippee!" Charlee hollered and raised a palm. "We lost them. High-five me."

Mason had never high-fived anyone in his privileged life, but he didn't hesitate for a second to slap his palm against Charlee's. His heart pounded, his gut turned upside down, but damn, he was having fun.

Their skin contacted with a solid splat.

And ripples of awareness blasted through his hand and up his arm.

He met her gaze. Her eyes rounded with surprise and he knew she felt it too. This surge, this splurge, this pure spill of thrill.

Ah, hell, this wasn't good.

Not good at all.

CHAPTER

7

I'm not falling for him, Charlee argued with herself as she propelled the Bentley toward Tucson. *I'm not.*

Liar, liar, panties on fire.

She'd only known the guy twenty-four hours. She couldn't be falling for him.

Maybe not, but every single time he leveled his brown eyes and cocked his dimples at her, she broke out in a cold sweat.

Ah, jeeze. She was screwed.

I won't fall for him. I won't, I won't, I won't. I don't care how cute and brown-eyed and long-legged the man is.

She had to keep her guard up and her tongue sharp if she hoped to survive this jaunt through the desert with her dignity intact. So what if he thought she was a bitch. It was better than getting her heart broken. Again.

Moistening her lips, Charlee inched her Ray Bans down on her nose with an index finger and sneaked a quick peek over at him.

Mason was leaning back in the plush leather seat, his long legs folded at an uncomfortable-looking angle. She found herself tracing a path from his expensive leather shoes up the length of his body to his broad chest. She caught her breath and flicked a look at his face.

Thank God his eyes were closed and he hadn't caught her giving him the once-over. His hands lay folded across his stomach and his chest rose and fell in a smooth, steady rhythm.

She studied his profile. Regal nose, solid jaw, high cheekbones. She felt kind of soupy inside, like she'd drunk too much water too quickly. She recalled when they'd high-fived each other and a fresh shiver of something nice mixed with something very scary tangoed through her.

After the great escape back there on the freeway, Mason had pulled over, taken the keys from the ignition, dropped them into her hand, and said, "Take over, Champagne. I'm not cut out for high-speed chase stuff."

Amazed, she simply accepted the keys and switched places with him again, but she couldn't help pondering his change of heart. After he'd successfully eluded the Malibu, he was downright triumphant. He'd grinned like a kid, his eyes feverish with the thrill.

He'd *enjoyed* it.

Perhaps, Charlee postulated, that's what bugged him. He didn't know how to cut loose and have a good time. Mr. Buttoned-down pops a button and doesn't know how to handle himself.

And don't be getting any wise ideas about becoming his teacher.

Oh, but wouldn't he make a glorious teacher's pet.

Stop it!

Her palms grew sweaty on the wheel and her heart reeled drunkenly against the wall of her chest. She was headed for deep trouble, entertaining such thoughts. She was not going to fall again. No way, no how. No, no, no.

Who was she kidding? It was all she could do not to pull the car over and jump his bones right here and now.

Damn her hide but she'd always been attracted to sophisticated men who were so far out of her league she couldn't reach them with a high bounce on a trampoline. She knew better than to tumble for another rich brown-eyed handsome man.

They were opposites in every way. He was the kind of guy who'd dip a toe in the water, testing the temperature before going for a swim. She dove right in and took what she got. He was a linen napkin kind of guy. She was paper towels. His life was planned, well ordered. Hers was chaos and she liked it that way.

Unfortunately, something about him whispered to the soft feminine side of her she'd stuffed down deep a long time ago. He made her feel smart and savvy and admirable. He respected her. That was a first from guys like him.

And he made her want things she had no business wanting.

Rather than think about the potent male beside her, Charlee jammed her sunglasses back into place and returned her focus to the road. White-hot heat poured from the cloudless blue sky and bounced a shimmer of radiant waves up from the asphalt. She studied the desert, the wide expanse of dry barren land most people eschewed but which an intrepid few embraced.

While some might find the desert a lonely, desolate place, she felt differently. The desert was alive with nature. You just had to know where to look for it. To Charlee the desert was home. What made her feel lonely and desolate was not water-starved land but the emptiness gnawing at her when she was in a roomful of people.

She imagined Mason's busy life was jam-packed with people. His parents, his brother, his grandfather, his friends. His business partners, his colleagues, and high-society debs. He hailed from a foreign place where she did not belong and could never fit.

Shaking her head, she forced herself to think about something else and speculated on the men in the Malibu. Who were they and why had they been following them? She tried to tie everything together — their grandparents, the half mil Mason's grandfather embezzled, her father, the men in the Malibu, Maybelline's ransacked trailer, the bullet through the trailer, Elwood's apartment fire, but no matter how hard she tried, Charlee couldn't paste together the link. Too many pieces of the puzzle were missing.

What concerned her right now was their destination. Were they on a wild-goose chase? Since Mason had turned the keys over to her, she'd driven a steady eighty-five miles an hour hoping against hope to spot the red and white camper.

Maybe Elwood and their grandparents weren't on this road, she fretted. What then? They might not even be in Arizona.

Charlee nibbled her bottom lip. Up ahead she spied a small crossroads with a gas station and a convenience store. Noticing the gas gauge had slipped to almost a quarter of a tank, she pulled over.

Mason didn't wake up when she stopped. Poor guy

must be exhausted. She filled up the tank, and then sauntered into the convenience store. She grabbed a couple of packages of Twinkies and snagged a six-pack of iced Pepsis from a barrel next to the checkout counter.

"Hey," Charlee asked the pimply-faced clerk as he rang up her purchases. It was a long shot, but what the hell? "By any chance has a red and white camper stopped by here in the last few hours?"

"Some guy in an Elvis suit at the wheel?"

"Yeah." Charlee arched her eyebrows in surprise. "You saw him?"

"Who could miss him?" The clerk shrugged. "He paid for his gas with quarter rolls."

"About how long?"

The clerk scratched his goateed chin. "Maybe three, four hours ago."

"Hey, thanks. Keep the change." Charlee gathered up her drinks and Twinkies and started for the door.

"He didn't get back on the road to Tucson though," the clerk said, stopping her in mid-exit.

"No?"

He shook his head. "Nope. Took the back road up to the old movie studio lot."

"What movie studio lot?" Charlee frowned.

"They used to make westerns there in the forties and fifties. My grandmother claims John Wayne was once a regular around these parts. He even autographed the back of a movie ticket for her. *Rio Lobo* I think it was."

"No kidding?"

"Studio lot is closed down now. Abandoned. Boarded up. Except local kids go up there sometimes to drink, smoke weed, and get laid. Don't know why the Elvis guy went up that way. Road dead-ends in the studio lot. Nothing else up there but rattlesnakes and tumbleweeds."

When Charlee got back to the car, Mason was awake. She climbed in and tossed him a Twinkie.

"What's this?" He held the cellophane wrapper gingerly between his index finger and thumb as if it would jump up and bite him.

"Thought you might be hungry." She ripped into her own Twinkie and sank her teeth into the sponge cake. "Yummm."

"These things are filled with preservatives and bleached white flour."

"So?"

"They are not part of a healthy diet."

"Oh, my, call the food police."

"Go ahead, make fun."

"Jeeze, Gentry, lighten up. One Twinkie isn't going to kill you."

"I think I'll pass." He sat the snack cake on the console between them.

"Okay fine. I'll eat it."

He narrowed his eyes. "How in the hell do you stay so slender eating junk?"

Charlee brushed cream filling off her chin with the back of her hand and grinned. "Lucky I guess. I'm blessed with a high metabolism."

"I need real food," he grumbled.

"Well, Joe's Stop and Sack isn't the place for five star cuisine, sorry. It's Twinkies or nothing until we hit Tucson. Unless you want me to go back in and get you a bag of pork skins."

"No thanks. I can wait."

"Suit yourself." She spun the Bentley out of the parking lot and took off down the narrow dirt road a few yards to the right of the store, a rooster tail of red dust kicking up beneath the tires.

"Hey." Mason sat up straighter. "Where are we going?"

She told him what she had found out from the clerk.

"Why would your father whisk our grandparents away to an abandoned movie set?" He scowled.

"I've been thinking about that."

"Come up with anything?"

"Well . . ." Her suspicions weren't pretty and she didn't want to alarm Mason but he had a right to know. "I'm thinking he might be holding them for ransom."

"You're kidding?"

"It crossed my mind. He's kidnapped before."

"What!"

"Settle down. It's not as bad as it sounds. He snatched a Vegas headliner's Yorkie. The little dog was vicious, chewed his fingers up. He had to go to the emergency room and of course that's when he got caught. The Yorkie's owner dropped the charges for old times' sake because she and Elwood used to be lovers way back when, so he never did any time or anything."

"Why didn't you tell me before?"

"I didn't want you to bust a gut. Like you are now. Besides, it was just a dog. Not a person."

"Well, it looks like he's made the jump from kidnapping canines to holding humans hostage."

"Don't worry. Elwood's not violent or anything. He won't hurt them."

"How can you say that? My grandfather's life is at stake!" Mason hollered.

"So is my grandmother's and you didn't hear me raising my voice or the veins on my forehead getting purply and popping out."

"For all I know"—Mason glowered—"you and your grandmother are in on the scheme. Nothing but bad things have happened to me ever since I met you."

"I resent that. You're the one who turned my life topsy-turvy. I was perfectly happy sitting in *my* office minding my own business until *you* strutted into my life."

He paused. "All right. I was out of line with that last comment. I really don't believe you and your grandmother are in on it."

"Thank you."

She really did like the way he could admit when he was wrong. Most of the men of her acquaintance were busy trying to find someone else—usually her—to blame for their unhappy circumstances.

Mason reached over and lightly touched her arm. "I can get rather aggressive if I think my family is in danger."

Yeow! His touch sent a brush fire of emotions sweeping through her body. Desire, excitement, restlessness, and fear. Yep. Mostly fear.

"Mmmm," she mumbled, unable to speak past the lump of terror in her throat. He was touching her again and she was feeling way too susceptible.

Whatever you do, Charlee Desiree Champagne, do not make eye contact with those dreamy brown peepers of his. Don't you dare.

She wished he would take his hand away but he kept touching her. She felt that sudden, wild, almost irrepressible urge again to pull the car over, fling herself into his arms, and kiss him like there was no tomorrow.

It had been a very long time since she'd been with a man. His touch made her desperate to feel something hot and wild and womanly. She'd been hiding her femininity under her boots and jeans and cowboy hat for quite some time and her hormones were rebelling.

She batted his hand away roughly.

"You're mad at me."

"I'm not."

"You are. I can tell by the way you shoved me away."

"I'm not mad. Your hand was just hot. This car is hot." She fiddled with the air-conditioner vents. "Are you sure this heap has freon?"

"Charlee," he said, his voice sounding extra deep and throaty. "Would you look at me, please?"

No! No!

"I apologize if I offended you in any way."

"I accept your apology," she whispered. "Okay?"

"I can't believe you until I can see your eyes."

"Look, Gentry," she snapped as panic surged through her. "I'm driving here. I'm not in any mood to gaze into your eyes."

"All right."

Thank God. Charlee sighed in relief as he let the issue go.

She gripped the steering wheel so hard her fingers cramped. Flexing first one hand and then the other, she realized they had driven almost thirteen miles with nothing in sight but cactus and rocks and a Gila monster or two.

"Are you sure the clerk wasn't pulling your leg?" Mason asked.

"Maybe it's on the other side of the mesa."

"How far are you going to drive before you admit defeat?"

Charlee hardened her jaw. "I never admit defeat."

"Never?"

"Ever."

"Determination is an admirable quality, Charlee, but sometimes you gotta cut your . . ." Mason's voice trailed off as they rounded the mesa and the road dead-ended at a padlocked iron gate.

They spotted a weathered, barely readable sign proclaiming: TWILIGHT STUDIOS. Then below it, a smaller, newer sign printed in thick block letters. PRIVATE PROPERTY, KEEP OUT. TRESPASSERS WILL BE PROSECUTED.

They looked at each other.

Twilight Studios. The same movie studio Nolan and Maybelline had once worked for.

Happenstance?

Charlee didn't think so. But what was the bond? Why had Elwood brought them here?

A high wooden fence divided the studio lot, but time and the desert had eroded the once stately planks into slumping, thin gray posts staggering across the red dirt like teeth sliding forward in an aging mouth. Several boards were missing from one area and a narrow trail told the story. Someone or something entered frequently through the opening.

Charlee parked the Bentley beside the fence.

"If your father brought our grandparents here, then where is the camper?"

"Inside the studio lot?"

"How did they get in? The padlock is rusted shut."

"Maybe Elwood knew another way in."

"What now?" Mason asked.

"We go in."

"The sign says no trespassing."

She stared at him. "What planet are you from?"

"Are we going in on foot?"

"Unless you've been holding out on me and you've got a magic carpet in your back pocket, yes, we're going to trespass on foot." Charlee opened the car door.

"But I'm wearing loafers and I left my sunscreen back at the hotel."

"That's why I have on cowboy boots and a hat," she replied tartly.

"Oh, yeah?" he retorted. "I thought it was because you wanted to look tough."

"That too," she confessed. "Come on." She was halfway to the hole in the fence before he even got out of the car.

He shut the door, shaded his brow with his hand, and looked around. "Do you think the Bentley will be safe parked here?"

"I don't think any gangbangers will be stealing your mag wheels if that's what you're asking."

"No, it's just if anything were to happen we'd be stranded."

"What about your cell phone?"

"That's assuming I can pick up a tower."

"You're unnaturally attached to your car, you know that, don't you?"

"Yes," he grumbled. "I'm aware I place too much value on a car. Can we get on with this, please?"

"Oooh, hit a touchy spot."

"Do you want me to bring up your towed Corvette?"

She raised her palms. "I surrender. No more cracks about the car."

"Thank you. I appreciate that."

Charlee led the way through the fence and into the lot. They walked side by side into the false facade of an Old West town. The first building they came to was an aged saloon with the obligatory hitching post, as dusty and weather-beaten as a real saloon might have been a hundred and twenty years before. The sheriff's office came complete with tumbleweeds and had the window-panes knocked out while the nearby livery stable hosted a rusted anvil and bent horseshoes. The town ended at the dry goods store with barrels of fake food sitting out front.

"I think I've seen this set in an old western or two," Charlee mused. "Ever see *Shane*?"

"Twilight didn't produce *Shane*."

"They could have used the set."

"Don't think so. According to Gramps, back in those days the studios were pretty territorial. They practically owned the actors."

"Yeah, Maybelline mentioned something like that."

The sun lasered down. Sweat collected along Charlee's collar and a vague uneasiness settled in her belly. The place was dead quiet. Not even the scratch of a scurrying lizard. The eerie theme song from *The Good, the Bad and the Ugly* drifted through her head.

"No one's here," Mason said.

A dread of dizziness washed over Charlee. Something wasn't right. If Elwood brought their grandparents here, then where were they? What if her father had crossed the line from small-time-get-rich-quick schemer to big-time felon?

She simply couldn't believe that. Regardless of his numerous faults, her father, no matter how much trouble he was in, would never hurt his own mother.

But what if there were other people involved? Don't forget the goons in the white Chevy. She didn't know if they had anything to do with Elwood kidnapping Nolan and Maybelline or if they had been following the Bentley for some other reason.

What if the Malibu goons were debt collectors and they'd been tracking her in order to get to Elwood? The possibility was a very real one. It wouldn't be the first time her father had owed money to the wrong people. Once, he'd even ended up in the hospital following a debt-related beating. Her uneasiness grew.

Elwood was here. He had to be. They needed to keep looking. She took off down movie-land street.

"Where are you going?" Mason asked.

"Every good western has a farmer's barn. It's gotta be around here somewhere."

They found the barn squatting at the end of the lot next to the facade of a farm house. The barn was for real, however, and the donkey's bray that broke the silence was just as authentic.

Charlee jerked her head around in time to see someone disappearing around the corner of the barn.

Without dithering, she went in hot pursuit.

She could hear Mason's footsteps pounding close behind her. She rounded the barn in time to see a man desperately trying to scale the mesa. She tackled him at a dead run and knocked him to the ground. That's when Charlee realized the guy was at least sixty and wearing ratty gold prospector clothes.

"Please don't hurt me, sister," the old man panted. "I

swear I don't know nothing about these weird goings-on."

Mason, Charlee, and the old prospector, whose name turned out to be, oddly enough, Waylon Jennings, sat on moldy hay in the barn out of the direct heat of the relentless sun, sharing the Pepsis Charlee had bought at the convenience store.

"Yep," Waylon said, "I thought I was seeing things when Elvis Presley got out of the camper. Seein' mirages are pretty common when you spend a lot of time alone in the desert but I couldn't figure out why in the hell I'd be having a vision about the King. I never cared much for his music and as for his movies, well they flat stank. 'Cept I kinda liked *King Creole*."

"Forget the movie criticisms," Mason interjected. "What happened?"

Waylon shot him the evil eye, then spit a stream of chewing tobacco juice at his shoes. Mason jumped aside and the old prospector turned his attention back to Charlee. "When Elvis pulls an older couple out of the back of his camper and I see he's got them tied up I start thinking maybe it's for real and I'm not imagining things, so me and Jackass—that's my donkey—come down off the mesa for a closer look."

Mason watched Charlee's face as she studied the old man. The woman was intensely focused. He could actually see her listening. He realized she was probably a very good private investigator.

Somewhere along the way, however, his attention shifted from respecting Charlee's interrogation skills to admiring the way her faded jeans curved tight over her perfect butt.

Maybe it was the desert heat, maybe it was lack of sleep and food, maybe it was sheer desire, but without warning, Mason was lost in a very sexy vision of his own and it startled him. He wasn't driven by sexual impulse. At least not usually. But something about tough, irreverent Charlee Champagne tapped into his baser instincts and made him want to throw back his head and howl with lust like a lonesome desert wolf.

What in the hell was the matter with him? Why, after twenty-seven years, had his libido chosen this particular moment to go haywire?

But even more disturbing than his physical desire for her were the other, more subtle feelings she roused in him. Affection. Tenderness. Happiness.

Dear God, he realized with a jolt. He was happier when he was around her. Happier than he'd been in years. Even when they argued, even when things went haywire, even when she was so stubborn he wanted to wring her sweet neck, he was happy.

Stunned, he could only gaze at her in wonderment. Surely he was mistaken. It had to be something else.

"Pepsi tastes real good," Waylon said. "Ain't had a soda pop in close to five years. The stuff costs too much."

"The older couple," Charlee gently nudged him back on topic. "And Elvis?"

"Oh, yeah. Where was I?"

"Elvis took them out of the camper."

"Yeah and the lady was saying he better untie them or he'd be sorry and you could tell Elvis wasn't about to untie her 'cause she looked like she was going to put her foot to his backside real hard. Feisty she was."

Mason wanted to yell at the old man to "get on with

it" even though he wasn't in the mood to dodge more tobacco juice. In his normal life, he was a take-charge guy, accustomed to maintaining a tight rein over both his job and his body, but out here, tempted by Charlee's unexpected appeal, away from the defining manners and mores of his world, he was clearly a guppy on parched soil gasping for oxygen and he hated feeling out of control.

But Charlee was running the show and she merely nodded patiently at Waylon. "Go on."

"The lady and Elvis got into a shouting match and when Elvis wasn't looking, the older man got loose from his ropes, sneaked up on him, and cracked Elvis on the head with one of those big Igloo thermoses from the back of the camper. Elvis went down like a sack of sand."

Way to go, Gramps! Mason mentally cheered.

Charlee winced. "That must have hurt. What then?"

"Well, sir, I mean, ma'am . . . the older man untied the woman and then they hopped into the camper. They spotted me as they were driving off and they stopped and asked me if I needed a ride. Said they was on their way to L.A. Hell, I ain't got any use for that city. Left there in nineteen and eight-one when my ex-wife kicked me out and I ain't regretted it for a second. I told that nice couple thanks, but no thanks."

"What happened with Elvis?" she asked.

"Well, not long after the couple left, Elvis came to, got on his cell phone, and called somebody. I guess it was about an hour later, though it might have been longer, this black limousine pulls up and guess who gets out?"

"Who?"

"Go on, guess."

Charlee shrugged. "I don't know."

"Take a guess."

"Marilyn Monroe," Mason spouted and got to his feet.

Waylon frowned at him. "Don't be dense. Marilyn Monroe is dead."

"So is Elvis."

Waylon needed a minute to process that before resuming his dialogue. "Anyway, one of them old-time western movie stars gets out of the limo. I can't remember his name but I know his face."

"John Wayne?"

Charlee glared at Mason. What was she getting testy about? She was the one who had sacked the old guy and now she was acting like they were best buds. "Don't pay him any mind. He's from a big city and doesn't know any better."

"No, not John Wayne," Waylon said, a waspish note in his voice. "You think I don't know the Duke?"

"Okay, if it wasn't John Wayne, who was it then?" Mason asked.

The old coot had spent way too many years baking his brains in the Arizona sun searching for some nonexistent gold mine. He didn't know if they could trust a single word the guy said.

Waylon snapped his grizzled fingers three times, trying to jog his memory. "He was in that movie with Walter Brennan. He played a gunslinger."

"Oh, that narrows it down," Mason said.

Charlee speared him with a do-you-mind expression. Actually, he did mind. He was hungry and hot and horny beyond all common sense. He needed a meal, a bath, and a bed. But mostly, he needed to find his grandfather and get the hell back home where he belonged before he did something irrevocably stupid like have crazed monkey sex with Charlee and ruin his family's best-laid plans for his future.

"It's okay, Waylon," she said. "You don't have to remember the guy's name. It's not important."

"Give me a minute, I know I can think of it."

"Let's just say some famous movie star showed up in a limousine to pick up Elvis and then they drove away together. Is that how it happened?"

Waylon nodded his shaggy, unwashed head. "Yep. That's it exactly."

"You know." Mason glanced at his watch and tapped his foot impatiently. "Now we know our grandparents have eluded Elwood and are on their way to L.A., we should get back on the road. Let's roll."

Forward motion. He had to regain control. Move things along. He'd allowed Charlee free rein but now it was time he took charge. If he didn't . . . Helplessly, Mason found his gaze drawn back to Charlee's curvy rump.

Forget distractions. He had a goal. Find Gramps. Nothing else mattered.

Determined, Mason started for the car without even waiting to see if Charlee was going to follow.

Nowhere Junction Next Exit. Last Chance for Food And Gas Next One Hundred Miles.

Nowhere Junction. Now that was truth in advertising. Mason figured the only place more isolated than here was the dead center of Antarctica.

"We gotta stop," Charlee said as she blew past the sign at a good ninety miles an hour. "My stomach is about to eat a hole through the bottom of my feet and my bladder's threatening to explode."

Mason gripped the armrest with both hands and clenched his teeth. He shouldn't have let her behind the wheel again after they left the abandoned movie studio lot, but she'd had the keys in her pocket and she'd simply slid into the driver's seat without asking if he wanted to drive. He was conflicted about that on so many levels.

On the one hand he did hate driving without a license. Breaking laws, even small ones, went against everything he stood for. On the other hand, she drove like a banshee with a firecracker clenched between her teeth. But when he'd outrun the Malibu, the capricious thrill blasting through him unnerved Mason so deeply he had insisted she drive.

He didn't like unplanned emotions. He was a cool, calculating guy, known in business for his unruffled aplomb. Faced with the evidence he could get just as embroiled in a car chase as some joyriding teenager had been a startling revelation to say the least. He thought he'd outgrown that irresponsible wildness after Kip's death.

But now, because of Charlee, he found himself longing for freedom. She made him want to break with tradition. She made him want to stand up to his folks and tell them he was tired of living the life they'd chiseled for him. Dammit, but she made him want to have fun.

"Ah hell," Mason muttered when he spotted the giant fiberglass hamburger perched atop a square little diner located next to a truck stop.

He was irritated with himself for his lack of self-control and annoyed with her for making him want to embrace that recklessness. His fickleness put him in a bad mood.

The pungent aroma of diesel fumes mixed with the smell of lard long past its prime filled the air. And all the vehicles in the parking lot were either pickup trucks or eighteen-wheelers.

"What?"

"This is the last food for one hundred miles? Deep-fried grease?"

"You were expecting maybe the Russian Tearoom?"

"I was hopeful to find something with fresh vegetables."

"This *is* the desert, Gentry." Charlee pulled into the parking lot.

"You can't park here."

"Why not?" She blinked at him.

"It's in the direct sun."

"Everything in Arizona is in the direct sun."

"Park under the shade cast by that giant hamburger." He pointed.

"Sheesh, Gentry, sometimes you can be a real pain in the butt. Anybody ever tell you that?" Charlee complained but backed up the Bentley and moved it under the shade of the hamburger.

Actually no one had ever spoken to him so frankly and he appreciated her for it. She deflated his ego with one prick of her sharp observations and unstuffed his stuffiness with her down-to-earth common sense. Mason unclenched his jaw. Maybe he was acting too persnickety. Lighten up.

"Thank you for moving the car," he said contritely.

Charlee seemed surprised by his apology. "You're welcome."

The wind gusted, sandblasting them with red Arizona topsoil as they got out of the car and entered the diner. Men in dusty jeans, boots, and cowboy hats sat on stainless-steel stools at the front counter. A fry cook in a dirty white apron doubling as a waiter leaned against the counter, a spatula gripped in one hammy hand. A country and western song twanged from the jukebox in the corner.

Every eye in the room turned to give them the once-over as the door closed behind them. The locals sent Charlee an appreciative stare, sizing her up as one of their own.

"I gotta go to the bathroom," she whispered, leaning

in so close he caught a whiff of her unique scent. "Be right back."

Charlee took off for the ladies' room. The men's gazes narrowed on Mason and classified him for what he was—rich, well heeled, and as out of place as Shaquille O'Neal at a midget wrestling match.

Ignoring them, he picked out a red plastic booth in front of the big picture window. He wanted to sit where he could keep an eye on Matilda. He noticed the men had spun around on their stools and were gawking at the Bentley.

A few minutes later Charlee returned and slid across from him, the chipped Formica tabletop sandwiched between them. She'd taken her braids down and her dark hair spread across her shoulders in a cascade of curls. She plunked her hat on the seat beside her.

He stared, dumbfounded. She was bewitchingly beautiful and he couldn't stop eyeballing her.

She flicked a long dark corkscrew of hair off her shoulder in a gesture so feminine he wondered if she was subconsciously flirting with him. He'd read somewhere when women were interested in a man they fiddled with their hair. Some kind of primal mating call.

"What?" She rubbed at her cheeks. "Have I got something on my face?"

"No, no." Mason forced himself to look away.

The fry cook wandered over and thrust two grease-stained menus at them. "What'll ya have to drink?"

"Coffee," Charlee said.

"Water. Lots of ice." Mason opened the menu.

The fry cook/waiter grunted and went after their beverages.

"Gotta have some java," Charlee confessed and suppressed a yawn. "I'm having trouble staying awake after not getting any sleep last night."

"Now you tell me. I should have driven."

She shrugged. "I like driving the Bentley." She consulted the menu. "I think I'm going to have the cheeseburger basket. What about you?"

Mason searched the list of options looking for anything remotely healthy, finally admitted defeat, followed suit and ordered the cheeseburger basket when the fry cook arrived to deliver their drinks.

Charlee stretched out her feet and her boots collided with his shin. "I'm sorry," she mumbled and jerked her legs away.

But the damage was done. The contact, even through the dual barrier of her boots and his pants leg, launched a rocket of desire straight through him.

Restlessly, she shook a package of Sweet 'n Low into her coffee. "So," she said after taking a long sip of what looked as if it could have passed for forty-weight motor oil. "Do you have any idea why our grandparents are going to L.A.?"

Mason shook his head. "No. Only thing I can think of is our family owns controlling interest in an accounting firm in Hollywood. But why Gramps would go there I have no idea. He's been retired for two years."

"That's the same accounting firm that's responsible for counting the Oscar votes."

"Yes. How did you know?"

Charlee gave him a smug smile. "I'm a private investigator, remember."

"You ran a profile on me."

She shrugged. "I had to make sure you were who you said you were. A girl's gotta protect herself."

Mason smiled. Smart and pretty. A deadly recipe. He was going to have to watch out for this one or end up regretting their trip through the desert.

And he never wanted to regret having known her.

"Okay," she said, resting her elbows on the table and propping her chin in her hands. "Let's suppose your grandfather *is* going to check on the accounting firm, although it's highly possible something completely unrelated is going on."

"Agreed."

"What does that have to do with my grandmother? I mean, why is she involved?"

"I don't know."

"We've assumed that they met each other years ago when they both worked at Twilight Studios. Then my father kidnaps them and takes them to an abandoned Twilight Studios movie lot. Doesn't that seem awfully coincidental to you?"

"You're saying there's a connection."

"Seems odd is all I'm saying."

He tended to agree, but for the life of him he couldn't figure out what Twilight Studios had to do with his grandfather embezzling half a million dollars from Gentry Enterprises and taking off to Vegas to meet Charlee's grandmother without a word to anyone. It was totally out of character for Nolan. Maybe his father and Hunter were right. Maybe Gramps was simply going senile.

Yeah? Then explain the men in the Malibu.

Maybe they hadn't been following him, but Charlee. Maybe the gunshot through the window had been meant for her. It made perfect sense. She was a private detective and over the years she had probably collected more than her fair share of enemies. Maybe chaos theory did indeed rule and nothing was connected.

Too bad he was so tired and hungry. He was missing something here and in his dulled haze of sleep-deprived starvation he couldn't think straight. Food. He needed food. Even a greasy hamburger would help.

Mason rubbed his eyes and stared out the window, checking on Matilda. The wind tossed dust eddies across the desert. He cringed as a small whirlwind passed over the Bentley. First chance he got, they were pulling into a carwash.

"When did your grandfather disappear?"

"What's today? I've lost track of time."

"Thursday."

He looked at his watch. Five-thirty in the evening. The trip to the movie studio had cost them a good three-hour detour. "My brother Hunter discovered the missing funds on Monday evening. When we went to confront Gramps on Tuesday, we discovered he was gone. I left for Vegas right away."

"Driving instead of flying so obviously you didn't feel as if the matter was that urgent." She peered at him over the rim of her cup.

"I told you I don't like to fly. And we did figure Gramps was probably just letting off some steam. Retirement doesn't suit him."

"So why not just leave him be?"

"He did steal half a million dollars from the family business."

"And then you arrived in my office yesterday afternoon," she said.

Had it only been a little more than twenty-four hours since he'd first laid eyes on Charlee Champagne? It seemed he had known her for years. Of course they had been together pretty well nonstop for the last twenty-four hours. If you averaged that up in dating time, saying a typical date lasted four hours, they would be on their sixth date.

Date? What the hell are you talking about, Gentry?

He had to stop this. His hormones were messing with his emotions. He was letting the circumstances wreak havoc on his brain. He needed to stop reacting from his gut and his heart and start thinking with his brain.

Pronto.

"Okay, so your grandfather takes off and in his room you find my grandmother's name and address."

"Well, actually, it was the address to the detective agency."

"Come to think of it, Tuesday morning was when Maybelline said she was leaving for her fishing retreat. Usually, she spends weeks preparing and talking about it and then, just out of the blue, she tells me to hold down the fort and takes off."

"I'm thinking that Gramps had hired her to work on a case for him."

"But what case?"

Mason shook his head. "I have no idea."

"Of course now there's a bigger question."

"Which is?"

"How do we find them once we get to L.A.?"

He paused a moment, pondering the question. "Gramps has a few old friends there. He doesn't see them much anymore, but we could give them a call and find out if they've heard from him. In fact, when we get back to the car I'll give them a ring. I can also phone home to see if Gramps has touched base with the family. Plus I'll check my voice mail to see if he's tried to contact me."

"It's a start," Charlee said. "I can check my answering machine too. And once we get into L.A. I can start calling hotels, see if our grandparents checked in anywhere. I'm assuming they'll stay somewhere upscale if your grandfather is anything like you."

"He's got five hundred thousand dollars in cash, he can pretty much stay at the most expensive hotel in town if he chooses." Mason's eyes met Charlee's and he could tell she was thinking the same thing he was. Their plan was lame but it was all they had.

"Maybe they're on some kind of trip through memory lane," she mused. "Recalling their misspent youth."

"Maybe. But that doesn't explain why Gramps stole the money or why your father kidnapped them or why the guys in the Malibu were following us or why some old western actor showed up in the desert in a limousine to give Elwood a lift."

"Touché."

"Something big is at stake."

"Yeah, like half a million dollars."

"It feels bigger than that. The whole thing makes me uneasy."

"How come your family sent you to Vegas?" Charlee asked. "Especially since you're not keen on flying."

"Pardon?"

"Why didn't your brother come after your grandfather or even your father?"

Mason shifted against the hard plastic bench and toyed with the paper wrapper from his white plastic dinnerware. "Because it's my job."

"It's your job to baby-sit your grandfather?"

"No. It's my job to play cleanup. Hunter is the front man. The mover, the shaker, the deal maker. I tie up the loose ends. It's up to me to maintain customer service. Make sure everyone is happy."

He tried hard to keep the bitterness from his voice. He was resigned to his position in the family hierarchy, but sometimes he couldn't help but begrudge the fact that he'd been relegated to second place simply by birth order. No matter how hard he tried, Mason always seemed to fall short in comparison to his older brother.

"So essentially you're the family janitor. Mop up the messes and whatnot."

"It's not like that," he protested.

She raised an eyebrow.

"It's not." He could hear the defensive tone in his voice. Who was he trying to convince? Charlee or himself?

"And what about you?" she prodded.

"What about me?"

"Are you happy, Mason?" She peered deeply into his eyes in a maneuver that made his gut hitch. "Do you like being the janitor?"

When I'm with you, I am.

Her perceptive question took him off guard. He had no idea how to answer. "Sure I'm happy. Why do you think I'm not happy?"

"Well, for one thing you're glowering."

"I'm not glowering," he denied and smiled purposefully.

"Now that's just plain wrong."

"What is?"

"Denying how you feel. Pretending to be happy when

you're not. What happens in your family when you express your displeasure?"

"What is this? Twenty questions? We're talking about our grandparents here, not me."

"What happens?" she persisted.

"I don't know."

"You don't know? What does that mean?"

Good Lord, the woman could worry a wart off a frog. "I've never openly expressed my displeasure."

"For real?"

"My parents aren't emotional people. We Gentrys prefer to stay reserved. It facilitates peace."

"Peace at all cost, huh. Explains a lot."

"Explains what?"

"Why you're so screwed up."

"I'm not screwed up." Annoyance surged inside him at her half-baked psychobabble. "You think I'm screwed up?"

"How old are you?"

"What's that got to do with anything?"

"Thirty-two, thirty-three?"

"I'm twenty-seven."

"Oh. Sorry." She looked chagrined. "You seem much older."

Before she could elaborate on her theory concerning his supposed screwed-up-ness, their cheeseburger baskets arrived, sidetracking them from further talk.

In spite of himself, the aroma of grilled onions made his mouth water and when he bit into the cheeseburger he sighed involuntarily at the delicious flavor.

"Good, isn't it?" Charlee grinned and dunked a french fry in ketchup.

Good? The fatty cheeseburger was sheer heaven but

he wasn't about to admit that to her. Not after all the bitching he'd done. Feeling contrite, he dabbed his chin with a paper napkin.

"Mmmm." Charlee's soft little moan of pleasure just about stopped his heart.

He looked up and the expression of delight on her face caused his breath to come in short, ragged gulps. Charlee's lips glistened in the cheap fluorescent lighting and her eyes glowed luminescent.

And when she slowly licked a morsel of melted cheese from her finger his entire body tightened and the swell of heat swamping his groin was almost more than he could bear.

Jesus. What in the hell was the matter with him? Talk about your mental turmoil.

He was not the kind of guy who vacillated. He didn't have conflicted feelings. Mostly, he ignored his feelings. So why couldn't he do that now? Why the constant struggle? He wanted her so badly and yet he didn't want to want her. He was screwing up his life. Ruining everything he'd built. Letting himself be tempted by a litany of "what ifs?"

This was wrong.

And yet the notion of kissing those provocative lips felt so damned right.

He was going to have to break up with Daphne and that's all there was to it. He'd barely thought about his girlfriend in the last twenty-four hours. And how could he commit to Daphne when he couldn't stop fantasizing about bedding a certain very sexy private eye?

The wind howled around the corner of the diner, escalating as sharply and rapidly as his desires. Dust bathed Matilda's windshield. Overhead the ceiling creaked and groaned.

"Let's get out of here." He wiped his hands on a napkin and then reached for his wallet. "I'll get the check."

Belatedly, he realized he had no wallet and no money.

Instead of heading on into Tucson where he'd had his secretary wire him money, they had immediately headed for L.A. after Waylon Jennings told them Maybelline and Nolan were headed there. He was still without cash flow and he hated being broke.

"You're broke, Gentry," Charlee pointed out, a little too gleefully for his tastes. She had an uncanny ability for pushing his buttons and shooting down his pretensions. "My treat." She pulled a wad of ones from her jeans and approached the cashier.

Damn if he could stop himself from eyeing the incendiary swish of her back pockets.

She paid for their meal and came back to retrieve her hat from the seat. She plunked the straw Stetson down on her head and turned to gaze at the windstorm.

"Maybe we ought to lie low until the dust devil passes," she said.

"No, no. It'll be all right." Mason wanted to get on the road. The sooner they got out of here, the sooner they'd get to L.A., and the sooner they were in L.A., the sooner he and Charlee could go their separate ways. "Give me the keys." He held out a palm. "I'll drive from here on out."

"Whatever." Charlee dropped the keys into his hand.

The metal roof groaned again, louder and more insistently. He took Charlee's elbow and guided her toward the door.

Was it his imagination or did she tense beneath his touch? Too bad. He'd been raised a gentleman. She was stuck with his deeply ingrained manners, like it or not. Besides, he liked touching her.

He leaned forward and reached to push open the front door of the diner, but the wind snatched it from his hand. At the same moment the roof stopped its low-level groaning and instead let loose with a sharp, metallic, bone-chilling shriek.

The whole building shook as the shriek gave way to a deep, heavy rumbling.

And then came a crash loud enough to rival a wrecking ball smashing into a dilapidated building.

Bam. Boom. Splat.

In unison, the truckers and cowboys seated at the tables and counters jumped up and ran to the window.

"Holy shit," someone exclaimed.

Charlee gasped and clutched Mason's shoulders, her fingernails digging into his flesh.

Mason froze, his mind refusing to accept what his ears had witnessed.

"I'm so sorry," Charlee murmured.

Slowly, in millimeter increments, he turned his head.

The giant fiberglass hamburger that forty minutes earlier had been perched jauntily up on the roof of the diner now lay squarely on top of Matilda, squashing her flatter than aluminum foil.

CHAPTER
9

"The thermostat is busted." Maybelline wiped her oil-stained fingers on a white paper napkin and slammed down the hood of the camper.

"So we're stuck here." Nolan splayed a palm to his forehead. He regretted leaving his cell phone at home. He hadn't brought it with him because he was afraid his family would call and he wouldn't be able to resist answering the damned thing.

"Until I can jury-rig something and we can make it to the next gas station, yes."

Nolan sank his hands on his hips and let his breath out slowly. "May, it's imperative we get to L.A. before the Oscars on Sunday night."

"I'm aware of that, but it is only Thursday evening. Relax. We'll get there."

"I'm worried about Elwood finding us again."

"Yeah, me too."

"The sooner we get to Hollywood the better. I need time to plan an offensive counterattack."

"I'm doing my best," she said calmly, took a map

from the glove compartment, then leaned against the hood and opened it up. "Our current location isn't even on the map."

They had decided to stay off the main roads after ditching Elwood at the abandoned Twilight Studios lot. Unfortunately, staying off the beaten path had been a calculated risk that wasn't paying out.

"As the crow flies, we're only a few miles from the interstate and a place called Nowhere Junction. Maybe we could hitch a ride there."

"Except when was the last time we saw another car on this road?"

Maybelline sighed and folded up the map. "Not for hours."

"Face it, we're stranded."

The sun squatted on the horizon. Nothing could be done tonight.

No point taking his prickliness out on Maybelline. At least she knew enough about engines to try to repair the broken thermostat. His manhood took a ding on that one but it couldn't be helped. The gizmos underneath the hood of a car were a complete mystery to him. Might as well make the best of a bad mess.

Fifteen minutes later they were ensconced in the back of the camper. They sat side by side on the bare mattress, their backs pressed against the cab. Nolan took an orange from the sack of supplies Elwood had left stashed in the front seat of the camper, peeled the skin away, and broke off segments for Maybelline. The tangy sweet smell of citrus fruit filled the small confines.

"Not exactly the way I imagined spending the night with you," he murmured.

"You imagined spending the night with me?"

"Hell, yes," he growled. "About a thousand times on the plane trip to Vegas and about ten thousand since then."

She leaned against his shoulder. "I never knew you thought of me like that."

"Like what?" he asked out of pure devilment. He wanted to hear her say it.

"You know. Sexually."

"I married you, didn't I?"

"That was in name only. You were just trying to protect me. I never thought you actually wanted to *sleep with me*, sleep with me."

"Christ, woman, what is the matter with you? The whole time we were married and living in that bungalow on the Twilight Studios lot and you were six months pregnant, I wanted you."

"I never knew."

"Come on. You never had an inkling?" He put his arm around her shoulder, drew her closer, and fed her an orange wedge. When her lips brushed against his fingertips, his old heart sang.

"I thought you were just a really sweet guy from back home who married me to save my reputation."

"Well, you were wrong."

"The whole three months we were married you never once even tried to kiss me." Maybelline leaned up and traced his chin with her finger.

"You were pregnant with another man's baby and I thought you were in love with him."

"I might have been. Once. Or I was in love with the image of who I thought he was. Until I discovered the cheating bastard was married."

"You were going to fling yourself off the HOLLY-WOOD sign over him. What was I supposed to think?"

"That I was pregnant and unwed back in the fifties when girls were judged rather harshly for that sin."

"What about you? Not once did you let on that you thought of me as anything more than a friend. And when you filed for the annulment . . ."

"Oh, come on, Nolan."

"What?"

"I knew I wasn't good enough for the likes of Nolan Gentry. Your daddy made that fact clear enough the time he threw a hissy fit when he caught us together at the soda fountain."

"My daddy was an ass."

"No. He was right. He knew you were Dom Perignon and I was Ripple."

"Dammit, don't put yourself down like that."

"I know who I am, Nolan. I've never labored under the illusion that I belonged in your world. The only reason I agreed to the marriage in the first place was because I would have lost my job at the studio if they'd discovered I was unwed and pregnant."

"It hurt me, May, when you got that annulment behind my back and took off without a word."

"I couldn't stay married to you when your family was planning on you walking down the aisle with Elispeth Hunt. I wasn't about to ruin your life just because I'd ruined mine. And when that gossip columnist started snooping around the set and asking questions, I knew I had to do something to protect you. I could just imagine what would happen if your father found out you'd married me out of pity."

"I didn't marry you out of pity, dammit. I married you because I loved you."

"If that was true, Nolan, why did you make everyone on the set swear to keep our marriage a secret? Thinking back on things it was a miracle no one gave us up to the gossip rags."

He swallowed hard. "I was a coward."

"No you weren't."

"I let the love of my life walk away because of my family."

"I hid from you."

"I should have searched harder."

"Your father had a heart attack. What else could you do but go home? And let's call a spade a spade. You married me because you wanted to feel like a hero."

"That's not true, but I am sorry," Nolan said vehemently, "if I ever made you feel like you were anything less than special to me."

"You never made me feel bad. I just knew we weren't right for each other."

"You were wrong about that."

Maybelline said nothing. He peered down at her in the gathering gloom. It was almost too dark to see her face but when he put out a hand, he felt the dampness of her cheek and knew she was crying.

"Ah," he said. "Ah, sweetheart, don't."

And then he was squeezing her tight, pulling her close to his chest, and kissing her like he should have kissed her forty-seven years ago.

Charlee stared at the car in horror.

"Matilda." Mason's voice cracked as he stood beside

the massacred Bentley. The plaintive sound sliced a hole through her heart.

"Mason, I'm so, so sorry."

He dropped to his knees and ran a hand over the piece of bright red metal that used to be a fender, poking from beneath the giant murderous hamburger.

"It's my fault," she said. "If I hadn't insisted we pull over for a meal. . . ."

"She's the only car I ever had," he murmured in the hushed reverential tones reserved for funerals.

The diner patrons stood in a circle around them, mumbling their sympathies.

"I lost my virginity in the backseat," Mason continued. "To Blair Sydney. She was home on spring break from Vassar the summer I turned seventeen."

Charlee squatted beside him, laid a hand on his shoulder. She felt lousy as hell. She was the one who had parked the car directly underneath the burger, even if it was at his demand. She should have ignored him and parked where she wanted.

"You shouldn't torture yourself."

"You don't understand. Matilda represented something important to me. Freedom from my family. A piece of my own identity."

"A shit load of money is what she represented," one of the cowboys muttered. "I'd hate to have his insurance premiums."

Charlee shot the loud mouth a quelling frown and the cowboy had the good grace to look embarrassed. "Come on, Mason, let's go back inside. Nothing can be accomplished out here."

He appeared to be in a trance, staring at the violated car as if he were peering into a crystal ball and seeing an unpleasant future. He sat for the longest time not saying a word. Just when Charlee thought she was going to have to pinch him to remind him he was alive, Mason spoke. "I should have listened to you. I should have left Matilda in Phoenix with your friend."

God, she hated being right. Hated seeing him so disheartened. She imagined her cherry red Corvette compacted beneath the oversized sesame seed bun and empathy pains knotted her stomach.

This wasn't good at all.

She had to snap him out of his funk.

Twilight deepened and the lights from the gas station next door came on. The other diner patrons meandered off, but Mason just kept sitting on the ground, shaking his head and reciting a litany of memories associated with the car—his college graduation, summer vacations, and cross-country trips. He was holding a wake for Matilda. The only thing missing was whiskey and Irish lament songs.

He worried her. Big time.

Allowing him to descend into self-pity—however understandable under the circumstances—was a luxury they couldn't afford. They had to get their heads straight and come up with a way out of here, ASAP. They had no car, very little money and now even his cell phone was D.O.A in the wreckage of Matilda.

Tough love. That was the answer. She made the conscious choice to aggravate him.

"You gonna sit there and feel sorry for yourself all night, Gentry?" She cocked her head and leveled him a stern stare.

He didn't even look up at her, which scared her even more.

"What? You want me to go find a preacher to eulogize the car?" She was desperate. If she couldn't break through to him she had no idea what to do.

He didn't move.

She snorted, exaggerating the sound for his benefit. "Great. Just what I might have expected from a spoiled, pampered, rich blue blood." She laid it on thick, gesturing with her arms and raising her voice in a desperate attempt to attract his interest.

"Having a frickin' pity party over a car. Boo-hoo, poor baby." She paced behind him, hands on her hips. "I got news for you, pretty boy, while you're indulging yourself, our grandparents are God knows where, maybe even being chased by nasty, menacing people while you sit on your duff and . . ."

"That's enough!" Mason snarled, leaped to his feet, and whirled around to face her in a movement so sudden and fluid Charlee choked on her words.

Ulp.

"Not another peep out of you."

For a long moment, she just stood there in disbelief, like the time when she was a kid and she'd been petting her hamster and it bit her so hard her thumb bled.

Mason's chocolate eyes smoldered with a perilous fire. His jaw was set, every muscle in his body tensed. His dimples, which were beguiling when he smiled, dug into his face like ominous burrows when he glowered. He stalked toward her with a loose hip stride that promised more trouble.

He looked very, very dangerous.

Charlee gulped and took a step backward, stunned by the changes in him. Was this the same man she'd just driven four hundred miles beside? Where was the self-controlled, self-contained guy she'd met in her office yesterday afternoon? Gone was all semblance of civility. In Mason's place stood a total stranger.

"I've had it up to here." He sliced his hand across his neck. "You push and you push and you push. A man has limits, Charlee Champagne, and I want you to know I've reached the edge of mine."

Okay, she'd snapped him out of his near catatonia but this certainly wasn't what she'd bargained for. He kept coming, his features a mask of unadulterated ferocity. Her stomach careened up to her throat.

And Charlee kept backing up, her eyes growing wider with surprise. She raised her palms in a defensive gesture.

"Now, Mason . . ." She started to explain why she had been so hard on him but he wasn't in the mood to listen. "Take a deep breath."

"I don't want to hear it." Gravel crunched beneath his feet. *Crunch, crunch, crunch.*

Her heart slammed against her rib cage like an unseat-belted crash-test dummy bashing repeatedly into the windshield of a Yugo.

His teeth were clenched. A vein at his forehead throbbed.

Charlee slowly edged one foot behind her hoping that if she moved without haste she would defuse his anger. "Settle down."

"I don't want to settle down." He was utterly pissed. He looked as if he wanted to tear her to shreds with his bare hands, bit by tiny bit. "I'm tired of settling down. I've been settled down for twenty-seven years and where has it gotten me? Stuck in the middle of the Arizona desert with an infuriatingly aggravating woman, that's where."

Another sliding step back. Another and another.

And then her boot heel hit smack-dab up against the outside wall of the diner.

Nowhere to run.

Charlee held her breath.

He slapped his palms against the wall on either side of her head, effectively pinning her in.

Uh-oh.

A tiny burst of panic exploded inside her. She'd created a monster. She could feel his pain, see it in his eyes, but there was something more than hurt and anger lurking in those blazing brown depths.

Passion, desire, and hungry sexual need smoldered there too.

Oh, God, oh, God, oh, God, she was in trouble.

Her blood ran hot and her insides were all jittery and jammed up. She couldn't let him know how she felt. Vulnerable and willing and turned on like a faucet. She sank her top teeth into her bottom lip and curled her fingertips into her palms to stay the rush of her surging emotions.

She had to lighten the mood. She had to think unsexy thoughts. She had to get her mind off the fantasy of making love to this brown-eyed handsome man. Going on the offensive had only provoked his ire. It was time to try something else. Humor maybe?

"Ever since I met you nothing but bad things have happened," he continued to rant. "I've been shot at, made fun of by creeps in a bar, had my wallet stolen, been in a crazed car chase, and now the vehicle that's dear to my heart has been smashed by a giant hamburger."

Charlee's upper lip twitched and an almost irrepressible urge to laugh pushed through her. When you thought about it, their circumstances were really sort of funny. Laughter might offer a wonderful release valve for her, but she had the distinct impression Mason would not appreciate a hysterical giggling fit.

"But none of those things were my fault," she squeaked as her mind frantically raced to think of something sarcastic and witty and fitting but she came up empty-handed. The drastic change in him was just too intimidating.

"Maybe not, but you attract trouble like a television screen attracts dust. I can deal with all that chaos. I can even deal with my car getting crushed. What I can't deal with is being insulted by a smart-mouthed private detective who thinks she knows it all because she grew up the hard way."

"I don't think I know it all," she denied.

He ignored her refutation. "Yes, I was raised in the lap of luxury. So sue me. It doesn't make me a bad person. I don't have to put up with your derision and your sarcasm and your holier-than-thou attitude."

"I . . . I didn't . . . I don't . . . That's not . . ." she stammered, hardly able to form a coherent thought.

He narrowed his eyes to slits and he leaned in closer. His lips were almost touching hers. His masculine scent invaded her nose.

Her breath came in hot, rapid gasps. The pulse in the hollow of her throat throbbed erratically. Heat swamped her body. The flavor of raw sexual desire filled her mouth.

God, but she was so aroused.

Charlee had never wanted anyone more than she wanted him right now. Her fingers itched to rip the shirt from his body. Her lips ached to ravish his. Her legs quivered with the urge to wrap themselves around his muscled waist.

And then, over his shoulder, she caught a glimpse of something that instantly dampened her raging libido.

A white Chevy Malibu pulling into the gas station behind him.

Oh, no. Not now. Not when her brain was swamped in hormones and not functioning properly.

What to do? What to do?

Think.

She had to create a diversion. Had to do something to make sure they weren't immediately spotted by the Malibu goons. She had to buy them some time.

But how?

Only one idea occurred to her. One single, awful idea that promised to plunge her even deeper into emotional danger, but it was all she had.

The men were getting out of the Malibu. The one from the passenger side was glancing around.

If he spotted them . . .

Not knowing what else to do, Charlee grabbed Mason by the collar and pulled his face close to hers.

"Kiss me," she demanded.

"What?" He looked as if she'd asked him to jump into the Grand Canyon buck naked.

"Kiss me now. Kiss me hard. Kiss me like you mean it."

"Huh?"

"Just do it, dammit."

Mason stared at her, his mind a chaotic jumble. Charlee's chest rose and fell in rapid succession, her breasts rubbing lightly against his inner forearms. Her lips glistened moistly. Her gaze was desperate.

Was she as turned on as he?

Her sense of sexual urgency surprised him, igniting a fire in him like a blowtorch to ten-year-old kindling. When had his sorrow over losing Matilda turned into all-out desire for the dark-haired, green-eyed woman captured between his arms?

He pillaged her lips. He was a plunderous pirate claiming his booty. He was a ruthless bounty hunter bringing his prisoner to justice. He was a cold-blooded cutthroat taking what didn't belong to him.

From the very moment he had clamped eyes on her in that small dusty detective office, he had yearned to kiss her.

Years of pent-up feelings surged through Mason. A river of underground sensation. Too long he'd suppressed his basic emotions and now they were tumbling out of him in a pure, explosive purge. Anger mixed with raw sexual desire mixed with sheer shameless need. Burning euphoria mixed with voracious carnal hunger.

She wrapped her arms around his neck and pulled him closer. Her hair brushed against his face and he just about came unraveled.

Mason thrust his tongue past her parted teeth and damn if she didn't moan and wriggle against him. She tasted like hamburger heaven.

He stroked the inside of her mouth with his tongue, surprising himself with his bold technique. He ran his hands down her feminine hips to cup her butt in his palms. As he enjoyed what was happening between them, he forgot about everything else.

The rest of the world was a blur. He forgot about Daphne, his job, his parents. He didn't think about Matilda or Gramps or the fact that a dozen truckers and cowboys were staring at them through the diner's plate-glass window.

He ignored the chugging, wheezing sounds and the choky diesel odors of the eighteen-wheeler engines idling at the gas station behind them. He didn't care that they were stranded in Nowhere Junction with no way out of here or that he had no money, no ID, not even a change of clothes.

Time hung suspended and nothing mattered but the silky slide of Charlee's lips against his. He felt liberated and feral and authentic, as if he had at last unearthed the real Mason. He felt consumed by a shadow self who had been prowling in his subconscious for years, just waiting for the chance to pounce free.

Charlee moaned into his mouth and her tongue took off on an adventure of its own. His body reacted vehemently, pulling him deeper into treacherous territory.

He allowed his hands to glide down her spine to her waist and then lower still. Her smallness surprised him. Because she acted so tough, toting that gun and spouting strong talk, she seemed larger-than-life. But right here, right now, in his arms, she felt soft and willing and womanly and surprisingly delicate.

His fingertips reached the waistband of her jeans and his groin ached with the desire to yank down her zipper and shuck those denim britches right over her hips.

Just when he was at the point of suggesting something so completely out of character that anyone who knew him would have sworn pod people had taken over his body, Charlee wrenched her mouth from his.

"Okay. You can quit now," she said. "They went inside the gas station."

"Who did?" Lust-addled, Mason could only stare at her.

"The men in the Chevy Malibu."

"What?"

She nodded toward the gas station behind them. Slowly, Mason turned his head and spotted the Malibu. Understanding dawned. Charlee hadn't asked him to kiss her because she was overcome by passion. She'd just been trying to avoid being spotted by the guys in the white Chevy.

He felt stupid and foolish and thick-witted. To think he'd actually believed Charlee had wanted to kiss him. But it had been nothing but a ruse, a ploy, a plot to keep them from being identified by their pursuers. His pulse kicked hard against his neck vein, embarrassed, ashamed.

Chagrined, he stepped back from her, lightly fingering his lips.

"The hamburger is hiding the Bentley from their view but I don't think it'll take them long to figure out we're here." Charlee gripped his arm.

"They're coming after us," Mason said flatly and stuffed down his mortification. He felt the way you did when someone waved at you from across the room and you waved wildly back, happy to be recognized, only to realize the person was waving at someone behind you.

"I'm afraid so."

"What do we do now?"

"I don't know. I gotta think." Charlee bit down on her thumbnail.

At that moment a chartered tour bus — with the destination sign mounted over the cab spelling out Los Angeles — rumbled into the parking lot. The bus pulled to a stop between the diner and gas station, blocking their sight of the Malibu.

"Maybe we could talk one of those truckers into giving us a ride," Charlee said.

The door to the tour bus whooshed open and the driver got off but Mason didn't really pay much attention.

"We could pay someone to give us a ride." Instinctively, his hand went to his pocket before he remembered again that his wallet had been stolen. He swore under his breath.

"Oops, looks like your money isn't going to help us get out of this one."

What was the matter with her? What did she have against money? Or against him for that matter?

"Don't worry, big spender. I've got it covered." Charlee unbuttoned two more buttons on her shirt, revealing an eye-popping amount of skin.

She handed him her straw cowboy hat, then bent over from the waist to brush her fingers through her hair. When she straightened, her curls had a wild, tousled just-rolled-out-of-bed look. She licked her lips to moisten them.

"What in the hell do you think you're doing?" he growled and grabbed her elbow as she started to stroll away.

"Just like you told me. Trying to catch flies with honey."

With breasts like that on display and that madcap hair corkscrewing everywhere she could snag every fly on every pair of blue jeans in the diner. Jealousy, mean and hungry, chomped into him at the thought of those men ogling his Charlee.

"Over my dead body. I'm not going to let you expose yourself in exchange for a ride."

"Got any other bright ideas? If so I'd like to hear 'em. I'm open. Oh, and hurry. I did happen to notice when those goons got out of the Malibu that they were wearing shoulder holsters under their jackets."

"You're saying they're dangerous."

"I'm saying they've got guns and we don't."

"Excuse me, folks."

Charlee and Mason glanced over to see the beefy, ruddy-faced tour bus driver standing next to them, a clipboard clutched in his hand and a harried frown pulling at his brow.

"Yes?" she asked.

"Are you Skeet and Violet Hammersmitz?"

Mason opened his mouth to deny it and Charlee promptly trod on his toe.

"Ow." He glared at her. If he wasn't so jealous and upset and embarrassed and confused, he might have been quicker on the uptake.

"Excuse us." She fluttered her eyelashes at the driver who was busily checking out the cleavage she'd forgotten to button back up. Mason had an irresistible urge to plant his fist in the guy's face and the intensity of his response shocked him. "My husband and I are having a little tiff. What did you say?"

Husband? What was the little minx up to?

"Are you the couple who missed the bus in Tucson

and called in to say you'd meet up with us here in Nowhere Junction?" the driver asked.

"See any other couples around here?" Charlee waved a hand.

"Well come on then, get on the bus. We're running late as it is and we got a schedule to keep. We're supposed to be in L.A. before midnight and it looks like we're not going to make it before two." The driver turned and headed back to the tour bus.

"What in the hell do you think you're doing?" Mason hissed once the man was out of earshot. "Telling that guy I'm your husband? I don't like lying."

"I'm getting us a ride to L.A., doofus."

"Oh." He paused a minute. "But, Charlee, that's not right. What about the other couple? What happens when they get here and the bus has left without them?"

"Let's forgo the ethics for once, Eagle Scout."

"There's nothing wrong with having standards."

"Yeah, yeah, it's admirable and all that but let's be sensible for once. The other couple doesn't have armed thugs following them. Plus obviously they've got another ride, or how else would they get out here? Don't worry about Skeet and Violet. They'll be just fine."

"Good point." He conceded.

The driver tooted the horn and motioned for them to get a move on.

"Well?" Charlee angled her head toward the bus. "Which is it? A free ride out of here or a showdown with those two *Soprano* wanna-bes?"

Just as she asked the question, the two men from the Malibu stalked into view, heading straight for the diner. With a jolt, Mason recognized them.

"Hey," he said. "They are the same guys from the airport. The ones who stole my wallet." Angrily, he started forward, his intent to challenge them.

Charlee grabbed him by the belt loop. "Whoa there, where do you think you're going?"

"They've got my wallet."

"And if you confront them you're gonna end up in the trunk of their car. Trust me on this. I know unsavory characters, and those two are as sleazy as they come. They've already stolen your wallet, you wanna add your life to their list of accomplishments?"

"No." He hated to let this go. Every male instinct urged him to fight for what he knew was right.

Charlee inclined her head. "The bus?"

When she put it like that, the choice was easy. Pretend to be Charlee's husband on a bus trip to L.A. or end up in some shallow grave in the desert.

He shot a backward glance at Matilda and his heart tugged. Nothing more he could do for her anyway. Squaring his shoulders, he followed Charlee to the bus.

CHAPTER
10

*C*harlee climbed the bus steps, Mason right behind her. His warm breath tickled the back of her head and the hand he placed at her waist, well wowza. Her head still swam from the power of his kiss. Her lips and cheeks and chin still burned from the abrasion of his beard stubble.

She wanted to snap at him to move his hand away, but she was pretending he was her husband so she had no recourse. She was stuck with his proprietary gesture.

"Violet! Skeet! Welcome, welcome, we were so worried you would miss the bus again." A short, plump, middle-aged woman with a perpetual smile locked into place enveloped Charlee in a lilac-scented hug and then stepped back to pump Mason's hand after they'd climbed aboard the bus. "I'm Edith Beth McCreath, your tour director."

"Nice to meet you, Edith Beth," Mason enunciated carefully, obviously trying hard not to lisp on the woman's unfortunate name.

"Gosh," Edith Beth said, craning her neck upward.

"You're a tall one. Must come in handy when you're reaching for shoe boxes on those high stockroom shelves."

"Excuse me?" Mason frowned.

Edith Beth looked stricken for a moment, plucked a day planner from her pocket, and started ruffling through the pages. "You are a shoe salesman, right, Skeet?"

"Yes, right. Sure. A shoe salesman."

Charlee rolled her eyes. She'd never seen a lousier liar.

Edith Beth jabbed at an entry in her journal with a stubby index finger. "Yes you are. It says so right here in my trusty notes. A shoe salesman from Des Moines. And, Violet, you sculpture fingernails for a living. Let me see those hands."

Before Charlee could stop her, Edith Beth grabbed her hands and stared down at her ragged fingernails. "Oh."

She jerked her hands away and hid them behind her back.

Edith Beth laughed. "Must be a case of the cobbler's children going without shoes, eh?"

The tour director glanced from Mason's dirty Gucci loafers to Charlee's scuffed cowboy boots. She tried to gauge what the woman was thinking but Edith Beth was well schooled in the art of displaying a perky grin in lieu of real emotions.

"Put 'em in a seat, Edith Beth," the bus driver growled. "I'm pulling out."

"Yes, yes," Edith Beth twittered and escorted them to the last empty seat on the bus. "Don't mind Gus. He's a bit grumpy, but he's a very good driver."

Once they were seated, Edith Beth stepped to the

front and picked up a microphone. "Everyone, let's have a hearty 'welcome aboard' for Skeet and Violet."

"Welcome aboard, Skeet and Violet," the other passengers recited.

"A shoe salesman?" Mason whispered to Charlee. "I'm a shoe salesman from Des Moines?"

"Could be worse, could be an undertaker from Chattanooga."

"But a shoe salesman? I don't know anything about shoes."

"Yeah, well, try being a nail technician who bites her fingernails." Charlee sat on her hands.

"I bet you make a horrible living, Violet dear. Good thing you married me so I can support you selling Hush Puppies and Reeboks."

Charlee peeked over at Mason. He seemed to have gotten over Matilda and was actually trying to crack a joke. Thank God.

"I can't tell a lie. You are my Prince Charming, Skeet."

She felt a tug on her shoulder and looked across the aisle at the petite blonde seated across from her.

"Hiya." The woman grinned. "I'm Francie Pulluski and this is my husband, Jerry." She wrapped an arm around the big bear of a man sitting next to her, who grinned and shook first Charlee's hand and then Mason's. "We just got married Sunday before last. How long have you guys been hitched?"

"A month," Charlee said at the same time Mason said, "Three weeks."

Francie chuckled. "Well, which is it? A month or three weeks?"

"Um, well, we eloped a month ago, but then his family insisted we have a regular ceremony," Charlee lied smoothly. "So Skeet considers that date our real anniversary, don't you, honey?"

"That's right, sweet 'ems." Mason gave her a tight-lipped what-in-the-hell-did-you-get-us-into grin.

Charlee almost laughed. She'd bet her last dollar the man had never before said "sweet 'ems" in his entire life.

"Did you see my ring?" Francie flashed her a modest diamond and Charlee made the obligatory oohing and aahing noises. "Now let me see yours."

"Um, it's at the jeweler's. Skeet bought it too big. You know how men tend to overestimate size."

Francie tittered. "I hear ya."

"So how did you two meet?" Jerry asked Mason.

Mason arched an eyebrow and she could tell by the look on his face it was payback time for that crack about men overestimating size.

"Why, the minute I saw the bartenders at Quintero's pub hose down Violet at the Wednesday night wet T-shirt contest I knew she was the gal for me."

"You were in a wet T-shirt contest?" Francie's eyes widened. "You brave girl! I could never do anything like that."

"She wasn't wearing a bra either." Mason winked. "It was true love at first sight."

"Drunk," Charlee said, giving Mason the evil eye. "I was totally drunk. I don't even remember meeting Skeet that night."

Mason's gaze locked with hers. "Oh, but you sure remembered me when you woke up in my bed the next morning licking my . . . er . . . toes."

To her utter shock, Charlee felt her cheeks heat as if

she actually had been in a drunken, bra-less, wet T-shirt contest and gone home with him for a night of debauchery.

"Got yourself a wild one there," Jerry said, a touch of envy in his voice.

Francie frowned, apparently not wanting her new husband to dwell on the mental picture of Charlee in a wet T-shirt, and she changed the subject. "Aren't you guys just excited to death to be going on the twenty-first-century version of the *Newlywed Game*?"

Um, the *Newlywed Game*? What was Francie talking about?

"You betcha," Mason said, really getting into his Skeet role. "We can't wait."

"You're gonna have to work really hard to beat us, though." Francie patted Jerry's thigh. "We know everything there is to know about each other, don't we, baby."

Jerry looked a little uneasy. "Uh, everything," he echoed, giving Charlee the distinct impression the guy had kept a secret or two from his new bride.

"No way are you winning," the husband of the couple seated behind Jerry and Francie exclaimed. "We're gonna take the grand prize. We couldn't afford a honeymoon and this is our chance."

Charlee looked around at the other passengers and realized everyone on board were young couples. She counted sixteen pairs, including her and Mason. Were they all *Newlywed Game* contestants? She asked Francie covert questions and discovered the bus was on a public relations jaunt. It had started in New York and was making media stops at various central locations around the country and picking up contestants as they went. The last stop before L.A. was Tucson. She was unable to ascertain, without making Francie suspicious, why Skeet and Violet from Des Moines were picking up the tour in Tucson.

She felt guilty then at the thought of robbing Skeet and Violet of their chance to out-couple the other couples on national television. She tucked her remorse to the back of her mind. It couldn't be helped. They'd done what they had to do to get out of Nowhere Junction.

"Don't worry"—Mason leaned over to whisper in her ear—"when all this is over I'm going to hunt up Skeet and Violet and surprise them with a second honeymoon."

It was as if he'd read her thoughts. Charlee smiled at him and something in her heart gave a strange tug. He might be a rich, spoiled, stubborn control freak, but he was also a nice guy.

Warning, warning! Danger, danger!

Stop having warm fuzzy thoughts about him. You know how much trouble you get into when you let yourself think pleasant things about wealthy, long-legged, brown-eyed, handsome men with matinee-idol smiles. Wise up!

"Everyone!" Edith Beth boomed over the microphone. "Time for travel games."

"Travel games?" Mason asked. "What are we? On the bus to summer camp?"

"Oh, it's fun," Francie said. "Just wait and see. We've been playing on and off since we left Tucson."

Edith Beth explained the rules. It was a memory game where one person started with a word and the next person had to come up with a word that used the last letter of the first word. The following person had to recite those two words, then come up with a third and so on.

The upshot being whenever anyone missed a word, the entire bus had to kiss their mate.

Oh, crap. No way. Charlee caught her breath at the thought of having to kiss Mason again. The last kiss had short-circuited her brain and got her feeling all soft and mushy toward him. No more. No can do. Nuh-uh.

She had to find a way out of this or face some pretty dire consequences.

Like the loss of all common sense when it came to drop-dead-gorgeous George Clooneyesque men.

Amid much giggling, the game started. When the sixth person forgot a word, Edith Beth tinkled a cow-bell. "Everyone kiss!"

How the hell had she gotten herself into this situation? Mason looked at Charlee and gave a little shrug. He leaned over to kiss her.

She doubled her fist. "You do and you die."

"It's all for the good of the cause. We wouldn't want to get found out as impostors and risk getting thrown off the bus."

"You're just trying to take advantage of the situation." She narrowed her eyes at him.

He smirked and flashed her those sinful dimples.

"You can pretend to kiss me," she said. "For the good of the cause. But that's it."

"Whatever you say." Mason leaned perilously close to her lips and almost, nearly, barely, touched her mouth with his. His gaze was locked on hers, his eyes burning a daring challenge.

The air in that tight space between them vibrated with tension and anticipation.

Gak! This was worse than kissing him. She felt keyed up, on edge, hypersensitive.

The game went on and they got away with feigning their kisses. Until it was Charlee's turn.

She tried to remember the cycle of words but Mason's body heat distracted her and she flubbed.

Edith Beth rang the cowbell.

Once again Mason almost, nearly, barely brushed her lips with his.

Charlee shivered.

"Oh, no, no, no," Edith Beth said, walking down the aisle to their seat and shaking her head. "That will never do. You're kissing her like she's your sister, Skeet. This woman is your wife. Lay a big wet one on her."

"Don't even think about it," Charlee whispered fiercely through clenched teeth.

Mason shifted away from her and confessed to Edith Beth, "I'm sorry, but I've never been comfortable with public displays of affection."

Thank heavens he'd heeded her words. He was trying to get them out of this. Heck, he probably didn't want to kiss her any more than she wanted to kiss him.

Yeah? So how come she felt a little disappointed?

"We're not the public," Edith Beth said. "These are your fellow *Newlywed Game* contestants. Come on, Skeet, plant a kiss on Violet she'll never forget."

"Kiss, kiss, kiss," everyone chanted.

"You guys," Charlee pleaded with the group. "Skeet had onions on his hamburger back at the diner and his breath is really pungent."

"I've got a mint," Francie offered and dug in her purse for a peppermint.

"Aren't you helpful," Charlee said and it was all she could do to keep the sarcasm from her voice.

Mason popped the mint and grinned at her. *All for the good of the cause*, his expression declared.

Charlee squirmed. She felt trapped and panicky and freaked out. She feared if he kissed her, really kissed her, the way he had back there in the truck stop parking lot, that every bit of rational self-control she possessed would fly right out the window and she'd turn into a quivering pile of estrogen Jell-O.

"I'm not moving until you give her a real kiss, Skeet Hammersmitz." Edith Beth folded her arms over her chest and tapped her foot against the floor.

"You do and so help me God, you'll pay for it," Charlee murmured in his ear.

"Tit for tat, sweetheart," he murmured back. "You started this back there at the diner."

He had a point. She had no one to blame but herself. Oh, and the goons in the Malibu.

His eyes met Charlee's and her stomach took the express elevator straight to her boots. Her heart pitter-pattered.

The last time she'd kissed a wealthy, brown-eyed, handsome man she'd gotten her heart shattered into a gazillion little pieces.

Buck up. You're older now. Less gullible. You can handle this. It's just a friggin' kiss, Charlee.

He hesitated.

Edith Beth clapped her hands and got a rousing round of "Skeet, Skeet, Skeet, Skeet" going.

Charlee didn't want him to kiss her against his will. She raised her voice to be heard over the chanting. "It's okay, folks. Skeet doesn't have to kiss me in front of everyone. I know he loves me."

"Prove it," someone from the back of the bus shouted.

"Kiss her, Skeet, kiss her, Skeet, kiss her, Skeet!"

"Oh, just go on and get it over with," she snapped.

And then Mason was kissing her even more passionately than he'd kissed her in the diner parking lot and that kiss had been pretty darned passionate. He curled her into the crook of his arms, bringing her close to his warm, firm chest. She felt the heady lub-dubbing of his heart through the soft material of his shirt.

Don't give in. Fight the feeling. It's just lips.

Correction. Not just lips. Hot, moist, demanding lips. Lips that tasted of peppermint. Lips that glided like silk over hers. Lips that took her breath and refused to give it back.

Lips that belonged to a wealthy, long-legged, brown-eyed, handsome man with matinee-idol smiles and a day's growth of beard stubble.

She was screwed and she knew it.

His kiss, his touch, his smell, all felt too good, too irresistible.

What the hell. She threw in the towel and succumbed to the moment.

Her eyes shuttered closed and she allowed herself to drift into uncharted waters, to fully experience the promise of his mouth. This was different than the rough, demanding way he'd kissed her before. This kiss was both hungry and tender. At once lazily languid and intensely urgent.

A hot, overwhelming rush of desire thundered through her. His tongue thrust past her lips and delved deeply into the warm recesses of her mouth.

Sensation stormed through her body. Waves of it,

crashing one on top of each other in a blind, mad rush. Sweetness and heat and pressure. Moistness and pleasure and pure, honeyed desire.

"Woooooooo," the whole bus chimed in unison.

Happy now, everyone?

"Okay," Edith Beth interrupted. "You get a gold star, Skeet. Let's move on. Your turn to recite the memory string."

But Mason completely ignored Edith Beth, his focus — and his mouth — centered on Charlee.

"Ahem," Edith Beth cleared her throat.

Charlee pried open one eye and saw him waving the tour director away. His own eyes were closed as he too savored the moment. Charlee's belly tightened.

"Somebody hand me a water hose," Edith Beth joked.

"A water hose was what got them into this," Francie said with a giggle.

"How come you never kiss me like that," Charlee heard one newlywed wife whisper to her husband.

Mason grinned against her mouth and she found herself grinning right back.

"All rightee then," Edith Beth said, admitting defeat. "We'll leave Skeet and Violet to it and get on with the game. Next!"

"What are you doing?" Charlee whispered into his mouth after Edith Beth had moved on but Mason continued to kiss her. "You can stop now."

"I'm enjoying the benefits of being your husband. Believe me, there's enough negatives in this relationship, I'm taking the good where I can."

"You're not really my husband and we don't have a relationship."

"You want to call Edith Beth back over here and explain that to her?"

"No. I guess you'll just have to go on kissing me."

"Guess so."

She knew they were using Edith Beth's game as an excuse to capitalize on the sexual allure that had been simmering between them from the very moment they had met. She knew she was susceptible to the charms of rich, brown-eyed, handsome, long-legged men. She knew she was careening straight for Heartbreak Hotel. But no matter how hard she tried to pull away, once started, she simply could not stop kissing him.

He was like a horrible, horrible addiction and she couldn't get enough, so she convinced herself there was nothing wrong with satisfying her physical craving as long as she didn't get her mind or heart or soul involved. She could kiss and simply walk away. This didn't have to mean anything more than sumptuous bodily pleasures.

Denial. The junkie's tool in trade.

The bus traveled on into the night and long after Edith Beth's game had ended, Mason and Charlee continued to kiss. They were like fourteen-year-olds sitting in the back row at the movies experimenting with their first flush of sexual desire. They slid down low and rested their heads against the back of the seat. Charlee was practically in his lap, her legs dangling over his knees.

Kissing was a heady, invigorating, and totally stupid thing to do.

They did it anyway.

Even when their lips started to chap they kept kissing.

Nothing was inside her head except the moment. She forgot about Maybelline and Elwood and Nolan. She forgot about the men in the Malibu. She forgot about the fact she had a terrible track record with men. She operated on pure animal instinct and indulged herself in the sensual pleasures of Mason's mouth.

Soon enough, reality would intrude. For now, they were on a honeymoon bus bound for Hollywood and the *Newlywed Game*. It was a world removed from where they'd come and where they were headed.

When they finally opened their eyes and came up for air, they noticed everyone around them was kissing. Mason grinned. "Look what we started."

"Forget the Love Boat. We've got the Love Bus."

"Wonder if this was what it was like back in the free love era of the sixties."

"Seems very decadent."

"And very arousing."

His brown eyes crinkled at the corners and he gave her a come-hither look that had her knees liquefying and her pulse leaping over tall buildings in a single hop.

You're digging yourself a deep one, Charlee. Remember Gregory. Everything was all fun and games with him too, in the beginning.

"We shouldn't be doing this," she said.

"No," he agreed. "We shouldn't."

And then he reached for her again.

Sometime around midnight, Mason woke with a start to find Charlee curled snugly against him, her head resting on his shoulder. His arm had gone to sleep and tingled with an achy numbness but he hated to disturb her slumber by moving.

The bus was silent except for the steady strumming of the tires rolling against the asphalt. Everyone around them was sacked out, cuddled together under sweaters or blankets. The sight was touching and darned romantic. For one brief moment he actually wished they were Skeet and Violet Hammersmitz on their way to compete in the *Newlywed Game*.

He studied Charlee's face in the light of moon glow slipping through the bus windows. She looked so relaxed, so peaceful. Her lips were parted slightly and her dark hair spilled over her shoulders in an inky cascade. He shifted, turning to relieve the numbness in his arm without waking her. Snuggling with her had its advantages and disadvantages.

It felt so right to have her tucked into him, to feel her soft, warm breath fanning the hairs on his forearm, to experience the comfort of her body heat.

"Mason," she mumbled dreamily in her sleep and wrapped her arms around his waist.

Something tightened in his heart. An emotion he was afraid to name. Closing his eyes, he bit down on the inside of his cheek.

What was happening to him? He was a disciplined guy. He didn't allow unwanted emotions to rule his life. That was one of the things he liked about his relationship with Daphne. She never made him feel wild or crazy or out of control.

Daphne.

Guilt as tall as Hoover Dam stacked his conscience. He had never done anything remotely dishonest and now he was sneaking around behind his girlfriend's back kissing Charlee. He was being unfair to both women.

He had no excuse. He'd gotten caught up in the moment. All the old rules of order had been turned topsy-turvy. Add to that the powerful pull of sexual attraction between him and Charlee and well . . . he'd been weak.

But his greatest fear was that his attraction to Charlee went far beyond the physical. He was scared to explore the thoughts, nervous about prodding the emotions growing inside him. Most of all, he was afraid to trust his feelings. Afraid to let go.

The last thing he wanted was to hurt either her or Daphne. But the fact that he could feel something so intense for a woman he'd known less than two days told him what he'd already begun to suspect. He simply could not ask Daphne to marry him as he had planned.

And as for Charlee?

He owed her an apology. A big one.

Plus, he needed to keep his hands and his mouth to himself for the remainder of their trip. Easier said than done when her body was entangled with his.

"Charlee," he whispered and gently shook her shoulder.

"Hmmph."

"Could you let me out? I need to visit the facilities."

She sat up blinking and he felt weirdly sad once the weight of her was gone from his body. She stretched her hands over her head, giving him a delightful view of the soft curve of her upper arms. In spite of himself, he stared.

God, but she was compelling. Her hair was tousled and her eyes narrowed into a cute little squint. She splayed a palm over her mouth to suppress a yawn.

He climbed over her knees, his shins brushing against her jeans in the process. Sudden heat hit him like an explosion.

What was it about her that commanded such a spontaneous response in his unruly body? Perplexed, Mason rotated his numb shoulder, trying to shake out the pins and needles.

He stumbled toward the back of the jostling bus in the darkness and scrambled for a handhold when they smacked into a pothole. He missed the back of a seat he grabbed for and found himself propelled forward onto his knees.

His face made contact with the back window glass. The bus leveled out and he pulled himself to his feet but what he saw out the back window shoved his stomach right into his throat.

There. In the darkness. On a long, lonely stretch of arid desert highway, the bus was being followed.

By a white Chevy Malibu.

They arrived in Los Angeles a couple of hours later. Even at two-thirty in the morning, the indomitable Edith Beth was perky. If he'd had a gun, Mason would cheerfully have shot her.

"Good morning, everyone," she chirped over her microphone as Gus turned on the interior lights. "Welcome to the City of Angels."

Everyone squinted and grumbled.

"Wakey, wakey!" She clapped her hands like a seal on uppers. "We'll be at the studio lot soon. And I know it's the middle of the night, but we've got to get you sorted out into your bungalows where you can finish up your naps, shower, and change clothes before the welcome breakfast at seven-thirty."

"Will there be lots of coffee?" Jerry asked.

"Oh, six or seven different flavors." Edith Beth

beamed. "You're our stars. Twilight Studios has done an all-out media blitz promoting the contest and our *New Millennium Newlywed Game* contestants. We're expecting a huge media turnout because reporters from all around the country are already in Hollywood for the Academy Awards on Sunday night."

"Ah," Charlee whispered to Mason. "So we're the warm-up act for the Oscars."

"Looks like it."

Mason craned his neck toward the back of the bus to see if he could spot the Malibu, but their seats were too far away from the back window and if he made another trip to the bathroom Charlee was going to start thinking he had a bladder problem. Sooner or later, he would have to tell her they'd been tailed from Nowhere Junction.

"What's the matter?" she asked. "You look jittery. Nervous about being on the *Newlywed Game*?"

"We're not actually going on the game show, Charlee. Soon as we hit the studio lot we're getting a taxi out of there. ASAP."

"At two-thirty in the morning? Why can't we sleep at the bungalow for a little while first?"

"Because we don't have time."

"What aren't you telling me?" She narrowed her eyes at him.

He sighed. No pulling one over on her. She didn't miss a single thing. How was a guy supposed to protect a woman like that? So much for his vain attempt at handling the matter on his own.

"The Malibu is behind us." He jerked a finger at the back of the bus.

"They figured out we got on the bus."

"Well, I can't imagine it was that hard to put two and two together. Smashed Bentley, only couple at the truck stop, and then we disappear at the same time the tour bus does."

"I've got half a mind to walk right up to them and ask them who the hell they are and what they want."

"Don't you dare," he growled, but kept his voice low so the other passengers wouldn't overhear them. "They're armed and dangerous."

"You were all for tackling them when you realized they were the ones who stole your wallet."

"That was me, not you."

"Oooh, Gentry, you're getting all protective on me." She lightly traced a finger over his bicep. "That is sooo sexy."

"Knock off the teasing, Charlee. I'm serious."

"Me too." She gave him an impish grin.

Fresh guilt assaulted him. Obviously she'd read more into last night's kisses than he intended. He had to set things straight with her.

"About last night . . ." he started to say but then Francie leaned across the aisle and interrupted him.

"Aren't you just over the moon excited?" she enthused. "This is the most thrilling thing that's ever happened in my entire life. I bet I won't be able to sleep a wink after we get to the bungalow."

"What about our wedding night, babe, that was pretty thrilling," her husband Jerry interjected.

Francie waved a hand. "That was fine, sweetie, but this is live television. Imagine. Common ordinary everyday people like us on TV."

Charlee and Francie chatted up a storm and Mason never got the chance to apologize for kissing her. A few minutes later, the bus pulled up to the studio lot and checked in with the guard at the security gate.

A spotlight shone on a large banner spanning the entrance. It read: TWILIGHT STUDIOS CONGRATULATES BLADE BRADFORD ON HIS SECOND OSCAR NOMINATION.

Blade Bradford.

Hmm. Mason had completely forgotten that Blade Bradford, the actor who had beaten out Gramps for best actor, had recently made a silver screen comeback with a small budget film the previous year that had earned him a best supporting actor nomination.

Charlee nudged him. "Twilight Studios? Is this just happenstance or could this have something to do with Maybelline and Nolan?"

"It is weird but I don't see how this *Newlywed Game* thing and our grandparents are connected."

"I don't trust coincidences," Charlee said. "Keep your eyes open for a link."

Edith Beth got on the microphone and started in on her spiel. "Blade Bradford's Oscar nomination has resurrected not only his own flagging career but has been the saving grace of Twilight Studios that until the unexpected hit of *The Righteous* was on the verge of bankruptcy. Between Blade's coup and developing television shows like *The New Millennium Newlywed Game*, Twilight is poised to return to its glory days of the 1950s. So see, you guys are part of a history-making event. So give yourselves a big hand."

On cue, the bus broke out into applause.

Gus pulled the bus to a stop under bright security lights outside a collection of bungalows.

"Back in the early days, actors actually lived in these bungalows while they were making movies," said Edith

Beth. "You'll be rooming two couples to a bungalow. I'll call out your names and your bungalow numbers and give you the door key as you get off the bus."

Mason reached over and squeezed Charlee's hand. "Here's where we make a break for it."

Charlee giggled. "You sound like an escapee from some cheap prison flick."

"I *feel* like an actor with a third-rate script," he said. "Keep an eye out for the Malibu. I'm hoping they weren't allowed on the lot."

They stood in the aisle and waited their turn to disembark. Edith Beth herded everyone outside while Gus unloaded luggage from the right side of the bus.

"When you get off," Mason instructed, "head around the front of the bus and go left."

"Wow, Gentry, taking control. I like your macho side."

"Charlee, this is no joke."

"Sorry. Just trying to lighten the tension."

She was right. He was tense. If he clenched his jaw any tighter, he'd snap off a tooth. Charlee climbed off the bus in front of him and immediately darted to the left. Mason followed right behind.

"Skeet, Violet!" Edith Beth snapped her fingers. "This way. You're in bungalow five with Jerry and Francie."

"Hurry," Mason said. "Before Edith Beth gets hold of us."

Charlee sprinted ahead and rounded the corner of the closest bungalow before he did, but he hadn't taken more than two long strides when she did an abrupt U-turn and almost plowed smack-dab into him.

"What?" Startled, he put out an arm to stop her forward momentum and grabbed her wrists between his fingers.

"Go back, go back." Charlee moved her hands in a shooing motion. "They're here."

"Who are here?"

"Our Malibu buddies and they're coming toward us and they don't look happy. Move it."

That's all it took. He grabbed her arm and hustled her back round the front of the bus to face the frowning Edith Beth.

"You two enjoy being mavericks, don't you?" the tour director asked in a snippy tone. "Now pick up your suitcases and go to your bungalow."

Two suitcases remained on the curb. Everyone else was shuffling off in the dark toward the row of cottages. Charlee looked at Mason. "Do you suppose that's Violet and Skeet's luggage?"

"Who else would it belong to?"

"But how come their luggage got on and they didn't?"

Mason shrugged. "Who knows? People and their luggage get separated all the time."

"Maybe they were making out in the bathroom of the bus terminal."

"Maybe."

Mason hurried over to pick up the suitcases. When he bent down, he darted a quick glance under the bus and spied two pairs of legs on the other side.

"Skeet, Violet, hurry up," Jerry called. "We're waiting for you guys."

CHAPTER
11

$\mathcal{M}$ ake the best of a bad situation, Charlee told herself. As long as the Malibu goons were lurking outside, they might as well get some shut-eye. They could worry about escaping after daylight. Sensible advice until she saw the size of the bed she and Mason were expected to share.

"Oooh," Francie called out from the bungalow's other bedroom. "Aren't these beds nice and cozy. Just perfect for snuggling."

Cozy, hell, in that twin bed wanna-be, they'd be stacked on top of each other like Pringles in a can.

Mason dropped the suitcases on the floor and turned to look at Charlee who hung back in the doorway.

"We sleep in our clothes," she decreed.

"I'm not arguing."

"And no touching."

He cocked his head at the tiny bed. "Be reasonable."

"Okay then, we sleep back-to-back."

"Why? Afraid you'll be tempted?"

"Of what, kicking you out of bed?"

"You can relax, sweetheart. I'm much too tired to even think about molesting you, much less work up the energy to do it." He peeled off his shoes and flopped down on the bed.

The truth of the matter was, she was *very* tempted and a little disappointed he wasn't even going to try to molest her.

What in the hell is the matter with you?

It was the idea of lying next to him on that itty-bitty bed that had her thinking crazy thoughts. All she had to do was look at his long form stretched out on the mattress and her stomach performed a three-hundred-and-sixty-degree loop-de-loop.

She was *not* getting emotionally involved with him. She just thought he was kinda sexy and a very good kisser.

Well, stop thinking like that, she chided herself and edged cautiously toward the bed. She left the bedroom door open just in case Mason changed his mind in the night and decided to get frisky. She could make a quick getaway if necessary.

And speaking of getting away, concentrate on how you're going to get away from the Malibu goons. That's what's important.

She kicked off her cowboy boots, turned off the bedside lamp, and gingerly lay down next to Mason.

He didn't move. Propping herself up on her elbows, she peeked over at him. He appeared to be sound asleep already. Good. She would close her eyes for just a few minutes while she thought about how they were going to get out of this mess. She would plan for tomorrow. She'd plot a way to find Maybelline with or without Mason's help.

She was not going to think about how solid Mason's body felt pressed against hers or how the steady sound of his breathing reassured her. Not for one single minute was she going to notice how his long legs hung off the end of the bed or how his beard stubble gave him a roguish appearance in the muted glow of the night-light. She was not going to remember how vulnerable he'd been back in the diner parking lot when that hamburger had smashed Matilda to smithereens or how angry he had gotten just before he'd kissed her for the very first time.

No siree. He was completely out of her head. She was giving herself a mental Mason vaccination. From now on, she was one hundred percent immune to his charms.

Charlee paced the closet-sized dressing room where she and Mason had been told to cool their heels before the live broadcast began at nine.

Before leaving the bungalow that morning, Mason had tried to make a phone call to his brother only to discover the cottages weren't equipped with telephones. Charlee had peeked outside to see the Malibu still parked in the studio parking lot, although there were no signs of the two gun-toting men.

Not knowing what else to do and faced with Edith Beth shooing them along, they had followed Francie and Jerry and the other couples to the breakfast buffet. The media had interviewed them and then the couples had been ushered over to the studio.

And so, they waited.

Charlee was dressed in the least offensive outfit she could find in Violet Hammersmitz's suitcase. That meant she was stalking back and forth in a red flouncy-skirted micro-mini, a black faux leather shirt with shoulder pads and four-inch, scarlet, ankle-strap stilettos. She looked like a streetwalker version of Joan Crawford.

She was within inches of putting her sweaty, two-day-old jeans and T-shirt back on and saying to hell with it. Especially since the stilettos were a size too big and she kept falling off them.

Poor Mason hadn't fared much better. He had gotten stuck wearing Skeet's gaudy purple, hula girl print Hawaiian shirt, beige Bermuda walking shorts, and bright yellow canvas deck shoes.

Must be hard, she thought with a touch of sympathy, for a pampered blue-blood accustomed to the finest designer haute couture to find himself outfitted in Cheap-o-Mart red-light-special duds.

"I don't want to go on the show," he repeated for about the twentieth time in the last five minutes.

"It'll be fine."

"We'll be on national television. Representing ourselves as Skeet and Violet Hammersmitz."

"Don't sweat it. You'll live. I'll live. Skeet and Violet will live."

"You just don't understand. What if my family sees the show?"

"Something tells me the Gentrys from Houston Texas are not big fans of daytime television."

"Somebody my parents know might see us."

"And that would be the end of the world?"

"Three days ago, I would have thought so. But now, after all we've been through, what's a little parental disapproval in the grand scheme of things?"

"That's the spirit," she encouraged. "Rebel. Buck the system. I'd say you're about ten years overdue."

"You don't understand," he said darkly. "Gentry Enterprises is a high-profile company. We live in a fishbowl. People watch what we say and do. My family is very conscious of their public image."

"No kidding."

"You're awfully young to be so sarcastic."

"And you're awfully old to let your family pull you around by the nose."

They glared at each other.

"It's going to be a disaster," he muttered.

"Look, Mason, going on television beats the alternative. We either go on the show, which gives us time to come up with a plan for eluding Rocko and Bruiser out there, or we might as well just get fitted for cement shoes, go climb into the trunk of their Chevy right now, and be done with it. Come to think of it," she mused, "cement shoes have got to be more comfortable than these medieval torture devices." She bent to tug at the straps biting into her ankle.

"You don't wear high heels much." His gaze, tracking the length of her bare legs, sent heat waves shimmering through her.

"What was your first clue? The fact that I keep twisting my ankle?"

"There you go with that smart mouth again."

If he only knew what was going on inside her body. Her sharp tongue was her singular defense against the hot and bothered way he made her feel. The lone barrier that kept her heart safe.

"I'm also guessing you don't wear short dresses either considering the fact you're swishing that skirt around so hard you keep flashing me your panties."

"What!" Aghast, she plastered her hand to the back of her skirt. "Oh, crap, how am I ever going to be able to sit down without giving the audience squirrel shots?"

Mason laughed so hard he almost fell off his chair. "I can't believe you said that."

"What?" Charlee narrowed her eyes at him. "What's so funny?"

"I don't think I've ever heard a woman say 'squirrel shots' and not be discussing wildlife photography."

"That's because the only women you're ever around are those hoity-toity stuck-up society women. Squirrel shot is a perfectly legitimate term."

He was still laughing; his dimples tap dancing their way into her heart. So much for the mental Mason vaccination she'd given herself last night. Apparently his strain of charm was so virulent no adequate inoculation existed.

A heavy sense of inevitability weighted her. She felt like one of those shooting gallery ducks going around and around on the mechanical track, listening to the *ping-ping* of ricocheting bullets, never knowing when she was going to get hit but certain the blast was coming.

"Just keep your legs crossed very tightly and don't squirm. You'll be okay."

"I swear this was the longest skirt in Violet's suitcase. The woman is a floozy, I'm telling you." Charlee kept yanking at the hem, trying to make it stretch lower.

Mason eyed her legs again. "If Violet looks anything like you do in that outfit then Skeet is a lucky, lucky man."

"That does it. I'm going back to the bungalow and putting my blue jeans back on. I can't have you ogling me like a hunk of bologna."

"Sweetheart," Mason said and arched an eyebrow. That simple word sent an arrow of longing straight through her very soul. "Forget bologna. You're filet mignon all the way."

She thrust a thumbnail into her mouth and started to gnaw.

"Stop that."

"Stop what?"

Mason got up from the stool parked next to the lighted vanity table that hosted makeup, nail polish, cold cream, and other beauty supplies. He walked over to extract her thumb from her mouth.

"Sorry," she apologized. "It's a bad habit I can't seem to break."

"Sit down," he said and nodded at a chair on the other side of the tiny room.

"What for?"

"I'm going to paint your fingernails bright red and every time you start to bite them you'll see that flash of crimson and stop."

"Get out of here."

"I'm serious. Noshing your fingernails completely negates your tough girl image."

"I know."

"So sit." He pulled the chair next to the vanity and patted the seat while he plunked down on the stool.

Charlee eased down across from him. Mason rummaged through the bottles of nail polish and selected a screaming vermilion color.

"Give me your hand."

Reluctantly, she stuck out her hand. He shook the polish, and then uncapped it. Taking her hand in his, he stroked the brush over the nail of her pinkie.

She forced herself not to shiver at his touch and read the label on the polish bottle to distract herself. "Be Still My Heart."

"What?"

Her gaze leaped to his. He cocked a grin with his dimples on full-out assault.

"The polish," she said in a rush, not wanting him to think she was saying he caused her heart to stop. "That's the name of the color. Be Still My Heart."

"Oh." He lowered his head again, moved on to the next finger.

"Where did you learn to paint fingernails, Gentry? Don't tell me you have a secret life dressing up in women's clothing."

"No, nothing like that. I'm afraid the truth is much more mundane. I built model cars when I was a kid. Hundreds of them. I spent hours holed up in my room, gluing and painting."

"Really? Rich as your family is I would have supposed they'd have hired someone to build the models for you."

He flashed her another look. This time he was clearly irked. "Money isn't everything, Charlee."

"That sounds like someone who's never been broke."

"I don't want your sympathy, so don't think that's why I'm telling you this, but I was really a lonely kid. My folks weren't hands-on parents." He didn't sound bitter, just matter-of-fact. "That's what money will buy you. Nannies so that you don't have to fuss with the mess of daily child rearing. No kissing those skinned knees and risk mussing your makeup. No rushing home from parties to put your kids to bed. No tedious bedtime stories. Hired help will do it all for you." He laughed but Charlee realized that chuckle held a note of hurt. "But, hey, at least I had both my parents. You got cheated out of both of yours."

"Maybelline was enough." She stared in fascination as he finished painting her left hand and motioned for her to give him her right.

"What happened to your mother?"

Charlee shifted on the seat, uncomfortable with the conversation. She didn't like talking about herself. Exchanging personal information resulted in closeness and she'd already told Mason way too much about Elwood. That's as close as she wanted to get.

She said nothing.

"Come on, Champagne, it's your turn to share." He gazed at her. She saw intelligence, understanding, but worst of all an overriding compassion. She didn't want him feeling sorry for her.

Just tell him and get it over with.

"She was onstage one night and her headdress slipped. Didja know those things can weigh up to fifty pounds? She tripped on the stairs and broke her leg. She died in the hospital after a blood clot went to her heart." Charlee paused as the memory washed over her. "I was at Maybelline's watching cartoons and eating a peanut butter and jelly sandwich when she got the call."

"It must have been hard on you."

Charlee shrugged, pretending the pain didn't run river deep. "I don't remember her much."

He didn't say anything else and Charlee recognized

his technique. He was waiting for her to fill the silence. She refused.

The ticking of the wall clock sounded like a gong in her ears. The air in the room seemed stale. Dust motes cavorted on the shaft of sunlight slanting in the window blinds.

"There you go. All done," Mason said at last and capped the fingernail polish. He blew on her hand to dry her nails. His warm breath sent chills of anticipation skittering up her arm.

Charlee jerked her hand away, disconcerted by the emotions pumping through her. She stared at her vermilion fingernails. *Be Still My Heart*. Her hands looked as if they belonged to someone else. Someone soft and giggly and feminine, and she was none of those things.

"Your nails look nice. I'd love to do your toenails next. There's something incredibly sexy about painting a woman's toenails."

"Lord, don't tell me you have a foot fetish."

"I think I have a Charlee fetish." And then he did the unthinkable. He leaned over and ran a hand up the edge of her skirt, his fingertips brushing lightly over her upper thigh.

She slapped his hand away. "Knock it off," she growled.

He ignored her.

"Mason," she jabbed a stern note of warning in her voice.

"Yes?" He arched a devastating eyebrow and she couldn't find her tongue. Dammit, where had she put the stupid thing?

He pulled her off her chair and onto his lap and

peered down into her eyes with that knee-melting brown-eyed stare of his.

"Don't you dare," she threatened.

"Dare what?"

"Do what you're thinking."

"What am I thinking?" His eyes challenged her with a lusty gleam.

Her heart pounded and her palms grew wet. Ah hell, she grew wet in another place not too far away from where his hand lay.

"No more of that kissing nonsense we were doing last night."

He dipped his head lower and pursed his lips. "Why not? You really seemed to like it on the bus last night."

"That's exactly why not," she squeaked. "I did like it. Too much."

"I liked it too." His voice was deep and masculine and packed with sexual tension. "What's wrong with that?"

"We're wrong. You and me."

"If wanting you is wrong, I don't wanna be right."

Why did he have to say that?

Charlee, you're in deep trouble. Get up. Get out of his lap. Run away.

"We can't do this," she whispered. "My fingernails are wet."

"I don't intend on kissing your fingernails."

"Smart-ass."

She thought she could forget about last night and that heady, Edith-Beth-word-game-induced make-out session they'd indulged in. She thought how his kisses had made her feel special and cherished and appreciated.

She thought she could treat it lightly. She'd told herself repeatedly those kisses meant nothing.

Ha! She was falling faster than a barrel tumbling over Niagara Falls.

"I know why you're so cranky."

"I'm not cranky," she denied and tried to squirm out of his lap but he held her flush against him and the more she squirmed the more aroused he became, leaving no doubts as to where his perverted thoughts lay.

"You are definitely cranky."

"Am not."

"You've been hiding your femininity for so long behind that tough-talking attitude and your gun and those cowboy boots and faded blue jeans that you've completely forgotten what it feels like to be admired for the sexy, desirable woman you are."

"Oh, you're so full of it," she said, even though his words hit the bull's-eye with such unerring accuracy her throat clogged.

"You can't fool me, Charlee Champagne. I see right through your streetwise persona." He lowered his voice. "Deny it all you want but I know that deep down inside you're soft and vulnerable and tenderhearted."

"Stop grinning at me like that," she snapped, terrified he was going to spy the hungry longing reflected in her eyes for something she could never have.

How many times had she hoped that a man would gaze at her exactly the way he was gazing at her? How many times had she dreamed of strong loving arms around her? How many times had she longed to be swept off her feet and carried away into happily-ever-after?

She'd dreamed, yes, but she knew it was all a fantasy.

Real life simply didn't work that way. Hadn't May-belline drilled it into her head and hadn't Charlee's life experiences supported her own disappointment in love?

"I don't want this."

"Liar."

"You're becoming really pushy, Gentry. I'm not sure I like this new side of you. I'm not . . ."

Before she could finish castigating him for having the audacity to ogle her with such frank desire, he took her mouth hostage.

She wanted to tell him that she wasn't his for the tak-ing. That she wasn't some scullery maid eager to lift up her petticoats for the lord of the manor anytime his ap-petites led him to the kitchen. But she did not say a word. She breathed in the dark scent of him and savored the rich aroma. Damn her and her shortsighted weak-ness for brown-eyed handsome men.

Charlee succumbed, all fight and denial and fear van-ishing in the heated taste of his lips. She relaxed her neck against his forearm, the top of her head resting against the wall.

The pressure of his mouth was ticklishly light at first. Soft, warm, teasing.

Dizziness assailed her and she reached up to thread her trembling fingers through his hair and pulled his head down closer to hers. So what if she got fingernail polish in his hair, it would serve him right for starting this.

Last night's kisses had been no fluke of nature. The man could kiss with a mastery that took her breath.

Step by step he increased the pressure, cajoling her lips apart. The mild brush of his tongue was measured and indolent, seducing her in steadily escalating notches. Her head spun recklessly as he took the kiss deeper and deeper still.

His palm cupped the curve of her hip. An instant chemical reaction exploded inside her. The material of her borrowed black blouse grew damp from the anxious perspiration pooling between her breasts.

She tightened her fingers in his hair, pulling lightly, and heard him growl low in his throat as his breathing quickened.

She should put a stop to this. Right now. Get up. Move. Poke him in the eye. Anything to snap herself out of the languid dream state he'd woven over her.

But he smelled like orange juice and tasted like the sinfully delicious eggs Benedict they'd been served for breakfast.

She knew she was going to pay for her recklessness. It wouldn't be the first time she had paid a high price for her imprudent desires. She'd learned the hard way that nothing this sweet came without expensive strings attached.

Kiss in haste, repent for the rest of your days, Maybelline had drilled into her. And so far her grandmother had been right to warn her.

But Mason's mouth was moist and hot against hers, blurring the edges of reality and sucking her down into momentary bliss. Ah, what a foolish slave she was to her hormones.

He stroked her with firm, tender circles and she trembled beneath his touch, her body's response as unstoppable as an earthquake. From outside the dressing room came the sound of the *Newlywed Game* theme song played to an updated hip-hop beat. The steady pounding bass vibrated up through the floor and into the steamy air beneath them.

Her blood skipped through her veins with the strumming rhythm and gathered heavily in her groin. She ached to be filled with him.

Because of their circumstances she was safe from her own headlong recklessness. No matter how tempted she might be to take this lurking passion to its natural crescendo, she knew they couldn't get too carried away. Not when any moment they were expected onstage.

That remembered knowledge eased her earlier misgivings. She was free to explore this sweet interlude without fear of going further than she wished.

Or so she thought until Mason's hand slipped up her thigh and his fingers hooked inside her panties.

Charlee no, her mind warned but her body, oh-her-wicked wicked body was on fire for him and she writhed against his lap while his inquisitive fingers gently explored.

Too late for regrets.

Pure animal instinct took over when his lips left hers to trail a path of blazing heat over her chin and down her throat to the ticklish juncture where her collarbone intersected with her neck. She groaned at the tactile pleasure of his mouth against her skin.

He gave a low, throaty chuckle of pleasure and laved her with his tongue while his fingers continued to stroke the delicate tissue hidden by her panties. He sounded triumphant and a tad egotistical that he had dragged her down to such depths, but she was too lost in physical bliss to care.

One hand was undoing the buttons of her blouse, exposing her aching breasts to the hot air of his breath.

While her pulse leaped and revved in answer, his naughty hand slid under her back and she felt the hooks of her bra spring open. The guy knew what he was doing.

Charlee arched her back, practically beseeching him to take her nipples into his mouth. She rocked her pelvis against his hand begging for more. She shouldn't do this, but she was the helpless product of biology. Her body quivered and pulsated and yearned for more.

Forget common sense. Ignore prudence. Deny rational thought, whispered the pleasure centers of her brain. Stop thinking and simply enjoy.

When he sank a finger into her, she gasped and tightened her muscles around his warm, wet digit and almost came right then and there with his hand in her panties.

Moisture filled her mouth. She hadn't been this hungry for a man since, well, Gregory.

And look where that got you, whimpered the rational side of her brain, which had been all but bushwhacked by her wildfire libido.

Mason raised his head and peered down into her face, sensing her mood change. His dark eyes gleamed with not only lust, but with something deeper, something more. It wasn't the lust that scared her, but the something more. Was that tenderness skulking in his gaze?

Mesmerized, Charlee stared back, unable to look away, unable to stop herself from slipping pell-mell into the abyss of those dark brown eyes. They hung suspended like that for one long breathless moment. Their gaze locked, her blouse unbuttoned, her bra flapping loose, Mason's hand in her panties, his finger inside her, his erection impossibly huge and hard against her buttocks.

And she felt an inexplicable sadness as she imagined things that she could never have with him. A wedding night. A home. A baby.

A knock sounded at the door at the same time a fresh-faced young woman with exotic almond eyes and honey-colored skin poked her head around the door.

"Mr. and Mrs. Hammersmitz . . . oh, my . . . oh, no . . . I'm so sorry." Flustered and flushing to the roots of her glossy dark hair, the girl spun on her heels and turned her back to them.

Charlee jumped from Mason's lap, buttoning her blouse as she went.

"Stupid, stupid, stupid," the assistant muttered to herself. "You've got to learn to stop walking in on newlyweds."

"It's all right," Mason assured the woman. His voice seemed loud in the confines of the small room. "We're the ones who should apologize for not locking the door."

She peeked over at him and saw that his hair was sexily disheveled and his mouth was plastered with the vixen red lipstick the makeup artist had caked on her lips. And she saw that his eyes reflected an unexpected happiness. A happiness bordering on pure joy. She had caused that look.

Charlee caught her breath at the glorious realization of her power over him.

The young woman still did not look at them. "They're ready for you on the set now," she squeaked, then scurried away.

"I think we traumatized her for life," Mason joked.

"I think you traumatized me for life," Charlee confessed before she realized what she was going to say. The last thing on earth she wanted was for Mason Gentry to know exactly how vulnerable his happiness made her feel.

Lust was one thing. Love was something else entirely.

CHAPTER
12

*M*aybelline woke to find her bare legs entwined with Nolan's. When she turned her head, she was treated to a spectacular view of his broad, muscled back. Sometime before dawn he'd put his boxers back on, making him both modest and adorable.

Her cranky old heart careened into her chest as unbalanced as a drunk staggering out of a bar at two A.M. Last night had been incredible and she couldn't thank Nolan enough for making her feel like a desirable woman again. He'd given her a whole new lease on life and the fortitude to face what lay ahead of them.

What you're feeling is way more than gratitude, Maybelline, and you know it.

She was in love.

The dreamy teen who had hidden her love from him forty-seven years ago because his father had told her a white trash Sikes would never be good enough for a Gentry had sent her fleeing to Hollywood. And she'd ended up sleeping with a married man simply because he'd looked like Nolan.

That same young girl who'd had the stars smacked from her eyes by an unplanned pregnancy and a man unwilling to assume responsibility for his own son.

That spunky kid had carried a large burden on her small shoulders and she'd done the best she could. But Elwood's father had turned Maybelline hard and cynical inside when it came to love and romance.

She grieved now for her lost innocence. She felt guilty too, for coloring Charlee's view about men and life in general. She felt guilty about a lot of things. About the way Elwood had turned out. About the way he'd blackmailed Nolan.

Her lover had been wonderful, however, never blaming her for what Elwood had done.

Her lover.

Maybelline smiled up at the ceiling. She was sixty-three years old and Nolan Gentry was her lover at long last. The lover who made her feel like a giggly, girlish sixteen-year-old all over again.

Something good had come of Elwood's criminal behavior. Unfortunately, there was still a whole lot of bad they had to clean up before they could take their budding relationship one step farther. Too many things hung in the balance. Like the Gentry family fortune.

Maybe Nolan's father had been right. Maybe she did spell nothing but trouble for his son.

"Morning, sunshine. What's got you concentrating so hard?" Nolan reached over and rubbed the frown line between her eyebrows with the flat of his thumb.

She looked into his dark brown eyes and smiled. "You."

He tugged her into his arms and held her against his chest for the longest time. They lay not speaking, listening to the sound of their synchronized breathing and reveling in the rekindled love they'd found.

Finally, Nolan kissed her and said, "We have a long day ahead. We should get up, get started."

Maybelline nodded but neither of them moved. She feared that if they got out of bed she would realize it was all a dream.

He nuzzled her neck and planted small kisses along the underside of her jaw.

"Best not start something you don't plan on finishing," Maybelline whispered. "Because I can't be held responsible for what I do next."

"You issuing a threat, honey? Or a promise?"

"Why don't you take a chance and find out."

An hour and a half later, sexually sated and voraciously hungry, Maybelline and Nolan sat on the tailgate of the camper eating a bag of popcorn for breakfast. Maybelline kicked her legs back and forth, munching contentedly.

"You deserve brunch at the Four Seasons," Nolan said.

She waved a hand. "That sort of thing means nothing to me."

"Oh, just wait until you come to Texas. I'm going to spoil you something rotten."

"Well, old man, don't count your chickens before they hatch. We've got a lot of damage control to do before we can start making plans for the future."

Nolan frowned. "I was trying not to think about all that for a few minutes."

"That's because you're the idealist and I'm the realist."

"How did I manage for so long without you?" he asked.

She grinned. "You did pretty well by yourself. A high-society wife, a son, a huge investment firm. I wouldn't have been an asset in your world, Nolan, and you know it. Your daddy certainly knew it."

"Well, my daddy's gone and my world has changed. I'm not the easily influenced young kid I once was."

"Let's not talk about this right now," Maybelline said. "You keep an eye out for passing cars while I take another look at that thermostat."

She had been tinkering under the hood of the camper for about twenty minutes, alternating cussing out the thermostat and sweetly cajoling it to work, when Nolan called out, "Car's coming."

Maybelline straightened and tucked the one tool she had—a toothbrush-sized wrench she kept in her purse for emergencies—into her back pocket. Nolan was standing at the edge of the road, windmilling his hands in an attempt to get the car to stop.

She wiped her hands on a napkin and narrowed her eyes at the vehicle. Damn if it wasn't a big black stretch limousine, right out here smack-dab in the middle of the Arizona desert. It looked as incongruous as a gold prospector at a high school prom.

As the limo drew closer she could see the windows were tinted. It pulled to a stop at Nolan's feet. Maybelline sauntered over to stand beside Nolan, a queer anxiety shooting through her veins.

Slowly the electric windows rolled down and she found herself staring not only into the face of the man who'd impregnated her forty-seven years ago, but down the barrel of a bull-nosed thirty-eight as well.

* * *

Mason's blood raced through his veins. He felt like a caged beast. Restless, pacing, hungry to be free.

Calm down. It's just stress.

Stress. Yes.

That was the only excuse. Ever since losing Matilda he'd been acting crazy, out of character and out of control. Once the trip was over, once he'd found Gramps and ironed out this obvious misunderstanding, he would go back to being his old self.

Except oddly enough, some not-so-small part of him did not want to go back to his life the way it had been before he'd met Charlee Champagne.

Before Charlee everything had been nice and safe and predictable. *He'd* been nice and safe and predictable. The good son, doing what he was told, scheduled to marry a woman his parents approved of, doing the job they'd picked for him.

He'd been living someone else's life.

And now?

Well now, things were in utter chaos. But in a weird, wonderful way, the chaos felt great.

Charlee made him itch for all the childish, carefree things he'd missed in life. Things he'd never even known he'd missed until he met her. Undisciplined, unruly, impetuous things like making out in the balcony of the movie theater or skinny-dipping in the lake at midnight under a full moon or feeding each other a banana split at Baskin-Robbins.

He glanced over at her. God, but she was extraordinary. Impulsive, yes, but cautious too. She made decisions quickly—like getting them on the bus—but she was vigilant with her emotions, never letting him know exactly what she was feeling. She was smart and witty and determined. She was confident and generous and brave.

And in that sexy little outfit that had once belonged to Violet Hammersmitz she absolutely took his breath away. He was halfway in love with her already.

They were on a sound stage seated in a cheap plywood box, decorated with wedding bells and doves, that probably looked very nice on television, but in reality Mason feared getting splinters from the unfinished boards.

Francie and Jerry sat in the box next to them. All four of them had just won the first game and had advanced to the play-off round. This, in spite of the fact that he and Charlee had done everything within their power to answer the questions incorrectly.

It seemed some weird cosmic synchronicity compelled them both to choose the same wrong answers. Call it fate, call it destiny, call it kismet. New Agey as it sounded, Mason feared the universe was hell-bent on shoving them into each other's arms, no matter how they struggled against it.

He was surprised to discover the notion didn't scare him. Not in the least. In fact, he craved the heady excitement of falling in love and he knew this was what had been missing from his relationship with Daphne.

Francie wriggled her fingers and mouthed, "Good luck," at the same time the music swelled and a spotlight came on to showcase the Bob Eubanks look-alike who came popping out from behind the curtain.

The live audience broke into immediate applause.

"Good morning, folks! And we're back for the grand prize round. I'm Manny Mann, your host for Twilight

Studios' *New Millennium Newlywed Game*. Let's give a
big hand to couple number one Skeet and Violet Hammersmitz from the heart of America, Des Moines,
Iowa!"

The spotlight shone on him and Charlee. Obediently
the crowd clapped and Manny Mann went on to introduce the remaining couples.

Mason peered over at Charlee again. She looked
more nervous now than she had in the first round, poor
kid. Winning had kicked the stakes up a notch. They
simply had to lose this time.

She was so tough and self-reliant he kept forgetting
she was covering a soft, vulnerable core and that she
hadn't had the advantages in life that he'd enjoyed. Advantages like private tutors, Harvard Business School, a
life coach, a media coach, and a mentor. Smiling his encouragement, he reached over and squeezed her hand as
the production crew cut to a commercial and the emcee
joked with the audience.

"You're doing just fine," he whispered. "I know we'll
lose this time."

She nodded but instead of his touch reassuring her, he
was surprised to find she trembled even harder.

"Charlee? Are you okay?"

Before she could answer, the same young assistant
who had interrupted them in the dressing room came
over to escort the ladies offstage to a soundproof room.

Thirty seconds later, they were back from commercial
and the Bob Eubanks clone, Manny Mann, jumped right
into the program.

"Husbands, here's your first question." He paused
while dramatic music played. "Would you say your

wife's chest is more like a watermelon, a grapefruit, a peach, or a strawberry?"

The audience twittered.

"Skeet?" Manny prompted him with a smug smirk. "What fruit are Violet's breasts most like?"

The spotlight shone on Mason. What a stupid question. He forced a smile. He was stuck here, he might as well play along.

"Are we talking size here, Manny, or flavor?"

The crowd hooted and guffawed enthusiastically at his response.

"Either or, Skeet. Just answer the question."

"A peach." He'd just discovered firsthand that Charlee's breasts were round, soft, and perfect. Just the right size for cupping into a man's palm.

And on went the stupid questions. Mason was never so relieved in his entire life when at the next commercial break they brought the wives back in.

Charlee seemed to have recovered from her stage fright. She was laughing and joking with the other women. That is until she sat next to him again. The smile left her face and she nervously started to chew on her thumbnail but stopped herself before she could nibble off the flashy Be Still My Heart crimson polish.

Then a curious thought occurred to Mason. Maybe Charlee wasn't afraid of being on television or of winning the game. Maybe she was afraid of *him*.

Charlee afraid? Impossible. He thought of how she'd used her body to block his from the bullet shot into her grandmother's trailer. How she'd tackled the old gold prospector at the abandoned studio lot. How she'd boldly bluffed her way onto the tour bus. Charlee was the most courageous woman he'd ever known.

"Okay, ladies, now we'll see how well your answers matched your husbands'. Remember in this round each correct answer earns you five points. Violet, how do you suppose your husband answered?" Manny Mann asked and then repeated the ridiculous fruit question.

Charlee glanced at her chest, and put an exaggerated comic expression on her face. "Well, Manny, most people would probably say a strawberry, but my Skeet is really generous so I'm gonna say a peach."

A bell sounded. "That's absolutely correct. Skeet, hold up your card."

Mason raised the placard the assistant had placed in his lap at the break.

Charlee grinned.

"Aren't you going to kiss him for being so generous about your dimensions?" Manny asked a little too lewdly for Mason's taste. He noticed the emcee kept glancing at Charlee's chest and he frowned pointedly at the man.

"Oh, sure," Charlee said, then hastily leaned over and kissed Mason's cheek. The sweet smell of her lingered on his skin.

"Remember"—Mason leaned over to whisper to her once Manny had gone on to quiz Francie and Jerry—"we don't want to win this thing. Try to give wrong answers."

"I was," she protested. "I figured for sure you'd say strawberry."

"Oh, come on, Charlee, your breasts are perfect. Not too big, not too small. Firm and pert and . . ."

"Mason!"

Had he shocked her? It wasn't easy shocking Miss

Streetwise P.I., but yes, he did believe she was blushing. He grinned.

Manny was back with another question and damned if she didn't get that one right too. Even though it was a question about the nonexistent apartment they shared. By the time the five-point round was over, she'd answered all three of the questions correctly and they had more points than any of the other contestants.

Just before the assistant came over to escort the husbands offstage, Mason murmured in her ear, "Remember, answer the opposite of how you think I would answer."

"Okay, all right." She nodded. "I've got it under control."

"Violet," Manny said after the commercial break. "Can you tell us how old was your husband the very first time he made whoopee?"

Charlee hadn't meant to answer with the truth. Honestly, she hadn't. But her pride over the fact that she knew that Mason had lost his virginity in the backseat of the Bentley when he was seventeen with Blair Sydney took over and she blurted out exactly that and then belatedly slapped her hand over her mouth.

"No, Manny, that's not correct. I'm wrong. He wasn't seventeen."

"Too late, Violet." Manny winked. "You've already spilled Skeet's dirty secret. He's a late bloomer."

Charlee cringed. Mason was going to skin her alive. She imagined how embarrassed he would be if his most private sexual history got back to his parents.

God, she was an idiot. What possessed her to tell the truth?

Perhaps she'd subconsciously wanted to pay him

back for embarrassing her about her peachy breasts? Was she that petty?

"Violet," Manny returned to her after all the other women had answered the virginity question. "What was his parents' reaction the first time Skeet introduced you to them?"

Charlee tried to imagine meeting Mason's parents and almost snorted out loud. No doubt the Gentrys would hate her and everything about her just as Gregory's parents had hated her.

Think opposite of reality.

"Manny, Skeet's parents welcomed me with open arms and even asked me when we were planning on giving them grandchildren."

There. No way on earth would Mason get that question right.

"Ladies," Manny said after they had answered the remaining ten-point questions. "This is it. For twenty-five points, what is your husband's favorite food?"

Oh, getting this one wrong would be like falling off a log.

"Violet?"

"Cheeseburgers, Manny. And french fries. Skeet loves greasy fried foods."

Feeling self-satisfied that she'd done well, Charlee leaned back in her seat and gave Mason a thumbs up as the husbands filed onto the stage.

They were a team, she realized suddenly. Charlee admitted to herself she *liked* the feeling. She'd never felt this close to anyone, save her grandmother. It had always been her and Maybelline against the world.

Until her grandmother had run off with Mason's grandfather.

The shift in her thinking was disconcerting. All her life she had believed that she had no one on her side except for Maybelline. Certainly not her irresponsible father. And losing her mother at such a young age had only strengthened that belief.

Fool. You're setting yourself up for disaster. You know better than to fall for this guy.

She knew better and yet she could do nothing to temper the sweet, mushy feelings sprouting inside her the minute Mason took his place as her pretend husband.

It's just lust, she assured herself. *He's one helluva hottie and a crackerjack kisser. Nothing wrong with physical attraction as long as you don't let it become something more.*

When Manny asked Mason the virginity question and he got it right, Mason shot Charlee a look of alarm.

What in the hell? his expression said.

Charlee shrugged and looked apologetic. How could she explain her need to let the world know she was privy to Mason's secret when she didn't understand the motivation herself?

"Skeet, what was your parents' reaction the first time they met Violet?"

Mason looked uneasy. "Well, Manny, they welcomed her with open arms and even asked when we were going to start a family."

Ding, ding, ding, went the bell.

"That's correct, Skeet, earning you another ten points." Charlee offered him an I'm-so-sorry-I-screwed-up smile. Her stomach churned. Was he mad? Her anxiety level skyrocketed.

"And now, gentlemen. For that all-important twenty-five-point question. The question that can make or break you. What is your favorite meal, Jerry?"

"This is a cinch," said Jerry, rocking back in his seat and puffing out his chest with absolute self-assurance. "My favorite food is lasagna."

The buzzer sounded, signaling a wrong answer. Jerry blinked and shook his head. "What? What?" He glared at Francie.

"No, Jerry, your wife Francie says your favorite meal is pizza."

"Pizza, lasagna, they're both Italian food. Come on, Manny, cut us some slack," Jerry begged. "Francie gets pizza and lasagna mixed up. Come on over to our house the next time she makes pizza and see for yourself."

The buzzer blasted another raspberry.

"Sorry, Jerry, you're out of the running."

The next two couples managed to get the answer right, tying them up with Charlee and Mason.

"Skeet and Violet Hammersmitz, if you answer this question correctly, you'll not only be our grand prize winner but you will have proven you know each other more intimately than any of the other fifteen couples in the contest."

Please get it wrong, Charlee prayed and clenched her fist. *I know you hate hamburgers.*

"For a total score of sixty points, Skeet, and a two-night stay at the famous Beverly Hills Grand Piazza Hotel along with special VIP tickets to this year's Academy Awards ceremony on Sunday night courtesy of Twilight Studios, what is your favorite meal?"

The crowd and Charlee held their collective breaths. She crossed her fingers and her toes and closed her eyes tight.

Say sushi, say Chateaubriand, say anything besides hamburger.

Because her heart hung in the balance. For the life of her she couldn't imagine anything worse than spending the night with Mason in a luxury hotel.

Just the two of them.

All alone.

In a fancy hotel.

With champagne and room service.

Given those circumstances Charlee knew she was not strong enough to resist him or if she even wanted to. Not when all it would take to get her stripped naked was one flash from those darling dimples.

"Well," Mason drawled in that sexy Texas way of his that never failed to set her pulse flailing erratically, "Manny, I just love cheeseburgers and french fries."

Directly following the broadcast, Charlee and Mason found themselves surrounded by news media. In a blur of activity, they were interviewed and then whisked away in a limousine.

As their driver pulled out of the Twilight Studios parking lot, Charlee spied the thugs leaning against the white Chevy Malibu glaring at them.

She nudged Mason in the ribs and nodded out the window at the men. "Winning the contest was one way of getting away from those goons."

"They'll just follow us," Mason predicted gloomily and sure enough, not two minutes later, the Malibu pulled up behind them in the traffic on Sunset Strip. "We're stuck for now, but once we get to the hotel, I'll call my family and have them wire money."

A confident gleam sparked in his eyes as if he had everything figured out. He seemed different, more sure of himself. He sat up straighter and assumed a regal air in spite of Skeet's hideous tourist clothes. Mason was back in his milieu.

By the time they arrived at the Beverly Hills Grand Piazza he was back to being a Gentry again, the same controlled, calculating executive who'd marched into her office on Thursday afternoon.

Gone were all traces of the open, adventuresome man who had cut loose back there in the desert. The man who had kissed her all night long on the honeymoon bus. The man who said her breasts were perfect as ripe peaches.

That was a good thing. Right?

This way, she didn't have to worry so much about falling for him. Still she felt sorta sad that Skeet was gone for good and Mr. Straight-and-Narrow was back at the helm.

The minute the hotel valet opened the limo door, a second contingent of reporters and another perky representative from Twilight Studios were there to greet them.

The representative introduced herself as Pam Harrington and bustled them into a reception area.

"Are all these people for us?" Charlee stared in disbelief at the milling throng gathered in the hotel ballroom and lining up for a lavish buffet.

Pam smiled. "Well, we are waiting for Oscar nominee Blade Bradford. He was supposed to be here to congratulate you on winning the game but I guess he's running a little late."

Blade Bradford, huh? Blade was her grandmother's least favorite actor. She'd done makeup on him back when she worked for Twilight. Even though Maybelline wasn't one for trashing people, she'd only had bad things to say about the Oscar-winning actor.

And because of Maybelline's unhappy experiences in

Hollywood, Charlee herself had never been starstruck. As her granny was fond of telling her, movie stars put on their pants one leg at a time, just like everybody else.

Pam cast a nervous glance at her watch. "If you'll excuse me, I'll just go make a couple of phone calls. Help yourself to the buffet."

"Ah," Mason said after Pam had bustled away, his tone suggesting he'd just died and gone to heaven. "Caviar."

He went straight for the black fish eggs.

Fish eggs. She should have known that would be his favorite food.

Blech! She looked at the salmon pâté, the foie gras, the oysters on the half shell, and the sushi rolls spread out across the elaborate buffet.

She was hungry but not *that* hungry. She settled for a dry wheat cracker and ended up having to guzzle half a glass of champagne to wash it down.

Charlee snagged one of the tuxedo-clad waiters by the arm. "By any chance you wouldn't happen to have a jar of Skippy chunky peanut butter hidden away somewhere in the kitchen, would you?"

The waiter rolled a haughty expression down the end of his nose. "Madam, this is the Beverly Hills Grand Piazza."

"And?" Charlee one-upped his hoity-toity look with her own particular brand of a hard-edged stare she'd perfected in the dark alleys of Vegas.

He squirmed under the intensity of her glare but maintained his snooty countenance and added a flippant head toss. "I'm afraid we do not stock Skippy chunky peanut butter."

Charlee was about to tell the guy to pluck the stick

out of his ass when Mason glided over and smoothly intervened.

"But I'm sure you carry some brand of peanut butter. So run off to the kitchen and get some for the lady," he said pointedly in his most superior tone.

Apparently his commanding voice and the way Mason set his facial features overrode Skeet's garish outfit. Even when it was disguised in Cheap-o-Mart duds the waiter recognized aristocracy when he saw it.

"Yes, sir"—the waiter bowed contritely—"I will bring the lady her peanut butter."

"Thank you." Mason smiled like a shark on chum patrol.

"You didn't have to stick your nose in." Charlie sank her hands on her hips, irritated that he had gotten results from the wormy waiter where she'd failed.

"You looked like you needed the help."

"It must be nice," she said sarcastically, "having people fall all over themselves to do your bidding."

"Why are you mad at me? I got the peanut butter you wanted."

"I should have been able to get my own peanut butter off that lippy waiter."

"You're being unreasonable."

"Am I?"

"This is Beverly Hills."

"Meaning?"

"Different things work in different worlds."

"What are you talking about?"

"If I'd waltzed into Kelly's bar and ordered caviar what do you think would have happened?"

"Good point," she conceded.

The waiter reappeared, rushing over with a fat dollop

of peanut butter centered on a leaf of butter lettuce and riding atop a fine bone china plate.

"Is Madam pleased?" he asked her, but his eyes were on Mason.

"Madam is very pleased," Mason assured him. "You will be be commended to your supervisor."

The waiter nodded and hurried off.

"You're really great at this greasing-the-palm stuff, aren't you?"

"Makes the world go round, babe."

"Babe? Oh, horrors. Better watch out, you're slipping back into Skeet vernacular," she said.

"Thanks. I appreciate the warning." He flashed her an intriguing expression she couldn't interpret, but it made him look kinda sexy. Charlee downed the rest of her champagne in a desperate hope it would make him look less attractive.

Bad move.

He only looked cuter through the sweet sheen of high-dollar bubbly. When a waiter offered her another glass of champagne, she took it, even though her head was already helium-balloon floaty.

She could quaff a quart of rotgut whiskey just fine but champagne shot straight to her head. The more expensive the brand, the faster she succumbed.

According to Maybelline, Charlee's mother had been the same way and Bubbles adored bubbly so much she had even named herself after it. Judging from the way her head was reeling, the effervescent stuff must have set Twilight Studios back a pretty penny.

By the time the food was gone and Blade Bradford still hadn't appeared and the grumbling reporters began to clear out, Charlee was seriously regretting that second glass of champagne.

Pam walked over. "I'm so sorry. It seems Blade can't make the reception."

"Probably three sheets to the wind in some hooker's bed," mumbled the photographer trailing after Pam.

"But we're going to take a publicity photo anyway. I'll just stand in for Mr. Bradford." Forcing a smile, Pam sandwiched herself between Charlee and Mason and draped an arm over their shoulders for the photographer. Charlee smiled dopily for the camera and held up two fingers for bunny ears over Pam's head.

"What's going to happen," Charlee whispered to Mason after Pam had moved away to ply her public relations skills with the reporters, "when they figure out we're not Skeet and Violet?"

"We'll deal with that problem when it arises."

"Come, come, come." Pam was back, grinning and snapping her fingers. "Now for the moment you've been waiting for. Let's go see your honeymoon suite."

She escorted them through the lobby and toward the elevators. Charlee wobbled precariously on Violet's four-inch stilettos and at first she was grateful when Mason put a steadying hand to her elbow.

But his touch, combined with the dizzying effects of the champagne, made her feel all warm and fuzzy and receptive. And she hated soft, squooshy emotions like those.

Soft, squooshy, girlie emotions only got you into trouble.

Take a note. Remember that.

"Here we are." Pam slid a card key through the electronic eye sensor and pushed open the door.

Charlee had been in luxury suites many times when she'd worked as a hotel maid, but that was in Vegas where everything was ornate, flashy, and gaudily overdone. This room was pure elegance.

From the cherry wood canopied bed to the eggshell satin duvet to the silver champagne bucket with a bottle of iced Dom Perignon nestled on an antique teacart the place whispered money, money, money.

On the classy bureau sat a gigantic fruit basket. Beside the basket rested an artfully arranged bouquet of colorful spring flowers and a half-dozen flickering candles giving off the scent of honeysuckle.

"Wooo, fancy-schmancy," Charlee said.

"I'll just leave you two alone to enjoy your prize. If you need anything, here's my beeper number and your Oscar tickets." Pam handed Mason an envelope.

"Thank you." He stuffed the envelope in the back pocket of his shorts.

"The reporters will be back on Sunday afternoon to interview you before the Academy Awards. And tomorrow I'll take you shopping on Rodeo Drive for your Oscar ceremony clothes. All courtesy of Twilight Studios."

"No kidding," Charlee murmured. "New clothes too. What a kick."

Guilt needled her. This should be Violet Hammersmitz's big adventure, not hers, but in spite of herself she was enjoying this Cinderella gig.

"Have fun," Pam said, looking distracted, and left the room.

Once the door snapped closed behind her, Mason and Charlee turned to stare at each other.

"Wow, Gentry"—Charlee spun around the room, her head swirling—"do you live like this all the time?"

"What do you think of me? I don't live in a hotel. I have a house, I go to work, I volunteer my time to charities. I have a normal life."

"Yeah, but do you eat caviar and sleep on four-hundred-thread-count sheets and have people waiting on you hand and foot every day?"

"It's not that big of a deal."

"Oh, maybe not to you, but to me this whole thing seems surreal."

"It is surreal. The fact that you and I are stuck here pretending to be husband and wife has little basis in reality."

"Hmm, I don't know about that. I'm real and you're real and if I pinched you hard on the fanny I bet you would holler."

"I think it's time I made a few phone calls," he said, ignoring her "pinching him on the fanny" remark and heading straight for the white and gold phone centered on the Queen Anne writing desk.

Giggling, Charlee fell backward onto the satin duvet and immediately slid whiz-bang onto the floor. She sprawled on her spine, her neck resting awkwardly against the footboard.

"There's a trick to lying down on satin," Mason said without even looking up from punching his calling card number into the phone.

"So I gather." Charlee stared up at the ceiling and willed her head to stop whirling.

From this angle, she had a tantalizing view of the length of Mason's leg.

Man-o-man-o-man.

Her eyes tracked a path from his thigh to his knee and down to his muscled calf. An irresistible urge took hold of her. She wanted to scoot across the carpet and sink her teeth into the fleshy part of that calf to see if it tasted as juicy as it looked.

She licked her lips.

A prickliness crawled across the nape of her neck, light and ticklish. She reached a hand around to push her hair away.

The creepy-crawly sensation transferred from her neck to the back of her hand. She pulled her hand down and stared in horror at the black widow spider inching across her skin.

She literally froze.

Her throat constricted. Her tongue turned to cement. Her brain locked.

Help!

The old spider-bite wound in her backside throbbed. Her hand blanched pale as bleached linen, highlighting the black spider's dark journey across her wrist.

She couldn't breathe. She couldn't scream. She couldn't move. She was trapped in a terrifying nightmare.

Help! Help!

Mason was staring out the window, the telephone receiver cradled against his cheek. She had to get him to notice her before the deadly spider sank her vicious venom into her bloodstream.

Look at me, dammit! she mentally willed.

No such luck.

Meanwhile Miss Arachnid strolled leisurely toward her elbow.

Help! Help! Help!

Charlee flashed back to that night in the Wisconsin woods. She recalled the painful sting as the black widow bit into her tender behind. She remembered, in vivid detail, the agonizing therapy at the hospital and the skin grafts that followed.

She could not, she would not go through that terrible ordeal again.

Act. Move. Do something.

Mason!

Galvanized by the same fear that a second before had frozen her, Charlee threw back her head and let loose with a bloodcurdling shriek.

Mason came up out of the chair as if he had been zapped in the butt with a blowtorch. He jumped to his feet, flinging the telephone away from him and jerking his head around to find Charlee lying on the floor, the hem of her miniskirt hiked up to her panties, a terror-stricken expression on her face.

"What is it? What's happened?" He sprang to her side, his blood pumping through his veins like a fire hose in a five-alarm blaze.

"Aaa-aaa-aaa."

"Charlee, speak to me." Good God, what was wrong?

She stared him in the eyes, then shifted her gaze to the small black spider crawling up her shoulder.

"The spider? You're scared of the spider?"

Vigorously, she nodded. Relief washed through him. Thank God. He couldn't imagine what had caused her to scream like Marie Antoinette at the guillotine.

So the tough P.I. from Vegas was afraid of spiders. He tried not to smile at her fear as he leaned over to scoop the spider into his palm.

"Noooooo," she wailed.

He blinked at her. "What?"

"It's a black widow!"

"No, it's not. See."

He opened his palm and she reacted as if he held a live hand grenade, covering her head with her arms in the fatalistic manner of a soldier in a fox hole.

"Charlee," he coaxed. "It's okay to look."

Tentatively she lowered her arms and peeked over the side of his palm.

"See, sweetheart," he spoke softly. "No red hour-glass."

"Really?" Her eyes were wide and he spotted a tear glistening on her cheek.

He had never seen her like this, cowering defense-lessly. Her unexpected weakness tugged at something inside him. He got up, walked to the window, opened it, and deposited the spider on the outside ledge.

When he looked up and glanced over the parking lot, he winced to see the Chevy Malibu parked across from the hotel. At some point he would have to deal with that threat.

But for now, Charlee needed comforting.

After closing the window, he came back, reached down, and tugged her gently up off the floor.

She cringed in his arms, trembling like a rabbit trapped in a coyote's lair. "I was so scared, Mason."

When she whispered his name, he realized it was the first time she had called him by his given name rather than Gentry.

What did it mean? More importantly, what did he wish that it meant? That she was drawing closer to him? Letting down her guard? Starting to trust him?

"I thought for sure it was a black widow. I admit I'm

jumpy when it comes to spiders. I've been bitten and I know how bad it hurts."

He rested his chin against the top of her head, rubbed his hands up and down her arms. "Shhh, shhh. It's all right."

The sound of the phone off the hook buzzed its obnoxious message, but Mason ignored it. He held her close, comforting her, easing her fears.

The sweet smell of her invaded his nostrils and he marveled at his body's immediate response to their close contact. What was it about her that invariably brought out the horned, pitchfork-carrying devil in him?

If he kissed her, she would taste of expensive champagne, peanut butter, and ripe, delectable sin.

He wanted her.

Badly.

And it was all he could do to keep from carrying her to the bed and making love to her.

Before Charlee, he'd always been attracted to cool, detached petite blondes with an elegant style and impeccable breeding. But somehow, he found himself completely enchanted by this long-legged, black-haired dynamo with a tart tongue that covered up her tender heart.

She was the total opposite of everything he'd ever thought he wanted. She was bold when he'd thought he wanted demure. She was tall and muscular when he thought he wanted dainty and soft. She was sassy when he thought he wanted accommodating.

Charlee challenged him in ways he had never dreamed possible. She called to the wildness he'd buried along with Kip. She resurrected his lost sense of adventure and she had him questioning his blind insistence on following the straight and narrow path his parents had laid out for him.

For that gift he would be forever grateful.

He found her exciting and dramatic and totally captivating. He adored that she knew unequivocally who she was and what she wanted out of life. He admired the way she courageously stood up for what she believed in.

Most of all, he loved the fact that together they were an electric combination of will, drive, and determination. With her, he felt like more of a man.

And there was absolutely no way she would ever fit in with his world.

He struggled hard to imagine her entertaining his high-society friends or sipping tea with corporate wives, dishing idle chitchat or chairing charity auctions, and failed miserably.

He tried to envision her in designer outfits and diamonds instead of her neon blue cowboy boots and a battered straw Stetson. No. He couldn't see it. Not that she couldn't wear finery and jewels, those things just did not suit her.

In the soft cushion of his privileged world, safely cocooned from the realities of the rest of humanity, Charlee would either wilt like a hothouse flower or grow to hate herself for the compromises that life with him would force her to make.

Mason would rather die than risk ruining her zest for life.

No matter how much he wanted to have sex with her, to taste those delicious lips, to run his hands all over her naked body, to hear her whisper his name in the throes of ecstasy, he would not give in to his urges.

Charlee deserved far better than being a sexual conquest. She deserved someone who could love her for who she was and not expect her to compromise to meet some predetermined standard. She deserved the freedom to be herself.

And he simply could not offer her those things.

Reaching down deep inside him, he summoned the strength to ignore his driving biology. He could control himself. He would.

Tenderly, he brushed his lips across her forehead and then stepped back.

"I better finish making those phone calls," he said and turned away without meeting her gaze because he knew one look into those compelling green eyes and he was a goner.

♥ ♥ ♥

CHAPTER

14

*S*till light-headed from champagne, the adrenaline rush of spider freak-out, and the disturbing effects of being held in Mason's arms, Charlee had to take several long, slow, deep breaths before her pulse rate decelerated and her heart plunked back down into its regular place in her chest.

Easy. Steady. Calm.

Breathe deep from your diaphragm. Let it out through your mouth.

Her shoulders relaxed and she could hardly feel the lingering imprint of Mason's fingers on her skin.

Okay, good. Shake it off. Things were getting back to normal.

While Mason went to complete his telephone calls, Charlee inched over to the window and gazed out to study the black spider who was already busily spinning a web.

She admired the creature's capacity to adapt to her sudden change in environment and go about business as usual even though she had been rudely displaced. Bloom where you're planted.

Maybelline's insistence that they live in a travel trailer had taught Charlee the importance of that lesson. If you wanted to last in this world you had to be ready, willing, and able to square your shoulders, pull yourself up by your bootstraps, and relocate whenever circumstances changed.

Her lifelong motto: Dust yourself off. Pick yourself up. Move on.

But she was tired of moving on. Tired of fighting her desire. Tired of being good. She was afraid of losing control of her feelings, not of sleeping with him. Actually, sex sounded really fabulous. It had been such a long time for her. Could she throw herself into physical pleasure while keeping her emotions at bay? Was she willing to roll the dice, take the chance for a night of exquisite pleasure?

Oh, yes, yes, yes.

You can do it, Charlee. You can keep your emotions out of the fray. Go for it. Have wild circus sex and then discard him like those rich, handsome men have always discarded you.

The idea excited her so much that she turned and raced into the adjoining bathroom with the intention of splashing her face with cold water to cool her ardor. She was startled to find a Jacuzzi tub big enough to hold an entire wedding party.

Plush, white matching his and her bathrobes were laid out on the mauve marble steps. More scented candles burned in gold and silver candle holders, scenting the air with Jasmine perfume. Another basket sat on the elaborate dressing table. This one was filled with toiletries, toothbrushes, toothpaste, and . . . *ulp* . . . were those Trojans?

A luxurious heat swept through her body along with the dreaminess of the champagne lingering in her bloodstream and she had an almost irresistible urge to strip off her clothes, settle right into that tub, and call for Mason to come join her.

Her yen for sin scared the bejesus out of her and Charlee back-pedaled from the bathroom.

Fast.

Mason was hanging up the phone. A frown creased his brow. "I couldn't get hold of anyone."

"What's up?" she asked nonchalantly, doing her damnedest to quell the erotic thoughts circulating through her brain with absolutely no success.

"According to the housekeeper my parents went to Paris for the weekend."

"What about your brother?"

"Hunter wasn't home and when I called his cell phone I got his voice mail. I left the number here. I'm hoping he'll check his messages and call back soon."

Her treacherous body throbbed, agreeing completely with the pleasure center of her brain.

Yeah, yeah, go for it.

Standing so close to him in this stylish suite, hearing him speak in that forceful businessman tone, smelling the tangy aroma of his cologne made Charlee's knees loosen.

She was terrified her lips might join her knees in rubberdom and she would say something truly frightening, like, "Let's get it on, you long-legged, brown-eyed, handsome, matinee-idol-smiling, beard-stubble-sporting stud you."

Oh, she was weak and stupid.

And she was more turned on than she'd ever been in her entire life.

High-caliber folly, rolling the dice and taking a chance that she could seduce him and then just walk away with her heart in check.

Charlee realized then she was breathing heavier than a greyhound after a race.

"You're panting," he said.

"No, no, I'm not," she denied.

"Still upset over the spider?"

"I already forgot about that."

"Charlee, you sound like you just ran up six flights of stairs. If you're feeling faint or something let me know. The last thing I want is for you to pass out and crack your head on the floor."

"Well, that's a sexy thought. *Not.*"

"Sexy?" He gave her an odd look.

Oh, crap! Why had she said that? She didn't want him knowing she was thinking sexy thoughts. Not when she was still so conflicted about said sexy thoughts.

"Did I say sexy? Not sexy. I didn't mean sexy," she babbled.

"How much champagne did you have?" Mason narrowed his eyes.

She held up two fingers. He glanced at his watch. "Two glasses in under forty-five minutes. You're drunk."

"I'm not drunk," she insisted, leaning in closer to get a better whiff of his Mason smell. "Just feeling a little . . ."

"Amorous?" he suggested with a raised eyebrow when she ran a finger over his collar.

"I was going to say horny, but yeah, okay, amorous will do."

"You're letting this honeymoon stuff go to your head, sweetheart," he said gently. "And although I find you sexy as hell, we both know this is neither the time nor the place to lose control."

"We're in the honeymoon suite of the Beverly Hills Grand Piazza. We have no idea where to start searching for our grandparents. And besides we can't go anywhere because the media and a Twilight Studios assistant are virtually camped outside our door, not to mention those two goons in the Malibu across the street."

She paused and studied his face. Stone wall. Nada. Zip. He was giving her nothing to go on. She took a deep breath and went on.

"We don't have any money or a car and we have no idea when your brother will call. Name a better time and place."

"I can't take advantage of you." He disentangled her arms from around his neck and stepped away. "I won't. You've had too much to drink."

"Such a gentleman." She clicked her tongue.

"You wouldn't think I was such a gentleman if you knew the thoughts spinning through my head, lady," he growled. "Some of them are downright illegal."

"Oooh. I like the sound of that."

"I can't do this," he repeated, although the distinct bulge in his pants argued otherwise.

"Open that bottle of champagne and catch up with me." She waved a hand at the bucket of Dom Perignon and lost her balance. "Oops."

He reached out and grabbed her before she fell and she smiled up at him.

"You did that on purpose," he accused.

"Who? Me?" She blinked innocently.

"Charlee," he said. "Please don't give me the full court press. I'm only human."

The look in his eyes sent her temperature blasting into the danger zone. Did she dare force the issue? Did she dare seduce him?

Was she brave enough to face her fears right here, right now? Stab the vampire of her past rotten romantic experiences squarely in the heart and live to tell the tale?

Was she really as tough as she pretended or deep down inside, when push came to shove, was she all talk?

She leaned in close and kissed him, but because she was tipsy and wearing Violet's ridiculous stiletto ankle straps, her lips bounced off his mouth and skidded headlong into a dimple.

God, she was woefully inept at this sultry seductress stuff.

Luckily, Mason turned his cheek, removing the gouge of his dimple and presenting her with a second opportunity to capture his mouth.

He kissed her back, grabbing her shoulders in his hands and holding her steady on her shoes.

Eagerly, she ironed her body against his, reveling in the hard line of his muscles and bones.

Okay, this wasn't so scary. No big deal. Just hormones, right? Hormones and moving body parts and making each other feel good.

But a few minutes later, Mason pulled away, his breathing hot and spiky, a "what just happened" expression on his face. His hair was a sexy, disheveled mess, his lips damp with her moisture.

"That's enough, Charlee. This can't go any further."

Seeze who? She blinked at him.

"I can't. I won't do this."

"Okay." She shrugged and stepped away from him. "Suit yourself."

Then she slowly started undoing the buttons on her blouse as she turned and headed for the bathroom.

"What are you doing?" He sounded panicky.

"Taking matters in hand. If you catch my drift," she called to him over her shoulder and dropped Violet's black blouse onto the tiled floor.

With a flick of her thumb, she unsnapped her bra and tossed it beside the blouse.

She shot a quick glance toward the mirror. In the reflection she could see into the bedroom. She could also see that Mason was craning his neck, getting a good view of her backside.

She bent at the waist to turn on the Jacuzzi and then wriggled her hips as she inched the skirt down over her thighs. She heard him inhale sharply and then cough as if he'd swallowed his tongue.

Pretending that she wasn't watching him watching her, she used her hair as a curtain to shield her face from him and sat down on the edge of the marble tub wearing nothing but thong panties and the scarlet high heels.

Her heart thumped against her chest gone tight with mounting anticipation. The whirlpool gurgled and churned and a fine mist rose to enshroud her.

With trembling fingers, she reached down to unbuckle the ankle straps. She heard footsteps and her pulse accelerated.

She thought she heard heavy breathing as well but she couldn't be certain over the noise of the hot tub.

Cocking her head to one side until a sheaf of hair slanted forward, she peeped cautiously through the opening and peered out at him with a coy look.

Mason stood in the bathroom doorway. His face had reddened and his chest rose and fell with hard, jerky movements.

Most definitely heavy breathing.

And he wasn't the only one.

The way his gaze caressed her skin made her tingle with excitement. To think that she was responsible for that wild, lusty gleam in his eyes sent goose bumps bivouacking along her forearms.

She kicked off the stilettos. Then, with her head down and blood racing, shimmied out of her panties.

He made a noise of pure masculine arousal.

Charlee slid over the edge of the tub and into the hot, effervescent water. She leaned back against the headrest and closed her eyes tight but she was too tense to relax, too darned aware of Mason's blatant gaze roving over her body.

"That's not such a good idea," he said hoarsely.

"What's not?"

"Getting into the hot tub when you've been drinking." He clicked his tongue.

"I didn't drink that much."

"You drank enough to make you strip naked in front of me."

"If you hadn't been peeking 'round the corner you wouldn't have seen me naked."

She kept her eyes tightly closed. One look at him

would send her scrambling pell-mell for that monogrammed bathrobe.

"You wanted me to see you naked. Otherwise you would have shut the door behind you."

"So how does that make you feel?"

"Angry."

"Angry?" She opened one eye at the testy note in his voice.

"Angry for not being able to resist you."

Oh my, oh my, oh my.

His fist grabbed for the front of his shirt and he pulled hard, sending buttons pinging off the tile floor. Charlee gasped and sat up straight, her eyes rounding in surprise at the feral, untamed look on his face.

Gone was the polished, controlled businessman. In his place stood a chest-thumping caveman, stripped naked of everything except the bare essentials.

Man. Woman. Biology.

Her pulse hammered.

He heaved his shirt flying and then his fingers went to his zipper.

She sucked in her breath as she watched the zipper slide down.

In one smooth move, he dropped his pants and a soft sound of pleasure popped from her lips. Ah, a silk boxer man. It figured.

His gaze was hot on her face and she felt her skin flush. She knew he was watching her breasts bob jauntily atop the water.

And when the silk boxers followed the pants and she got her first good, up close and personal view of him, Charlee just about choked.

Here stood a broad-shouldered, blue-blooded Texas

businessman with chest hairs the color of dark Belgian chocolate and a very serious gleam in his eyes.

The sight of him left her nearly speechless.

"W-w-well," she stammered before getting hold of herself. "Are you going to strut like a proud turkey all day or shake your tail feathers and get in here with me?"

"Just a minute."

In two long-legged strides, he marched over to the dressing table, yanked the cellophane wrapper off the gift basket, plucked a condom from the plethora of products, tore the packet open, and rolled the Day-Glo green rubber onto his burgeoning erection.

"Now that's a picture."

"You haven't seen anything yet," he promised and strutted back over to the tub.

"Do those things work in water?" She was on the pill and she would bet anything he didn't have a sexually transmittable disease but still, no sense taking unnecessary chances.

"Don't know. Never used one in the Jacuzzi."

"Me either."

"So we're hot tub virgins together."

She liked the sound of that.

Mason slid down in the bubbling liquid and he looked across the tub at her, his breathing labored and his gaze turbulent.

The water churned and pulsated around them. She'd never been naked in a hot tub with a man before and that erotic reality along with the powerful water jets massaging and caressing sensitive areas of her body stoked her arousal.

"Come here," Mason said in a tone so husky it

scraped her ears like sandpaper. He stared her right in the eyes and crooked a finger.

And just like that, every bit of courage she possessed drained from her body.

She shook her head.

"Don't make me come over there," he said, his voice a silky threat.

Her body trembled as if her temperature were a hundred and ten.

"You started this, now I'm finishing it." He reached under the water, found her foot, and trolled her toward him. Her head went under briefly and she came up sputtering, her hair fanning out around her. He hauled her closer to him until she floated above his knees.

"Is drowning me all part of your master plan?"

"I warned you."

She brushed the water from her eyelashes and looked at him. He rewarded her with his dimpled grin and she just about came undone.

He had one hand still clamped tight around her ankle and his other hand was . . . *oh, my.*

Charlee's eyes rolled back in her head at the sheer pleasure of what he was doing.

His fingertips lightly stroked her bottom in a tormenting technique that left her breathless, bewildered, and craving more.

"What's this?" he asked, his fingers finding the scar from her long-ago spider bite.

"Origins of my black widow terror."

He made a sympathetic noise and his touch lightened. He inched her closer toward him, slowly separating her legs with his knees while his eyes never left her face. He tilted his head and lightly ran his tongue across her parted lips. Licking first her top lip and then her bottom. He tasted salty yet sweet.

Letting go of her ankle, he reached up his hand to cradle her cheek as he kissed her and then she giggled.

"What's so funny?" he growled.

"You. Me. Everything."

"I'm glad I amuse you."

"Amuse me some more," she murmured.

She was in his lap at this point, her legs splayed on either side of his waist, her bottom bobbing against him.

"I love your breasts," he broke the kiss to murmur.

He scooted her bottom onto his knees and lowered his head to gently bite one of the stiff, pink nipples jutting hungrily forward.

"Oooooh," she exclaimed.

"They're beautiful," he pronounced, then went for the other nipple.

"Just like a peach."

"That's right."

His mouth was so hot against her tender flesh a fiery sizzle of electricity shot straight through her tense body. She ached for him. If he could cause this explosion inside her just by nibbling her breasts, she thrilled to think what else he could do.

Clutching his shoulders, she arched against him, pressing her breasts right into his face.

His tongue flicked across her nipples, initially slow, then gradually speeding up, building and building and building the pressure inside her.

Blindly, she reached down into the water, past their thighs, and found what she was looking for. The moment she cupped him in her palm, Mason gasped in shocked surprise.

"Your touch . . ." he rasped, "it's incredible."

She was smoldering, burning, simmering with heat and tension and desire.

"I want it now," she whispered. "I want you inside me. I want it hard and I want it hot and I want it fast."

"Yes, ma'am," he croaked. "Anything you want."

Mason spanned her waist with his hands and lifted her up in the water and then tried to settle her down on his erection, but she slicked off of him and he ended up crashing into her.

"Ouch."

"I'm sorry. Didn't mean to do that."

"'Sokay. Let's try again."

He carefully placed her over the throbbing head of him and tried to ease her over his shaft. They made contact—he was butted up tight against her opening—but she couldn't slide down.

She was stuck.

See what happens when you go years without having sex? Use it or lose it.

"Now I know how a shish kabob feels," Charlee grumbled.

"Shh, don't make me laugh. Let me just wiggle around here for a better angle." He shifted his backside against the bottom of the hot tub.

He wriggled. She jiggled.

Nothing happened.

"You're too big."

"I have to say, no one's ever complained about that before."

"First time for everything."

"It's not my size," he argued. "It's the water. It swells

the tissues and washes away moisture making it hard for things . . . to . . . er . . . fit."

"They make it look so easy in the movies."

"That's because it's simulated sex, not the real deal. Give me a minute to figure this out."

He tried a few maneuvers. Nothing.

"Maybe it's the condom," he said.

"This isn't working. Let's forget the whole thing." She tried to scramble out of his arms, but he held her locked in to place.

In a rush of panic, she remembered why all this scared her. Even their silly fumbling, especially their silly fumbling, escalated the intimacy between them. They were sharing and caring and laughing together and it was all too much to handle.

Charlee had thought that by getting naked with him, having sex and enjoying it, that she could sate her biological needs without involving her heart.

She was wrong.

And now she was embarrassed. She ducked her head.

Mason crooked a forefinger under her chin and tugged her face upward, forcing her to look him in the eyes. He reached up and pushed back a strand of damp hair plastered against her cheek.

"Talk to me."

"What?"

"Something's going on in that sharp little brain of yours. Tell me what you're thinking."

"I'm not thinking about anything."

"Liar."

"Okay, I was thinking I suck at this."

"You don't."

"I do. I tried to seduce you and look." She spread her hands. "I can't even carry through."

"Sweetheart, it's not your seduction technique at fault here. It's the hot tub. We could move. Try it again on the bed."

"I feel like an idiot."

"You're not an idiot." He leaned in and kissed the nape of her neck, softly feathering his fingertips over her skin.

"Stop trying to make me feel better."

"Why? You like being miserable?"

"No," she said and smiled.

"There you go. That's my girl."

Then without any further discussion, Mason got out of the hot tub, scooped her into his arms, and carried her to bed.

CHAPTER 15

*W*hat was he doing? Their failure to make a connection in the Jacuzzi had given him an out. They hadn't gone too far yet. He hadn't crossed the line.

Okay, he'd pulverized the line to dust, but theoretically, they hadn't joined bodies so the line, however invisible, still remained uncrossed.

But Charlee was in his arms, feeling wet and wonderful and smelling like heaven. He wanted her. And she'd wanted him. Sex between two consenting adults.

Yeah, but you haven't broken up with Daphne yet.

A mere technicality, the pitchfork-toting devil on his shoulder assured him.

Did Charlee really want to make love to him or was it simply the champagne, the excitement of their road adventures, and the thrill of winning the *Newlywed Game* motivating her? Mason didn't want her doing anything she would regret later.

She wrapped her arms around his neck and leaned her head against his shoulder, her long hair slapping wetly against his thigh as he moved. Strong feelings punted his gut. She looked so defenseless, so trusting.

Until that moment with the spider, until she said she was bad in bed, he had believed her completely invincible. Until now, the way she handled herself told him she was a woman who didn't need anyone.

Forget rough, tough, street-talking Charlee. This woman cradled against his chest was quiet and amiable and susceptible.

For the first time, she had really needed him and it made him feel big and strong and protective.

Then, when he laid her carefully on the bed, and she looked up at him with those exotic green eyes glazed with desire, he just about came unraveled. She pulled his head down to hers and kissed him tentatively, exploring the change.

He kissed her back, holding nothing in reserve. He gave her every ounce of the passion that had been building inside him from the moment they'd met.

She pressed herself against him, moaning softly, getting aroused all over again.

God, he wanted her so badly he could barely breathe. He hadn't been this shaken up about sex since that first time with Blair Sydney in the back of the Bentley.

Take it easy. No hurry. You've got all night.

He was dying to take her hard and fast and hot like she'd told him she wanted, but he would not. This felt too special. Too good to rush.

No matter how much the ache in his groin was killing him, he was bound and determined to make this a night neither one of them would ever forget. He owed it to them both.

He pulled back and gazed at her, his eyes tracing the

lines of her body. Gorgeous. Simply gorgeous. Not small and petite and delicate but a sturdy woman, strong and capable and substantial.

She caught his eye and slowly ran a hand down her breasts over the flat of her belly to the soft curve of her inner thigh.

"Mason," she whispered his name. "I want you here."

Ah, hell.

He leaped onto the bed beside her and promptly slid off the slick satin and crashed onto the floor.

"Are you okay?" She leaned over the edge of the bed and peered down at him, mirth mingled with hot, frantic desire in her eyes.

"Fine," he mumbled.

"You're right, rich boy, there is an art to lying on satin. Unfortunately you don't seem to know the trick any better than I."

"Being around you makes me forget every damned trick I ever learned." He got to his feet and came back to bed.

"Oh, ho." She grinned when he crawled up beside her on the damp duvet.

"When I'm around you, Charlee, I can't think at all. You mess with my head, woman."

"In a good way or a bad way?"

"I'll let you figure that one out." He straddled her body with his and pushed her back against the covers.

For the first time in his life, Mason allowed his senses to run completely ungoverned, no holding back. He thrust his fingers through her hair, his skin exalting in the unfamiliar feel of her.

He plundered her mouth and air rushed from her

lungs in a red-hot blast. He felt her breath against his lips, tasted her sumptuous flavor.

He didn't think about the consequences. He didn't think about his grandfather or the rest of his family or Daphne. He didn't think about the men in the Malibu. He didn't think about anything at all. He merely responded with every red-blooded masculine instinct inside him at the wonderfully erotic stimulus of kissing Charlee.

She wrapped her arms around his neck, spread her legs wide, and drew his body down on top of hers.

He sank into her, sweet and deep.

And then stopped, suddenly immobilized by the knowledge he wasn't going to last five seconds. Mason closed his eyes tight, gritted his teeth, and struggled for control.

Think baseball scores. Think accounts receivable, think about anything except how good it feels to be inside her.

Charlee arched her pelvis against his. "Please," she begged, "please."

She kissed him, hard and fierce, letting him know just how much she wanted him. She wrapped her legs tight around his waist and pulled him in deeper.

He moved against her, the sound of their panting breaths filling his ears, the taste of her exploding in his mouth, the smell of her charming his nostrils with her fragrant womanly scent. He tried to savor the moment, to take it slow and to make it last despite Charlee's whimpered urgings.

But she was so hot and tight and sexy he knew he simply could not hold out for long.

There's always round two.

She raked her fingernails over his back, wild to the core, and cried his name with escalating insistence.

Faster he thrust. Harder. His body ached and throbbed and quivered for release.

She met his rhythm, stroke for stroke. She bucked and writhed and wriggled in just the right way. Her breathing spread a thready heat across his shoulders, her muscles clenching him tighter and tighter still.

Then he made the mistake of opening his eyes.

Charlee's eyes were open too and their gazes met in a moment of pure surprised wonder. Her pupils widened and he stared deep inside her.

He felt as if he were slipping into an ageless abyss, dark and endless and wonderful. They made a connection far deeper than bodies joining.

His heart chugged sluggishly in his chest. All sense of time disappeared. Seconds could have passed or centuries. It was just him and Charlee there together.

Joined. One.

Something changed. He saw the shift in her eyes just before she closed them.

"Don't stop," she cried out and that's when he realized in the marvel of the moment, he'd stopped moving. "Please, don't stop."

She pounded lightly on his shoulders with her fists, urging him back into the tempo. "More," she whimpered. "More." She planted her feet on his buttocks and pulled him down to meet her thrusting pelvis.

The magical mist evaporated and they were back to raw primal sex.

He thrust and thrust and thrust. Giving it to her the way she wanted it. Hard and fast and hungry.

Not long now. He couldn't hold out much longer.

But, he suspected, neither could she. They hung on the verge of climax together, both seeking that sweet physical release.

Then she screamed his name low in her throat and her body went rigid. Her muscles gripped him and he knew she was coming.

Just as he was coming.

He felt the phenomenal energy rise up in both of them as they tumbled over the edge together and pulsation after pulsation clenched their bodies. Mason shuddered as a blinding, red-hot heat blasted up him in a splendid splurge.

Gasping, they clung to each other as the last echoes of glorious ripples subsided. As they drifted down from the lofty heights of simultaneous orgasm, a rare headiness seeped through his spent limbs.

He rolled to one side, drawing Charlee into his arms as he went. She rested her head against his shoulder, her warm breath tickling his chest hairs damp with their combined sweat.

Like survivors of a siege they clung to each other, breathing in synchronized rhythm, happy to be alive and together. He didn't want to let her go. Ever.

He'd never felt this way with Daphne. Nor any of the other women he'd known. He'd never experienced such crazy, out-of-control feelings. Why was Charlee different? What was it about her that made him feel differently?

Why, until now, had his past love relationships been more of a convenience than anything else? He had considered marrying Daphne because she was everything he had thought he'd wanted. Polished, accomplished, with all the right connections and credentials. Blue-blooded and cultured and sophisticated.

And the sex had been lousy.

Nothing like this knock-your-socks-off romp.

That's it, Gentry. It's the sex. That's why it feels different with Charlee. Apparently, stupendous sex mucked up a man's thinking.

Charlee awoke sometime later and lay awestruck in Mason's arms. She'd never experienced anything like what they had just shared. She'd had good sex before, sure, but nothing like this mind-blowing, toe-curling, explosive crescendo.

Mason's breathing lulled her and she tried her best to stay wrapped in the warm romantic afterglow of post coital bliss for as long as she could, but eventually, reality reared its ugly head.

She had to go to the bathroom.

Regretfully, she slipped from his arms and out of bed. Once her feet hit the floor, she turned to gaze over her shoulder at him.

He was already asleep. Poor dear. Plumb tuckered out. After a performance like that, he deserved to sleep uninterrupted for a week.

This had been a first for her. Mindless, uncontrolled sex merely for the sake of mindless, uncontrolled sex. She felt cleansed, purified. Reborn.

Charlee grinned. This having sex for sex's sake wasn't half bad. She liked using a man to sate her physical desires while keeping her heart cleanly out of the fray. That was the ticket. Have sex with your eyes open and your mind locked down tight.

It had worked. She didn't feel that same agonizing

tug of anxiety she had experienced after giving Gregory her virginity. No nagging questions like: why doesn't he take me out in public or introduce me to his parents? With her ex-lover she had waited for the other boot to drop, repeatedly wondering when he would realize she wasn't good enough for him.

Nothing to worry about. No commitment to fret over. Their mating had been about sex and putting her fears behind her and letting go of her unrealistic expectations about love and romance and intimacy.

Congratulating herself, she padded into the bathroom and then caught sight of her reflection in the mirror from the flicker of candlelight.

She stepped closer for a better look. Her eyes sparked, her skin radiated with a satisfied sheen, her hair was a sexy, mussed mess.

Casual sex looks good on you.

But bedroom escapades aside, together they mixed like . . . *well* . . . caviar and peanut butter. She'd learned the hard way—thank you very much for that painful lesson, Gregory—the class caste system was alive and well in the good old USA. Hadn't Maybelline always sworn this was gospel? Mason came from the haves and she came from the have-nots and never the twain shall meet.

Outside of hot sex that is.

And even if he couldn't see that, Charlee most certainly could.

She finished up in the bathroom, blew out the candles, and then tiptoed back to bed. Mason lay on his side facing toward her, his features relaxed in quiet repose. He looked so darned handsome she caught her breath and held it. She studied him a moment. Thick lashes shadowed his cheekbones and strands of short black hair spiked straight up. His tanned skin contrasted sharply with the white cotton sheets and caused her pulse to jump crazily. God, but he was the most gorgeous thing she'd ever had in her bed.

She felt like a proud huntress who'd brought home the juiciest cut of beef. She felt like Aphrodite churned from the sea. She felt like Venus de Milo with arms.

She'd claimed her sexuality and liberated her heart. Triumphant, Charlee crawled up into the bed beside him, spooned her fanny against him, and for the sweet short moment before she fell asleep convinced herself that everything was going to be just fine.

A few minutes later his fingers reached out and he gently caressed her cheek. The fine hairs on the nape of her neck lifted and her body heated as quick as microwaved leftovers. She threw in the towel. After all, they'd already made love once. At this point, how much more damage could another round do?

A repeated pounding on the door tugged Mason from an exquisite dream about Charlee. He yawned, stretched, rolled over, and collided with a warm, soft body.

Blinking, he rubbed his eyes and then took another look.

Charlee. Snoring softly and totally oblivious to the racket outside their room.

That was no dream. The movie playing over and over in his slumbering brain was the real deal.

They'd made love.

Not once.

Not twice.

But three incredible times.

The insistent pounding continued. Probably an overly ambitious member of the Grand Piazza's housekeeping staff, he decided and slid out on the other side of the bed. If Charlee could sleep through that racket, more power to her.

Yawning again, he retrieved a plush terry-cloth robe from the bathroom, tied the sash around his waist, and ran his fingers through his hair to tidy it before he went to open the door.

It took a good two seconds to register that his fiancée-to-be was standing on the other side looking rather disgruntled. Quickly, he moved to block her view of the bedroom and Charlee.

"Skeet Hammersmitz, I presume," Daphne said, her voice as cold and sharp as an ice pick.

Every hair on her head was perfectly arranged. Not a speck of lint dared to rest on her tailored suit. And even at eight thirty-five on a Saturday morning, her makeup was artfully applied.

"D-Daphne," he stammered, guilty as sin. "What are you doing here?"

"What are *you* doing here?"

They just stared at each other, her ice blue eyes the temperature of an igloo.

"I'm guessing you saw the *Newlywed Game*."

"Are you going to let me in, or do we have to discuss our relationship in the hallway?" Daphne raised one razor-thin eyebrow and crossed her arms over her chest.

"Mason?" Charlee called sleepily from behind him. "Is that room service? How sweet of you to order breakfast."

Ulp.

Every man's worst nightmare. The moment when

your soon-to-be ex-girlfriend comes face-to-face with the woman you can't get out of your mind.

"Aren't you going to introduce me to your new 'wife'?" Daphne asked in a voice as frosty as a Siberian tomb at the same time Charlee came up behind him tying the sash to her robe.

"I hope you ordered Belgian waffles. I love Belgian waffles." Her tone was as light and airy as Daphne's was heavy and frigid. She touched his waist and peered around his shoulder at Daphne. "Oh," she said. "You're not room service."

Daphne glared at Mason. "Do we have to do this in the corridor?" she repeated. "You know how I hate a public scene."

"What's happening?" Charlee looked at him, bewildered.

Mason could not hold her gaze. The consequences of what he'd done whacked him in the gut with the impact of a wrecking ball taking down a Vegas casino.

Must minimalize guilt, his basic male instinct screamed. *Pretend this is normal. Pretend you haven't just made love with the right woman for all the wrong reasons while you're almost engaged to the wrong woman for all the right reasons.*

Mason ushered Daphne across the threshold. "Daphne, this is Charlee Champagne. Charlee, Daphne Maxwell."

"I thought her name was Violet."

"No. It's a long story."

"I'm all ears," Daphne said.

"Who are you again?" Charlee asked.

"How do you do?" Daphne extended her hand to Charlee. "I'm Mason's fiancée."

Since he was intently studying the wainscoting along the ceiling, Mason felt rather than saw Charlee's jaw drop.

"F-f-fiancée?"

He swallowed hard, jammed his fingers through his hair, and forced himself to look at her. The pain he saw reflected in her eyes just about killed him.

"Daphne and I are not officially engaged," he denied, knowing he sounded for all the world like a kid who was trying to have his birthday cake and eat it too.

"We've been dating for three years," Daphne said. "We've talked about getting married. We've even priced houses together. I call his parents Mother and Father. You, my dear girl, are nothing but a road-trip fling and if you were fantasizing about landing yourself a rich man, then honey, you were sadly mistaken."

Mason braced himself for Charlee's outrage. Would she go for his jugular? Scratch his eyes from his head? Pull out her gun and shoot him? Actually, shooting was too good for him. He'd behaved badly and he knew it. He'd led her on, he'd allowed himself to give into his lust, he'd hurt her and there was nothing he could say or do to alter that fact.

"You don't owe me an explanation. I'm just the one-night stand." She blithely waved a hand.

"Charlee . . ." He opened his mouth but he had no idea what he was going to say. He couldn't promise her anything. His own life was in turmoil. His grandfather was missing and he was more confused than he'd ever been in his life. "You weren't a one-night stand."

"Hey, listen." Charlee shrugged. "It's no big deal. I mean, I gotta confess, you took me off guard. You didn't strike me as the sort of guy to cheat on your fiancée."

"Honey," Daphne said sarcastically, "all men are the sort to cheat on their fiancées."

"She's not my fiancée," Mason protested feebly.

"This fight really needs to be between the two of you." Charlee picked up Violet's suitcase. She opened it on the bed and started rummaging through the contents. "Last night was great, Mason, I gotta confess. Really righteous. But if you thought it meant more to me than just sex, then you're dead wrong."

On the surface she seemed extremely calm. Impulsive, headstrong Charlee composed and in control?

That's when he noticed her hand was trembling oh-so-slightly. It was eerie to witness and that tiny tremor told him far more than a temper tantrum would have. She was hurt. To the quick.

He felt sick to his stomach. He disgusted himself.

She retrieved an outfit from the suitcase and marched into the bathroom to get dressed. Mason watched her go, his heart sinking to his feet.

Daphne tapped him on the shoulder. He turned to look at her. She pursed her lips in a disapproving frown. He never noticed before how petulant she looked when things didn't go her way.

"If you come home with me to Houston right this very minute then I'm willing to forget all this ever happened. Every man deserves to sow his wild oats before settling down."

"Daphne, my grandfather is still missing."

"Well, that's not my problem now, is it?" She sank her hands on her hips. "I've already booked our return flight. The plane leaves in three hours."

"You had no right to do that."

"And you had no right to use your grandfather as an excuse for a quickee with trailer trash."

Mason fisted his hands. "Don't you dare call her that."

"What? The truth hurts? You go slumming, darling, you have to expect to acquire a few fleas."

Charlee popped back out of the bathroom wearing another one of Violet's short skirts, a very tight T-shirt embossed with the word "Hellraiser," and her own neon blue cowboy boots. Mason's eyes were immediately drawn to her long, shapely legs and his heart hitched when he saw her knees were trembling too.

What had he done?

"Good-bye you two." Charlee flung her purse over her shoulder. "Have a nice life."

"Charlee, wait." Mason started after her, totally forgetting he was in his bathrobe. "You can't go out there alone. Remember the armed men in the Malibu."

"If I can handle a night with you, I can handle those two," she said flippantly and tossed her hair over her shoulder.

Her casual dismissal sliced into him and left him hemorrhaging. Had he meant nothing more than a sexual conquest? And why did that thought upset him so? Wasn't it what he thought he'd wanted?

No, he realized miserably. It wasn't what he wanted. Not at all. He wanted more. So much more he couldn't keep all the thoughts in his head at once.

He had to talk to her. Tell her what he was feeling. Hash this thing out.

"Come back here," he demanded.

She ignored him, squared her shoulders in that defensive little gesture of hers, and sashayed out the door.

Mason grappled for the clothes he'd worn the day before, snatching Skeet's beige walking shorts up off the floor and trying to stuff both legs in at the same time. He ended up losing his balance and toppling over into the bed. The sheets still smelled erotically of the sex he had shared with Charlee.

"If you follow her," Daphne threatened, "not only is it over between us, but I'm pulling strings with Birkweilder. I have the influence to get him to cancel his account with Gentry Enterprises and you know it."

Mason met Daphne's cold, calculating stare. "You wouldn't dare."

"Oh, just try me. My contacts got you the deal, I can pull it whenever I want."

He clenched his teeth, surprised to discover he utterly did not care. "Do whatever you think you have to do, Daphne. I'm sorry, but it's over between us."

♥ ♥ ♥

CHAPTER
16

*S*he'd done it again. She'd fallen for another wealthy, long-legged, brown-eyed, handsome man.

Stupid, stupid, stupid. Would she *ever* learn her lesson? Was she doomed to keep tumbling for the wrong guys? What in the hell was the matter with her?

The tears she'd managed to hold at bay back there in the hotel room tracked miserably down her cheeks. Angrily, Charlee scrubbed at them with the back of her hand.

Last night she'd deluded herself. Pretending that it was just physical between them, that she could keep her feelings in check, when she had simply been repeating her same old destructive patterns of getting involved with unobtainable men.

Secretly she had allowed herself to believe that Mason was different from the other men she had known and now she'd found out the truth. He was worse than the rest. The man was engaged.

Well, not officially, protested a tiny voice in the back

of her head. The same stupid voice that had led her willy-nilly into his bed.

It didn't matter. He was a cheat and a liar. And he'd used her. Just like Gregory had.

Bastard.

Ahem, you seduced him.

Yeah but she'd been drunk on champagne.

Excuses, excuses.

She stalked down the palm-tree-lined street, her boot heels smacking against the sidewalk.

A group of guys in a Jeep drove by, honking at her and issuing crude catcalls, but she ignored them. Her anger was finely focused.

Jerk. Nimrod. Dillhole.

Her first impression of Mason had been the right one. Ruthless heartbreaker.

More tears streamed down her face. Dammit. Why couldn't she stop crying?

Because you fell in love with him.

No way. Nuh-huh. She was *not* in love with him.

In lust? Yes. Oh, baby, was she in lust. But she did not love him. She couldn't love him. She wouldn't let herself. She was not going through that kind of heartache again.

Not after being disappointed by her father and then treated badly by the likes of Tommy Ledbetter and Vincent Keneer and Gregory Blankensonship.

She was through. Done. Finished with men. Maybelline had the right idea all along. Men were worthless scoundrels, the lot of them.

Charlee was so busy mentally berating men in general and Mason Gentry in particular, she blocked out all external stimuli. She didn't hear the seagulls cawing overhead. She didn't smell the scent of coffee and pastries from the bakery she passed. She didn't taste the salt of her tears as they slipped over her lips. She didn't feel the breeze lifting the hairs on her arm.

And she didn't see the white Chevy Malibu slinking down the street behind her.

Mason tore out of the Beverly Hills Grand Piazza as if his hair had been dipped in kerosene and set ablaze. Charlee had a good three-minute lead on him. He swiveled his head right, then left, staring down the street in each direction for as far as he could see.

No sign of her.

Ah hell. Which way had she gone?

"Are you looking for your wife, Mr. Hammersmitz?" asked the ponytailed valet.

"Yes, yes. Did you see her?"

"Cute chick in the coolest blue boots and hot black T-shirt."

"That's her. Which way did she go?"

The valet held out his palm, the universal signal for you-want-information-it's-gonna-cost-you.

Mason stuck his hand in his pocket in search of a twenty-dollar bill to press into the man's greedy fist before remembering he was penniless.

"I'm sorry, man. I don't have any money on me."

The valet shrugged. "Dude, maybe I was mistaken. Maybe it wasn't her after all."

He was accustomed to money greasing wheels, making life easier. He'd never really thought much about it in his daily life. Money had always been a tool and he'd used it freely. It spoke for him so he didn't have to speak for himself.

The valet turned away.

Anger spurted through Mason. Anger at the system he had helped to engender. Anger at the blasé valet. Anger at Daphne.

But most of all, Mason was angry with himself.

Without even thinking, he did something he would never have done even four days earlier. The dark wildness he'd kept hidden for so long burst free in an unstoppable torrent and he turned into a complete and utter Neanderthal protecting his own.

He grabbed the impertinent valet by his lapel, lifted him off his feet, and slammed him against the brick building. "Tell me which direction my wife went and tell me now," he growled with so much intensity he startled even himself.

"Hey, man, okay, okay." The valet's eyes rounded with fear. "Don't have an aneurysm. She was headed toward Rodeo Drive."

"Appreciate the information." Mason let go of the man's jacket.

As he hurried away he heard the valet mutter, "White trash."

His gut constricted and he managed to keep himself from whirling around and giving the guy an earful by reminding himself Charlee was in jeopardy. She was out there on the streets of Beverly Hills alone with those two goons who had followed them from Vegas. He had to get to her before they did.

He took off at a dead sprint and turned right. A woman walking her dog glared at him. He jumped over a hedge to avoid her, got caught in the spray from a sprinkler system and kept on running without missing a beat.

Dread filled his mouth and he knew with a horrible certainty Charlee was in trouble.

And then he saw her.

Relief washed through him. Thank God, she was all right.

She was a football field length ahead of him, marching with her head held high. Her coal black hair swaying provocatively just above her gorgeous butt. Those jaunty cowboy boots blazing a neon blue path across Beverly Hills as defiantly as a nose thumbing.

Something pinched inside his chest. Something tight and heavy. The stab of pain came not from running but from the very sight of her. Damn, he loved those neon blue cowboy boots.

And he loved the way that little skirt flounced sassily over her thighs. Since he was coming clean with himself he might as well admit it. He loved a lot of things about her.

He loved her passion, her directness, her power. He loved the way she grabbed life in both fists and truly lived each moment to the fullest. But most of all he loved the way she made him feel like a better man for simply having known her.

Mason slowed to catch his breath, his heart thudding perilously loud in his ears. Charlee, Charlee, Charlee, his blood seemed to strum.

Mason was so compelled by the sight of her, his eyes feasting upon her luscious body, he didn't see the Chevy Malibu creeping along behind her until the back door was flung open.

"Charlee," he yelled.

But he was too late.

Just as she turned her head, one of the muscle-bound

thugs tumbled from the car, slapped one hand around her waist and the other around her mouth, and then pulled her into the backseat.

Before Mason could react, the door slammed and the Malibu sped away.

"Oww!" the thick-necked goon cried as Charlee sank her top teeth into the base of his thumb. "Stop that."

"Get your hands off me, you big ape." She fought him but he held her tight against his lap.

"You're feisty," he said. "I like that."

She elbowed him sharply in the ribs.

"Oww! Sal, make her stop hurting me."

The guy behind the wheel raised a handgun and pointed it over the seat at her. "Behave."

Charlee settled down. Not because she was afraid of them—if she had a dollar for every time someone had pointed a gun at her she would be on vacation in the Caymans right now instead of stuck here with these two—but because she could think better if she wasn't having to battle Mr. Personality here.

"Who are you guys?" she demanded. "And where are you taking me?"

"You'll find out soon enough," grunted Sal the driver who thankfully lowered his gun and returned his eyes to the road. "Shit! Look at the freeway. It's backed up for miles."

"Take PC1."

"I can't turn around now."

"Well, take the next exit."

"We're gonna be stuck in traffic for hours," Sal complained.

The thug beside her had retrieved his handgun from

his shoulder holster and held the nose of the thirty-eight pressed against her ribs. Charlee sighed and longed for her own gun.

"Who do you work for?" she asked him.

"None of your business."

"Why have you been following us since Vegas?"

He just grunted.

"You're the guy who shot through my grandmother's window, aren't you?"

"So what if I was?" he asked petulantly.

"Don't tell her anything," Sal commented.

"Did you ransack the trailer too? I saw your car at my grandmother's place."

"She had something we wanted."

"What?" Charlee demanded. "What's this all about?"

"Shut up." He prodded her with the gun.

"Were you the ones who set my father's apartment on fire? What was that about?"

"That wasn't us. We didn't start the fire. We were just looking for your old man."

"I said not to tell her anything," Sal snapped. "Are you listening?"

"He's right. Shut up." The other man dug the gun deeper into her side.

"Where are we going?" Charlee asked, figuring if she threw enough questions his way he'd answer some of them eventually.

"You don't take orders too good, do you?"

"Not from cretins who didn't finish high school."

"Hey! I got a GED, it's the same thing," the man beside her protested.

"Sure, go ahead, delude yourself," Charlee said.

"It is." He glared.

"Petey, she's giggin' you, man, don't fall for it," the driver said. "Just gag her and tie her up and be done with it."

Petey frowned. "You really think a GED isn't as good as a high school diploma?"

Frankly Charlee had no personal prejudice about anyone's level of education but Petey obviously had a problem with his credentials.

"Well, you did end up as hired muscle," she pointed out. "Probably wouldn't have happened if you had stayed in school. Who knows? You might even be running your very own Subway sandwich shop today if you had just gotten that diploma."

So much for her smart mouth, Charlee decided five minutes later when they hadn't budged two feet in wall-to-wall traffic and she was trussed up with more tape than a Miss America contestant in the swimsuit competition and lying facedown on the seat.

On the up side, she hadn't thought about Mason in a good ten minutes.

Mason.

Ah, hell, why had she thought about him?

"Hey," Petey said. "Don't cry. We're not going to kill you, I promise."

Tears rolled down her face.

"Come on now." Petey patted her awkwardly on the shoulder. "It's going to be okay."

She must look pretty bad if her kidnapper was trying to console her. That made her cry all the harder. Damn Mason Gentry.

And just like that, all the fight left her. What did it matter if Sal and Petey did kill her? At least she'd be out of her misery.

*　　*　　*

Mason sped down the Pacific Coast Highway in the rental car he'd commandeered from a disgruntled Daphne. By some miracle, the Malibu had gotten stuck in a traffic jam and he'd managed to catch up with them. But he only saw the two men in the car.

What had they done with Charlee?

Savage vengeance, unlike anything he'd ever felt, coursed through his veins. If they'd hurt one single hair on her head, he'd wring their necks with his bare hands.

What had happened to the controlled, success-oriented businessman who'd walked into her office a mere four days ago? Where was the guy whose family name meant everything to him? Who was he now?

Something hard, solid, and certain burned directly to the left of his breastbone.

He was in love with her. Stone cold in love and he had no idea what to do about it.

Romantic love made no sense to his logical investment banker's brain or the fact that it had happened so suddenly, so unexpectedly. But there it was.

She was his soul mate. His better half. He knew it with a certainty that rocked his world.

He felt like cracked lightning. Raw, stark, dangerous. Charlee had done this to him. She stripped off his controlled exterior and exposed the man beneath. The man who'd been shambling through life without really living it. The man who'd been afraid to break free and go for what he really wanted. The man who'd been almost dead inside until he'd met her.

She'd changed everything and now he was about to lose her.

This whole thing was his fault. If he'd just told her

about Daphne beforehand, they'd be safely ensconced in the hotel room waiting for Pam to come take them shopping for Oscar clothes.

Ha!

The thought of that leisurely afternoon spent watching Charlee try on designer outfits evaporated.

He gripped the steering wheel and moistened his lips. Once they'd gotten off the congested freeway and onto the Pacific Coast Highway, they'd been moving right along. Past Santa Monica, past Venice Beach, past LAX.

Where were they going and was Charlee still with them? And if she wasn't, what could they have done with her? Was she in the trunk of the car?

Was she dead?

Fear bit him. She wasn't dead. She couldn't be dead. He had so much to say to her, so much to explain.

He had to apologize and he had to tell her how he felt about her. It didn't matter if she didn't love him back. What mattered was that he was in love with her.

Steeling his jaw, he narrowed his eyes with resolve. He was sticking to the Malibu like Velcro. Nobody but nobody was going to abduct his Charlee and get away with it.

Nolan paced off the cramped confines of the mineshaft for the one-millionth time since Blade Bradford and his illegitimate son Elwood had abandoned them here the afternoon before. What in the hell were those two up to, he wondered.

A thin beam of light slanted through a hole in the ceiling, barely illuminating the constricted space. That dinner plate-sized hole was too far away to reach and every time he moved a fresh dusting of earth crumbled from the dirt wall.

What had once been two tunnels leading right and left from the underground room to the mines were now blocked with debris and rocks from a massive cave-in. Elwood and Bradford couldn't have entombed them any more effectively if they had actually buried them alive.

Come to think of it, this had all the makings of a Poe short story.

"Nolan," Maybelline chided, "please stop pacing."

"I'm trying to erode the damned wall."

"More likely you'll cause it to fall in on us." She waved at their precarious surroundings, then put the hand up to shield her nose and sneezed.

He paused. She was right. Plus he was kicking up enough dust to choke an asthmatic.

At first, Maybelline had been as antsy as he, pacing and cussing both her offspring and her ex-lover for dumping them here the day before. But during the last few hours she had grown so calm Nolan got worried. Maybelline wasn't the quiet type.

She sat with her back against the north wall, her eyes tightly closed.

"Are you okay?" He squatted beside her and ignored the creaking in his knees.

"I'm fine. I'm just trying to think."

Nolan exhaled sharply and sat down. He'd spent the last sixteen hours wracking his brain for a solution and he'd come up with nothing.

At gunpoint, Elwood and Blade had forced them into the mine shaft, slammed and bolted the rusted but solid metal door, and walked away. They'd had the decency to leave them three two-liter bottles of Evian, four apples, a bag of Doritos, and a Heath bar.

It wouldn't take long to go through their meager provisions. Well, except for the Heath bar. His teeth not being what they used to be, the chocolate-covered hard toffee was not his candy of choice.

He got to his feet, unable to sit still, and squinted up at the shaft of light taunting him from overhead. He looked back over at Maybelline and watched her press her tongue to her lips.

A trickle of perspiration pearled at the hollow of her throat and the quick kick of lust that had him wanting to lick away her salty sweat startled him. He was as randy as a young buck. Go figure.

"Thirsty?" he asked, reaching for the Evian. They had been careful to ration the water, not knowing how long they had to make it last.

Maybelline shook her head. "We need to conserve."

"Your lips are dry."

She opened one eye to peer up at him through the thick haze of dust motes. "I'll live."

"One sip," he urged, fretting over how pale she looked. His gut clenched. He thought of how they'd made love in the back of the camper. How good she'd made him feel. How much he enjoyed being with her. "One sip won't hurt."

"Okay," she gave in. Obviously she was pretty darned thirsty if she acquiesced this easily.

Nolan untwisted the lid and the round plastic ring separated from the cap and came off in his hand. He passed the water to Maybelline but found himself staring intently at the white plastic ring.

Rings were symbols.

Of unity. Of eternity.

Of marriage.

Deep, long-buried emotions swept through him. From the time he could remember he'd been accused of being a hopeless romantic and now he knew it was true. He believed they would get out of here. He believed they had many long and lusty years ahead of them. He believed they would solve the Oscar dilemma facing them.

But most of all, he believed, with all his heart, that he was in love with Maybelline Sikes and had been for the last forty-seven years.

And he was going to ask her to marry him again. This time for real. Right here, right now, with the white plastic ring.

Holding the ring between his forefinger and thumb, he got down on one knee.

The sound of his knee hitting the ground resonated wooden, hollow.

He and Maybelline looked at each other in surprise.

"Wood floor under the dirt," she said.

Simultaneously, they began to dig.

♥ ♥ ♥

CHAPTER
17

*M*ason sat in Daphne's rented Mercedes next to a vineyard outside Figero, California. It was a small town in the very corner of the state near the Arizona/Mexico border. He waited for the cover of darkness. The Malibu was parked in the driveway of a weather-scarred farmhouse a quarter mile from where he had stationed himself.

Apparently, the goons in the Malibu never realized they were being followed. When they'd pulled into the farmhouse, Mason had driven past, and then circled back. He'd caught a glimpse of the two men hustling Charlee inside.

Sitting still and doing nothing had never been so excruciating. The minutes ticked by. His stomach grumbled because he hadn't eaten since the seafood buffet at the hotel the night before, but he ignored the hunger pains. His own needs were inconsequential. Charlee was in trouble.

He wished for a pair of binoculars. He wished for a spy camera. He wished for a gun.

He'd thought briefly about going to the police but the idea of explaining everything and the fact that he had no identification on him, plus the terrible fear that if he left for even a moment the thugs might disappear with Charlee, kept him rooted to the spot.

He wished regretfully that he had commandeered Daphne's cell phone as well as her vehicle but unfortunately, the urgent need to follow the Malibu had overridden careful planning. He had to do the best with what he possessed.

Which meant he had his brains, his tae kwon do training, a tire iron, and the burning desire to make those guys pay for stealing his woman.

His woman.

He liked the sound of that. Liked it so much in fact that he grinned. He also liked the kick-ass, Vin Diesel attitude stoking through his veins.

He couldn't wait for nightfall.

Except he had no choice but to wait. Other than a dilapidated barn located a few hundred yards from the house, the surrounding field was vacant, barren land. They would see him approaching from all four sides. No bushes, no shrubs, no trees.

Darkness was his ally. Even though it was killing him, he would wait.

Briefly, he closed his eyes and saw Charlee. The way her face glowed when she laughed. The way she fit so snugly into the curve of his arm. The way she smelled like no other woman on earth. The way her lips tasted of honeyed sin. The way she teased and goaded him to fulfill his highest potential.

How had she managed to embed herself under his skin so quickly and so permanently? Instead of getting her out of his system as he'd hoped, making love to her had drawn him even closer to her.

He missed her with an ache so severe a fistful of Percodan wouldn't cure it.

His eyes flew open. Dammit. He had to see her. Had to touch her. He had to know she was all right. He clenched his fists to control his impulse to storm the farmhouse and risk killing them both.

Five minutes after sunset, he was out of the car, tire iron in hand, even though streaks of purple and orange still illuminated the sky behind him. The silence was eerie. He heard nothing except his pumping blood roaring through his ears.

Charlee. He had to rescue Charlee. Nothing else mattered. He'd die for her if he had to.

Driven by that one relentless thought, he crouched low and sprinted toward the run-down farmhouse. When he reached it, he paused to catch his breath and pressed his back flush against the wall.

Cocking the tire iron like a baseball bat, he waited, listening.

When enough time had passed so that he could be certain he hadn't been detected, Mason inched toward the bedroom window located a few feet to his left. Cautiously, he eased his head around and peeked through the curtainless window.

The room was empty.

Pulse strumming, he crept down the side of the house to the next window that turned out to be a bathroom with those watery panes you couldn't see through.

Sucking in his breath, he wiped his damp palms on the front of Skeet's purple hula girl shirt, reapplied his steel grip to the tire iron, and moved on.

Another bedroom.

He darted a glance inside the window.

And spotted Charlee.

Bound and gagged and reclining on her back in a pink and orange paisley plastic beanbag chair.

For one brief impossible second, his heart literally stopped.

She was alive. Thank God.

Now what? He paused to ponder his next move, his mind racing at a startling clip as he formed and rejected one plan after another.

"Ahem."

At the sound of a throat being cleared behind him, Mason froze.

Slowly, he turned his head and came face-to-face with one of his own ilk.

The tall, distinguished-looking gray-haired man wasn't one of the two goons who'd kidnapped Charlee. That much was clear. The man standing before him sported a hundred-dollar haircut, a thousand-dollar designer suit, and a very large handgun pointed right at Mason's head.

"Ah, the younger Mr. Gentry." The man gave him a cold, false smile. "I suggest you put down the tire iron and come with me."

Charlee had to pee bad. She'd been holding it for hours. If Sal and Petey didn't let her go to the bathroom soon she would have to wet her pants or suffer irreparable kidney damage.

Unfortunately, the two men were in the other room playing gin and she lay in the stinky beanbag chair that obviously had not been cleaned since 1975, her hands and feet bound and her mouth still covered with duct tape. Her captors had only been in to check on her once since they'd arrived at the farmhouse several hours earlier.

She knew she should be devising some clever plan for escape, hatching some kind of brilliant detectivish scheme, but no matter how hard she tried she couldn't seem to concentrate on anything except the persistent ache in her bladder. Not even when she tried to evoke Mason's visage just so she could hate him.

About the time she had decided to surrender to nature and just pee her pants, she heard the front door slam and a new voice inside the house. Someone else was here.

Her pulse rate spiked. Who could it be?

She heard the sounds of an argument but couldn't make out what was being said.

Then came the footsteps. Several of them, headed toward the bedroom.

Oh, crap. This was it. They'd brought in the terminator. Would they let her pee before they killed her? she wondered idly.

The door flew open and Mason stumbled inside, pushed ahead of a dapper man with a thin mustache, cruel black eyes that belied his oily smile, and a nasty-looking forty-five in his hand. Petey and Sal stood in the doorway behind him.

Mason!

Their eyes met. She saw relief and a sweet tenderness swimming in his chocolate eyes.

Her treacherous heart leaped with joy at the sight of him when it should have been condemning the wretched scumbag. She'd never been so happy to see anyone in her entire life.

Even though she shouldn't be, she was glad, glad, glad he was here and she wasn't alone anymore.

"Mmghphm," she mumbled through the duct tape.

"You"—the man motioned to Petey with his gun—"take the tape off and let her speak. And you"—he frowned at Sal—"tie this guy up."

Sal went to fetch some rope while Petey squatted beside her and ripped the tape off her mouth.

"Ouch!"

"Payback's a bitch," Petey said. "That's for biting my thumb."

Oh, well, at least she'd gotten a free lip waxing out of the deal.

"I need to pee," she squawked. "Now."

Petey looked to the man with the gun. He nodded. "But you go with her."

Charlee winced. She wasn't crazy about the idea of having Petey in the bathroom with her but at this point her eyeballs were swimming and her modesty had pretty much disappeared.

Petey untied the rope from around her ankles so she could walk, but the well-dressed man wouldn't let him untie her hands. She almost fell when she put weight on her feet but Petey caught her by the elbow and held her steady.

"How am I supposed to get my underwear down?" she grumbled.

"Just consider me your third hand." Petey grinned lewdly and wriggled his fingers at her.

Charlee wished she hadn't asked.

"If you do anything to her . . ." Mason started to threaten before the man in the suit shoved the gun against his temple and commanded, "Shut up."

When she returned from the bathroom with Petey, who'd actually been a perfect gentleman and averted his eyes after skimming her panties to her knees, she felt like a new woman. Pain-free and ready to start kicking some big thug butt.

Mason was tied up and sitting in the beanbag chair. Petey bound her ankles again and shoved her down on top of Mason.

She didn't want to take solace in his hard, masculine body but damn her, she did. Her short skirt exposed her thighs and the material of his shorts rubbed comfortingly against her skin.

The new guy was leaning against the windowsill, flanked by Petey and Sal. He cleared his voice. "Now that we have all the amenities taken care of, allow me to introduce myself. I'm Spencer Cahill, CEO of Twilight Studios."

Mason shifted beneath her and she sensed his confusion mirroring her own. Why had the head of Twilight Studios taken them hostage? Had he discovered they were masquerading as Skeet and Violet Hammersmitz and he was really pissed off about it?

But no, that couldn't be. His henchmen had been following them since Vegas. Spencer Cahill obviously knew who they were.

"Let me assure you, if you do as I say, you will come to no physical harm and following the Academy Awards tomorrow night you will be released."

"The Academy Awards?" Mason sounded as confused as she felt. What did the Academy Awards have to do with anything?

Cahill's eyes narrowed. "You don't know what this is all about, do you?"

"No."

"Ah, that's quite interesting."

"Interesting?"

"Humorous." Cahill laughed a dry laugh suggesting he wasn't the least bit amused.

"Let us in on the joke. We could use a good chuckle," Charlee said.

"I suppose I should take comfort in the fact your grandfather has kept his mouth shut. It bodes well for your chances of getting out of this alive."

"What are you talking about?" Mason's muscles tensed beneath her fanny and his voice bristled.

"By the way, where is your grandfather?"

"You tell me, Cahill. You seem to be the grand Pooh-Bah around here."

Cahill studied Mason for a long moment. "For all your traipsing from Las Vegas to Arizona to California you haven't located your grandfather?"

"How could we with Frick and Frack over there riding our bumper?" Mason nodded at Sal and Petey.

"Hey," Petey started, "I resent . . ." But Cahill cut him off short with a quelling glance.

"Never mind. We'll find him."

"I don't get it," Charlee said. "What's the big deal about the Academy Awards?"

"This has something to do with Blade Bradford," Mason said flatly.

"You're an astute young man."

"So clue me in, fellas," Charlee said. "I wanna know what's going on."

Cahill pushed off from the windowsill, clasped his hands behind his back, and walked closer to the beanbag chair. "I see no harm in telling you what you're up against. In fact, it might insure your cooperation."

"Just tell us what's going on," Mason seethed.

"As you're probably aware, Blade Bradford is up for his second Oscar for *The Righteous*, a film produced by Twilight Studios."

"Yes, they kept yammering on and on about it while we were on the studio lot filming the *Newlywed Game*." Charlee nodded.

"Oh, by the way," Cahill said. "I applaud your ingenuity. Getting yourselves on my *Newlywed Game* in order to elude my assistants." He shook his head. "Clever, very clever. And don't think I missed the irony. Here I was footing the bill for your stay at the Grand Piazza, which by the way runs a thousand dollars a night, and I couldn't touch you because of all the media coverage I'd arranged to promote the show."

She wasn't about to tell the guy they had stumbled into the deal. Let Cahill keep thinking they were brilliant strategists.

"A thousand dollars a night? You rich people are nuts." Charlee shook her head.

"Go on about Blade Bradford," Mason said. "What's this got to do with my grandfather?"

"Ah, yes. Last year, while going through some old records, I discovered quite by accident that Mr. Bradford did not legitimately win his first Oscar."

"No?"

"In fact, I've seen the original voting record from 1955. Your grandfather actually got the most votes."

"Someone cooked the books," Mason said.

"Of course," Cahill continued. "It seems the same year he was nominated for his first Oscar, Blade Bradford married Sheila Jenkins, the daughter of the man who once owned the accounting firm that audits the Oscars."

"The same accounting firm Gentry Enterprises now holds controlling interest in."

"Precisely. To make his new son-in-law's career, Max Jenkins cheated."

"What's that got to do with present circumstances?" Mason asked.

Cahill smiled. "I don't know if you're aware of this, but Twilight Studios has not been particularly financially viable in recent years. As CEO, I've had to make a few executive decisions."

"Such as?"

Charlee could feel the heat of Mason's breath burning along the nape of her neck and she shivered.

"Convincing Sheila Bradford, who is still on the board of directors at the accounting firm and has a very strong influence there, that a second fix might just be the thing both Blade and Twilight Studios needed to boost our flagging sales."

"So that's what this is all about? Cheating on the Oscars."

Cahill smiled again, uglier this time. "Cheating to get what you want is as American as apple pie."

"Not in my America, buddy." Mason's voice was hard, unflinching.

"I applaud your gung ho, Boy Scout attitude, Mr. Gentry, truly I do, but really it shows an appalling lack of sophistication. I might have expected such lowbrow sentiment from someone like Ms. Champagne here, but from a man such as yourself?" Cahill clicked his tongue like a disappointed parent.

Hey! She bristled. Had that creep just insulted her? She glared at him.

"Listen here, Cahill," Mason ground out. "Don't you say disparaging things about Charlee."

"Ah, I see the lay of the land." Cahill pursed his lips and smirked. "You and Ms. Champagne have obviously bonded. I'm assuming you made good use of the honeymoon suite intended for Skeet and Violet Hammersmitz."

"That's none of your business. Leave Charlee out of all of this."

My hero.

The words blazed across her mind like a neon billboard. Mason had defended her honor. Her chest swelled with pride, delight, and respect and then she got mad at herself for forgiving him so easily. She was not letting him off the hook without busting his chops first.

"I wish I could leave her out of it, but like it or not, Ms. Champagne *is* involved. You involved her when you left Vegas with her."

"I don't care what you say, I don't cheat and neither does my grandfather," Mason insisted.

Except on your fiancée, Charlee thought.

"And she's not my fiancée," he growled low in her ear, reading her mind so uncannily that Charlee jumped.

"I'm merely pointing out the obvious," Cahill continued. "But you of all people, Mr. Gentry, should understand how the real world runs. Don't tell me you've never ordered the books to be cooked to make your company's bottom line look better to investors."

"Never."

"And you call yourself an investment banker?" Cahill shook his head.

"You're sunk, Cahill. I'm damn well going to the television stations with what you've just told me. It's over."

"If I believed that, then I would have to let Sal and Petey kill you. Fortunately, I'm confident you won't go to the media."

"How can you be so sure?"

The intensity of Mason's anger generated so much body heat Charlee feared he'd sear a hole in her fanny. She had the sense that if Mason wasn't hog-tied, he would be performing a few of his more advanced tae kwon do moves on Cahill.

"I'm certain you won't go public. If I wasn't I wouldn't have told you a thing. See, we're now partners in conspiracy, you and I."

"The hell we are."

"Such vehemence. I remember what it's like to be young and passionate."

"I'm not like you. Not in the least."

"Perhaps you're right. However, one fact remains that ensures your silence and loyalty to my cause. Your family's auditing firm will be implicated if you go public with this information after Bradford receives the Academy Award."

"But you know my family wasn't involved," Mason protested. "We have no motive."

"It didn't matter with Arthur Anderson either. Only a few bad eggs were enough to topple one of the top four international auditing firms. Unluckily for you, Mr. Gentry, I'm your bad egg. You not only jeopardize yourself but your entire family fortune as well. Open your mouth and your life as you know it is over."

♥ ♥ ♥

CHAPTER
18

*M*ason didn't believe for a moment that Cahill would allow them to walk out of the farmhouse alive. The only reason he hadn't already killed them was because he was planning on using them as added leverage to keep Nolan quiet.

Cahill left the farmhouse, instructing Sal and Petey to watch over them. The two men had gone back to their gin game in the kitchen while Mason and Charlee remained piled on top of each other in the beanbag chair.

The weight of her body in his lap would have been uncomfortable were it not so erotic. Every time she squirmed, his body hardened.

"Sit still, dammit," he said, his teeth clenched.

"My leg is cramping up."

"That's not the only thing cramping up."

She gave a little gasp. "You're getting a boner."

"Yeah, so quit moving."

"I don't believe this. What are you, Gentry, some kind of sex machine? You've got two women and neither of us can keep you satisfied," she snapped.

"You're the only one who turns me on."

"I'm sure Daphne takes great comfort in that."

"Listen, Charlee, I'm so sorry about what happened."

"Save it for someone who cares."

Thank God, she stopped moving. They sat together in the darkness, her head tucked under his chin, her spine flush against his chest, his butt buried deep in the foul-smelling beanbag chair. They breathed together in a raspy, sweaty, rhythm and it took a while for him to calm down.

"I should have told you I was almost engaged," he said. "It was wrong of me not to."

"I don't give a damn, Gentry. Honest."

"You lie."

"Oh, please, don't flatter yourself."

"You're going to tell me last night meant nothing to you?"

"That's right."

He clenched his jaw and all the hopes and dreams he'd been spinning in his head about a future with Charlee shattered. Had he been so wrong? Had he just imagined the chemistry—both physical and mental—between them? Or was she simply being stubborn, denying her feelings in order to punish him for not telling her about Daphne?

"I'm going to let this issue drop for the time being. We've got a serious problem on our hands." He kept his voice to a whisper just in case Sal and Petey were straining their ears to listen in on their conversation. "But don't think the discussion is closed."

"Yes it is, because the goons are going to kill us." The calmness in her voice gave him strength. She wasn't afraid. She wouldn't panic like she had with the spider.

"It's a distinct possibility," he admitted.

"Just my luck I have to die with Don Juan Gentry."

"Don't make jokes about this and I'm not a Don Juan."

"You coulda fooled me."

"For what it's worth, I wish you weren't here either."

"Yes, yes. I'm fully aware you're regretting ever having met me."

"Nonsense," he shouted, then remembered to lower his voice. "I don't regret meeting you! You're the best thing that ever happened to me."

Charlee snorted, sending a puff of warm air rolling over his cheek. "Oh, yeah, right. I'm betting you said something suspiciously similar to Daphne once upon a time."

"Dammit, Charlee," he snarled. "Will you let go of your anger for two seconds? Not that your wrath isn't justified. In fact, I wouldn't blame you if you never spoke to me again after the stunt I pulled. What I meant by my remark was that I wish you were far away from here and safe."

"Do you mean it?" she asked after a long pause. "That I'm the best thing that ever happened to you?"

"I never meant anything more in my life."

"Seriously?"

"It doesn't get much more serious than this."

"How am I the best thing that ever happened to you?"

"Since I met you I've come alive. You jostled me out of my doldrums. You're the breath of fresh air in my stale, studied world. You turned me on my ear. Woman, you made me forget Daphne even existed."

"You don't think it's just the excitement of the car

chases and the goons waving guns at us and the hot sex, do you?" She sounded as nervous as he felt.

"I'll admit these past few days have been a thrill ride but they've been exciting because of you."

"Oh."

He could hear in her tone that she wanted to believe him. Please, let her believe him. He gave her time to mull things over before saying, "I feel like an ass. I was supposed to be rescuing you, but I mucked things up and got caught by Cahill."

"Hey, I let myself get snatched by Dumb and Dumber. Doesn't make me feel particularly bright."

"This is all my fault. You were upset. If you hadn't just found out about Daphne, you wouldn't have had your guard down."

"Don't flatter yourself, Gentry."

"You can't fool me, Charlee. Last night was special. I challenge you to deny it." He lifted his chin and nuzzled the curve of her neck.

"Well, I have to confess I enjoyed last night a little bit more than I'm enjoying tonight."

They fell silent.

That nasty old guilt nibbled at him. "I'm truly sorry I didn't tell you about Daphne before. I guess I never thought things between you and me were going to end up the way they did."

"I don't want to talk about this anymore. We need to concentrate on escaping. The sooner the better."

"You got any plans?"

"No, do you?"

"Not really."

"All rightee then."

More silence.

"I do have a rental car parked about a quarter of a mile away. If we could get loose we've got a ride back to L.A."

"Assuming Cahill doesn't find the car."

"Assuming."

"How did you get your hands on a rental car?"

"It was Daphne's."

"Oh, I bet that went over big."

"She's not an unreasonable woman."

"Which is what everyone looks for in a mate. Rich, sexy bachelor searching for wife. Must be sophisticated, beautiful, and oh, yes, above all, reasonable."

"You think I'm sexy?" he teased, grinning into her hair.

She poked him in the belly with her thumb.

"Ow, what was that for?"

"Being cocky."

"Babe, you have no idea."

"Knock off calling me babe. I'm not your babe or your sweetheart or your darling and I most certainly am not reasonable. If the tables were turned and Daphne had been kidnapped and you tried to borrow my car I wouldn't let you have it."

"You'd let the villains spirit her away?"

"Damned skippee."

"Lucky for you, Daphne's reasonable."

"No, lucky for you. If you were my fiancé and I caught you cheating on me, I'd castrate you with a pocketknife."

"For the last time, she isn't my fiancée. I never popped the question."

"Yeah, but you two obviously had an understanding."

"Things change, but I do regret the way it all transpired. I never meant to hurt either one of you." He lowered his voice, dipped his head, and blew on the back of her neck. Delight shafted through him when she shivered against the heat. "And if you were my fiancée, I would never cheat on you."

"Because I'd cut your balls off?"

"There is that. But mostly because I can't imagine any woman enticing me away from someone as spirited and exciting as you."

She said nothing for the longest moment but her breathing quickened. "Was that a compliment?"

"Yes."

"Well stop it."

"Why?"

"Because I don't want you to compliment me. I don't even want to like you."

"But you do."

"Yeah," she admitted after a long moment, "I do. Stupid me. I knew better, I warned myself, but I drank too much champagne and convinced myself I could separate sex from my emotions. I guess I was wrong. I've never been able to do that."

"What do you mean never?"

Charlee blew out her breath. She might as well tell him. She'd been avoiding facing her past for too long.

"It's a complicated story."

"I'm all ears."

She paused, searching for the words to begin. "When I was nineteen and working as a maid at the MGM Grand, I was courted by Gregory Blankensonship, one of the owners' sons."

"I've heard of the family," Mason said. "They're quite wealthy."

"I was leery. I'd already had a few bad experiences with wealthy guys. Including that senator I told you about, but Gregory was persistent. I would say I played hard to get, except I wasn't playing. I was attracted to him, oh, boy, was I attracted to him, but I was so scared of getting hurt that I resisted his attention."

"And that just escalated his interest in you."

"Uh-huh. He bought me gifts and took me on trips. I admit. He turned my head. It's an age-old story and foolishly I fell for it. When he told me he loved me, I slept with him. I gave him my virginity, Mason. I thought what we had was the real deal." Her voice caught and her throat clogged with tears at the painful memory. "I didn't care about his money, I swear. I was in love with him. Or the idea of who I thought he was."

"I hate the sound of where this story is going," he muttered darkly.

"The next day was Gregory's college graduation party. His parents were throwing him a huge shindig at their house in Tahoe. I thought he was going to introduce me to them at last. Even though I wasn't officially invited, I felt sure Gregory would want me there."

Charlee paused. Why did the memory still hurt so much? It wasn't the loss of Gregory that caused her so much distress. She'd never had him in the first place. What ate at her so cruelly was the humiliation.

"You don't have to go on, Charlee. It's none of my business."

"I just want you to understand," she said. "Why I came on to you last night and why I was so upset to find out about Daphne. Anyway, I bought a new outfit, purchased a plane ticket, and showed up at the party to surprise him."

"He wasn't expecting you to be there?"

"No. I walked into the party just as he was announcing his plans to marry this pretty young actress. I . . ." She couldn't go on. Tears splashed down her cheek.

"Ah, sweetheart, don't cry," Mason said.

"I'm not crying," she denied, sniffling.

"It's okay to cry."

"Hell, I don't want to cry over that creep. I'm still just so mad that I fell for his bullshit."

"What did you do?"

"I thought about causing a scene. I thought about dumping his champagne over his head or knocking food off the buffet or just clawing his eyes out but a weird sense of calm came over me. I introduced myself to the actress and his parents. Gregory's face went white as a sheet. He told them I was some weirdo who'd been stalking him. Imagine. The night before he'd told me he had loved me and he had taken my virginity and now he was denying he even knew me. Gregory had security guards throw me out of the house. And I'm afraid I've held a grudge against rich guys to this day."

"You used me to get even with this Blankensonship guy," Mason said flatly.

Pressed against him in the darkness, Charlee couldn't see his face, but she felt his body tense beneath hers, heard his heart rate speed up. She'd hurt him and the knowledge pricked her conscience. Had she used him? Were her motives that shallow?

"Not intentionally."

"Face it. Whether consciously or subconsciously, you used me."

"I didn't say it was right. I'm not proud of myself."

He exhaled sharply, the sound of it echoed in her

ears. "I suppose I deserve that. I should have told you about Daphne. I should have realized we were both feeling vulnerable after everything that had happened to us. I should never have made love to you."

"Mason, we didn't make love. We had sex. There's a huge difference." It wasn't true. Charlee *had* made love to him last night, even though she struggled to deny it.

Reject him before he rejects you, every protective instinct inside her cried. *Don't, under any circumstances, let him know how you really feel.*

"Yeah." Mason swallowed hard.

She heard the pain in that gulp and knew she'd caused it. Feeling incredibly wretched, she closed her eyes and pretended she was asleep.

Charlee jerked awake sometime later. While they slept she and Mason had managed to shift around so she was off his lap and butted up against him. They were face-to-face, in the beanbag chair, both their legs spilling off onto the bare wooden floor. The rope bindings around her wrists hurt like the dickens and her fingers were numb but her mind was clicking.

She'd dreamed of escape and the dream had given her the answer to their dilemma.

"Mason, wake up," she whispered, her ears tuned for sounds from the rest of the house.

He mumbled.

"Psst, wake up." She raised her knees and bumped against his.

He opened his eyes and looked at her. Damn, was he ever adorable with his hair mussed and that impossibly sexy beard stubble. "What is it?"

"I've got an idea," she said, and then told him about her plan.

Two minutes later, Mason started groaning loud enough to wake the dead three counties over.

Right on cue Petey and Sal burst into the room, guns drawn, looking bleary-eyed and smelling of beer and cigarette smoke.

"What is it?" Sal demanded, waving his Glock at Mason. "What's going on?"

"He's bad sick," Charlee said.

Mason upped the groaning.

"Oh, yeah, like you expect us to fall for that."

"I'm not kidding." Charlee put her toughest tone into her voice. "The guy's a diabetic. If he doesn't get something to eat soon he'll go into a coma."

"He don't look like no diabetic to me," Petey said.

"Yeah, like you know what a diabetic looks like. You didn't even finish high school."

"I got a GED," Petey shouted. "It's the same thing. And they don't teach you about diabetes in high school."

"How would you know? You didn't go," Charlee asked.

Petey leaned over the beanbag and shoved his gun in her face. Charlee stared back at him unblinking. He looked a little rattled by her lack of fear. "I've had about enough of you."

Mason made retching noises and he was so good at it that for a couple of seconds there Charlee thought he was actually going to throw up.

"Ew, ew, get him away from me before he vomits in my hair," she said.

"You're not scared of a gun but you're scared of a little vomit?" Petey shook his head in disbelief.

"They're playing us, man," Sal exclaimed.

Mason kept retching. His face turned red and the veins at his forehead popped out. Damn, but he was his grandfather's progeny all right. Give that boy an Oscar.

"Oh, God," Charlee screamed. "He's going to have a seizure. Untie him, untie him. If he dies, you guys know Cahill will finger you for the murder rap. Who are the police going to believe? A powerful CEO of a movie studio or two hired guns who didn't finish high school?"

"I got a GED," Petey howled, but he did reach down to cut the ropes binding Mason's arms with a knife he pulled from his pocket.

Sal put a hand to Petey's shoulder. "I'm telling you, it's a bluff."

"You willing to take that chance? She's right. The guy dies and Cahill's gonna have our heads."

Mason started bucking and his eyes rolled back in his head, then he flopped over onto his stomach.

"Shit, shit, shit," Petey exclaimed. "He is having a seizure."

"Untie him, untie him, untie him," Charlee repeated her mantra, hoping it would sink into Petey's thick skull and override Sal's objections.

Petey cut Mason's feet loose.

Mason's jerking intensified.

"His hands too! And turn him on his side," Charlee said.

"Yeah, man," Sal said. "If he pukes and inhales it he's gonna croak just like a rock star."

From the expression on Petey's face Charlee could

tell he was relieved to have his partner backing him up at last. He clipped the twine binding Mason's wrists.

And Charlee figured Petey regretted that move for the rest of his life.

Like Bruce Lee and Jackie Chan and Jean-Claude Van Damme and Chuck Norris combined into one malevolent force, Mason leaped to his feet and he started kicking ass and taking names. His performance was a thing of beauty to watch.

Blam, blam, blam.

Three quick blows and Petey was out. He smacked facedown on the floor like a felled redwood.

Timber.

Completely unnerved, Sal pointed his Glock at Mason's heart but his hands shook so badly one round-house kick from Mason sent the gun flying across the room.

"Your turn." Mason smiled and put Sal on top of his buddy.

He retrieved Petey's knife while the two men lay groaning, then quickly sliced through Charlee's bindings. He grabbed her hand and dragged her toward the door.

"Wait, wait." She pulled away from him just long enough to snatch up Sal's Glock on the fly.

They tore through the house in a blind panic, through the back door and into the peaceful, cool predawn darkness. Charlee paused to tuck the Glock into the waistband of her skirt.

"Come on, come on." Mason took her hand again and hustled her across the empty field toward the vineyard lying like a dark oasis a quarter mile away.

Good thing they were both in good physical shape.

Unfortunately cowboy boots didn't make for the best running shoes. Charlee's feet kept slipping in the sandy soil and she almost fell twice but Mason pulled her up and kept her from tumbling over.

"You can do it. We're almost there," he urged at the same moment the first shot rang out.

"They're shooting at us."

"I noticed. Better get a move on."

"We're out of range."

"They have a car. Won't take 'em long to catch up with us."

"Oh, yeah."

He tugged her around the edge of the vineyard and into the road but stopped abruptly.

"What is it?"

He swore. "The rental car's gone."

More shots resonated from behind them and then they heard the sound of a car engine firing up.

They looked at each other.

"Into the vineyard," Mason said.

She was beginning to feel like a yo-yo the way he kept jerking on her arm.

"Get low, get down."

"Too bad it's not a cornfield," she grumbled, dropping to her knees and following Mason as he crawled through the rows. "They can spot us easily in here."

"At least it's still dark."

"Not for long." Yellow strips of sunlight were already staining the eastern sky.

"Shh, let's listen. Flat on your belly. Head down." He reached out and splayed a palm to her back and pushed her into the sand with his fingertips.

"We never tried that position."

"This isn't the time for jokes, Charlee."

"No better time than when you're about to die."

"Well, if I have to die, I can't think of anyone I'd rather die with."

What? He sounded completely serious. Charlee swallowed, not knowing how to take his declaration. "I know being dramatic runs in your family, Gentry, but I'm not about to let the likes of Sal and Petey do us in."

"Shh. Listen."

Charlee lay breathing in the dirt, every muscle in her body tensed, her ears sharply attuned to the sounds of the Malibu inching slowly along the road.

The car stopped, engine idling.

Oh, dear.

She ached to turn her head and glance behind her to see how close the car was. Mason must have been feeling the same way too because he whispered, "Don't do it, Charlee. Don't move."

Like a kid playing statues, she froze. She didn't even blink. Blood rushed through her ears loud as a forty-piece tympani band. The Glock poked her uncomfortably in the ribs, but at least they had a weapon. Mason lay directly to her left, his fingers wrapped securely around her upper arm.

A car door shut.

"You see anything?" Sal's voice broke the silence.

She closed her eyes. Was Petey stumbling through the vineyard looking for them? Her pulse thumped in the hollow of her throat.

"It's too dark."

"Well, get the flashlight out of the trunk, dumb ass."

They heard the sound of the Malibu's trunk being unlatched and then slammed back down. One set of footsteps echoed on the asphalt.

They were totally screwed. Petey was bound to see them. She didn't want to die in a gun battle in some godforsaken spot in southern California.

If I have to die, I can't think of anyone I'd rather die with. Mason's words rang in her head.

It was the most romantic thing anyone had ever said to her, but she wasn't quite ready to die. Not yet. Not by a long shot. For one thing, she wanted more of Mason. Wanted more of his long, hot body in her bed. She wasn't going to let any half-brained thugs cheat her out of some seriously good sex.

Or a once-in-a-lifetime love, the little voice in the back of her head dared to whisper.

But Charlee wasn't ready to hear it. A panicky sensation that had nothing to do with the trouble they were in and everything to do with the terrifying thought that she might be falling in love with Mason squeezed her stomach with a sharp pressure.

"Damn. Batteries are dead." Petey's voice wrapped around them in the darkness. It sounded as if he were standing close enough for Charlee to encircle his wrist with her hand but she knew sound carried. He couldn't be as close as it seemed.

"There're more batteries in the glove compartment."

"Dammit, my nose is still frickin' bleedin'," Petey complained.

"It's your own fault. I told you they were up to something."

"Who woulda thought a rich guy would know that kung fu shit?"

"You're just pissed 'cause he kicked your ass."

"Shut up. He kicked your ass too."

"My nose isn't the one that's broken."

"Oh, yeah? They got *your* gun."

"Crawl on your belly," Mason told Charlee. "Fast as you can while Dumb and Dumber are busy arguing."

Charlee started crawling but the Glock jabbed her so hard she lost her breath. Quickly, she shifted the weapon to the back of her waistband. Mason was already several feet ahead of her.

"Stay with me."

"I'm coming," she said and then added mischievously, "And I don't mean that in a sexual way."

He merely grunted.

By the time the flashlight beam played over the grapevines above their heads, they'd traveled another few yards from the road. The sun had edged up a notch and when she turned her head to the left, Charlee could see the outline of a dilapidated barn squatting in the field several hundred yards away from the farmhouse and directly parallel to their current location.

The flashlight beam returned, this time sweeping lower to the ground.

"I see something," Petey called out.

"Is it them?"

"Can't tell."

"Hang on."

The car door slammed again. Sal and Petey were now both in the vineyard.

Charlee grabbed the Glock with both hands, rose to her feet, and spun around. As Maybelline always said, the best defense is a good offense.

"Charlee!" Mason cried out in despair. "What are you doing?"

The flashlight beam hit her in the face, blinding her, but she pretended she could see. She kept her wrist locked, the gun extended out in front of her.

She was taking a huge chance that he didn't have his own gun at the ready. "Back off, Petey, or I'll blow your head clean off your shoulders, I swear I will."

She heard him moving toward her. He kept the flashlight trained on her face. "Sorry, but I don't believe you."

Moistening her lips, she cocked the hammer. "Hear that?"

"I hear it, but do you have what it takes to kill someone? Come on, put the gun down, and play nice."

"Freeze. Don't take another step."

Petey kept moving toward her. "Oh, and by the way, since you've got a light in your eyes you probably aren't aware that I've got my gun trained on your head too and lucky for me, there's no light in my eyes. Guess we have ourselves a Mexican standoff."

"I don't want to kill you."

She stood with her legs splayed. Her heart rate curiously slow. She'd never been so calm in her life. She was vaguely aware of Mason having gotten to his feet behind her. She had no idea where Sal was at and that bothered her.

"You're not going to kill me," Petey said.

Charlee squinted against the powerful beam. Petey was just a few feet in front of her and sure enough, she saw that he held the thirty-eight in his right hand, the flashlight in his left.

Well, she thought. *It's come down to this. I'm going to kill a man tonight.*

She'd never killed anyone before.

First time for everything. It's either him or you and Mason.

She had to do something to gain the upper hand. Think! Think!

Then from behind her Mason flung sand in Petey's face and followed that with a fistful of grapes.

Chaos erupted.

Petey howled, dropped the flashlight and the gun as he raised his hands to his eyes.

At the same time, Sal came from behind Petey and dived for his gun.

Mason, who'd somehow gotten around to her side without Charlee being aware of it, kicked Petey's gun away just before Sal grabbed for it. Mason's foot made a solid whacking noise as it contacted against Sal's hand. The burly thug screamed like a girl.

Now or never.

She had to act before Sal or Petey found the gun. Charlee stared down the sight, aimed at Petey's right shoulder, and pulled the trigger.

Click.

"Bitch!" Petey screamed, enraged, and lumbered toward her. "You tried to kill me. I'll strangle you with my bare hands."

Desperately, she squeezed the trigger again.

Click. Click.

The gun was empty.

♥ ♥ ♥

CHAPTER
19

"Plan B." Mason grabbed her arm and she dropped the useless Glock.

"Plan B?"

"Tear ass for the barn."

"Right behind you."

They took off at a dead run, Sal and Petey cursing and hollering and thrashing around behind them. To Charlee it felt as if they were barely moving, slogging through syrup instead of sand. By the time they reached the barn door and shoved it open, they were panting so hard Charlee feared her lungs would leap right out of her chest.

"That . . ." Mason paused to heave in air, "was the most courageous, most foolhardy stunt I've ever seen anyone pull."

"See what happens when you live in an ivory tower? You don't get to meet many brave, foolhardy women."

"Charlee, I could search the world over and not find many women as bold as you."

"Me? What about you? Flinging sand and grapes in Petey's face. Stroke of genius, I might add."

"I certainly couldn't let him kill you and I didn't want you killing him either. It's a terrible thing carrying the burden of blame for someone's death."

Charlee met his dark, complicated eyes. It sounded as if he spoke from experience, but she had no time to explore his unexpected testimony.

"We've got to barricade the doors."

Her gaze scanned the barn. The usual garden stuff. Rusted rakes, hoes, and shovels. A Weed Eater, a collection of weathered two-by-fours, and baling wire. In the middle of the barn sat something large covered with a heavy gray tarp. A tractor maybe?

Grabbing the hoe, Charlee jammed the handle through the door latch while Mason wedged two-by-four braces between the door and the floor.

Mere seconds later Sal and Petey slammed into the door from the outside. It shuddered beneath the men's combined weight, but the blockade held despite their repeated battering.

In unison Mason and Charlee turned and spotted a large sliding metal door at the rear of the barn. He lunged for the rake and she grabbed a shovel.

"We're trapped, you realize," she said to Mason as they worked frantically to shore up the back door. "There's no way out of here. We've bested them twice, they know what we're capable of, we won't catch them with their guards down again. They're gonna get serious."

As if to prove her point, a bullet whizzed past Mason's ear and smashed into a support beam.

Another shot and then another. Bullets ricocheted

around the barn, zinging off the tin siding and spitting into the dirt floor.

Charlee covered her ears with her hands, eyed the tarp, and wondered if by some stroke of luck the tractor still ran. If they could get the thing started and crash through the back door . . . then what?

Petey and Sal had guns. They did not. And top tractor speed couldn't be more than twenty or thirty miles an hour. Not nearly fast enough to outrun a bullet.

But it was the only option her fevered brain could conjure. But what if it wasn't a tractor? Maybe it was a car. She could hotwire that puppy in sixty seconds flat.

Yeah, like what were the odds the thing would even run?

"Fine," Petey yelled at them. "I'm tired of wastin' my bullets on you. You can't get out. We've got you surrounded. We can wait."

Thank heavens. She could think more clearly without bullets bouncing around the room like pinballs.

"Charlee," Mason said, his voice gone deadly hollow, "do you smell gasoline?"

Their eyes met.

The air was hot and rich with the pungent odor of petroleum. Mason darted to the front door and peeked out through a bullet hole.

"They're pouring gasoline on the barn."

"Bastards," she said vehemently and stalked over to the tarp. Grasping the heavy gray canvas with both hands, she yanked hard.

And uncovered a single-engine Piper.

"Great. Just lovely. Isn't that our rotten luck?" She flung her hands in the air. "We find a plane and neither of us knows how to fly it. Why the hell couldn't it have been a car or a tractor? I'd have even taken a go-cart."

Mason didn't say a word.

The gasoline smell grew stronger, permeating the entire barn. It wouldn't take much to set this pile of kindling ablaze.

She looked over at him. His face was ashen and she was shocked to see his hands trembling. His gaze was fixed on the plane and he looked as scared as she'd felt when he had plucked the black spider off her shoulder.

"Mason! What is it?" She sprang to his side. "What's wrong?"

He swallowed hard.

"Talk to me." She grabbed his shoulders and shook him. "What is it?"

"I know how to fly that plane," he said.

"That's a good thing. Right?"

Mason shook his head and passed his palm over his chin. His pulse galloped a thousand miles an hour. Fear was a teamster's fist in his stomach. Just looking at the plane made him nauseous.

"I'm terrified of flying the same way you're terrified of black widow spiders."

"No."

"Yes."

"But that's crazy. If you're a pilot, how can you be afraid of flying?" Her voice pleaded for logic, for a lucid explanation.

"Crash," he said, his voice sounding eerily robotic. "College freshman. My roommate and I borrowed my father's plane without permission. Kip was at the controls but I was still responsible. My idea. A freak thunderstorm caught us. Brought the plane down. Kip was killed. My fault."

Charlee sucked in her breath. "I'm sorry for what happened to you, but we're wasting valuable time. You've got to fly us out of here or we're going to end up crispy critters."

"Can't."

He didn't want to be this way, but his limbs were paralyzed, useless. He tried to step toward the plane but even the sound of crackling wood and wisps of smoke seeping through the barn could not propel him forward.

Every terrifying moment leading up to the plane crash flashed through his mind. The huge fight he and his father had had over Mason's career path. His father demanding he drop his aviation courses and study finance. The plot he'd hatched to steal his father's plane to get even. Kip's enthusiastic support for the idiotic scheme. The savage storm. Kip's bravado that he could handle the weather. The bone-jarring impact as they hit the ground. The pain that shot through his shattered leg. Kip's blood on his hands. The cold, hard rain in his face.

He simply could not get into that plane.

"Okay," Charlee said. "I'm going to let you wrestle with those demons, while I hot-wire the engine. But you don't have long to make your decision. Basically here are your choices. Fly us out of here or die."

She was right. Simple as that.

Forget about Kip. Forget about the past. Forget your fear. Think about Charlee.

Without another word she marched over to the plane and started to climb in. She flung open the door, and then froze.

"Black widow," she said.

"I'll get it." For the first time he was able to walk toward the plane.

She squared her shoulders, tossed her head. "I can handle it." Then she picked up her foot and crushed the spider beneath the heel of her boot.

He stared at her, awestruck. The woman was truly and utterly amazing. He would do anything for her. Fight to the death if he had to. Fly that damned plane.

"Hot-wire the sucker," he said.

"About time." She coughed against the rising smoke.

She tinkered with the engine. Seconds ticked by. Then minutes.

Smoke thickened, swirled.

The engine caught, sputtered once and died. Charlee swore and tried again.

Flames licked across the floor, spreading closer, ever closer.

The engine sputtered again and lasted a little longer this time before it died.

Hurry, hurry.

The third time it worked. The engine turned over and purred.

The room was unbearably hot, the smoke so thick they could barely breathe.

"I'll open the back door," she wheezed. "As you taxi by I'll climb on."

Mason nodded and slid into the driver's seat. *It's just like riding a bicycle. You can do it.* If Charlee could squash that spider, he could fly the plane.

She yanked away the garden tools and shoved the door open while he set the plane in motion. The minute he committed himself, his fear evaporated and his long-forgotten joy in flying lifted inside him.

Charlee climbed into the passenger seat, grinning like he'd just won the powerball lottery. Hell, he felt as if he had just won the powerball lottery.

He gave the plane more gas, it jolted forward and they shot out the door. He pulled back on the throttle and they were airborne.

A triumphant cry burst from his lips. Ha! He had done it.

"Oops, here comes Dumb and Dumber."

Sal and Petey charged around the back of the burning barn but they were too late. The plane had already climbed thirty feet.

"Bye!" Charlee leaned out the window and waved.

For a minute there Mason thought Petey was going to shoot the plane, but obviously he thought better of firing a bullet straight into the air, because he holstered his gun.

Sal screamed at Petey. Petey flipped Sal off.

Mason grinned and grinned and grinned.

And then he got a bird's-eye view of the barn completely engulfed in flames and his heart rocketed into his throat. Dark, oily smoke spiraled skyward. If they had waited very much longer it would have been too late to escape.

At the thought of losing Charlee, his chest constricted.

"Yahoo!"

He glanced at her. She leaned over and kissed him lightly on the cheek. The warmth of her lips branded the moment in time.

"You were totally and completely awesome. I am so proud of you," she said.

"I've got to confess, if you hadn't had the courage to

stomp on that black widow I don't know if I could have snapped out of my terror."

"Oh, really?" She arched an eyebrow.

"You inspired me."

"I'm guessing this might be a bad time to tell you I faked it. There wasn't any black widow. I pretended to squash a spider. Pretty smart of me, huh?" She looked like a schoolkid who'd made the honor roll for the first time.

"Babe," he said, "you're unbelievable."

The sun was up and the sky was clear. Fire engines wailed in the distance. He spotted the Chevy Malibu tearing off down the road at a frantic clip. Sal and Petey on the lam.

Mason took the plane higher, ascending several hundred feet into the air and followed the road west, stunned at how good he felt. How alive.

He'd been taken prisoner, tied up, shot at, burned out, and forced to face his greatest fear. And he had never been happier in his entire life. How sick was that?

All thanks to Charlee.

She was the magnet that picked up the shattered, scattered filaments of the daring youth he'd once been and she'd put him back together again. He felt reborn. A new man. A new start. A new life.

A life he ached to share with Charlee. But was he in love alone?

Glancing over at her, he experienced the strangest tightening in his chest. He studied her profile, admired the way her cheek curved, the way her glossy black hair fell to her shoulders and beyond. She was dirty and soot-stained and her blouse was torn but he had never seen a prettier sight.

"You're gorgeous."

"Watch what you're doing, cowboy. From what you told me back there I'm assuming your flying skills are rusty."

"I mean it, you're drop-dead gorgeous."

"Ha. I'm not sleek and petite like Daphne."

"Thank God."

"What's that supposed to mean?"

"You're you. Every wonderful inch of you."

She gave him a look.

"What? You *are* wonderful."

"And you're drunk on courage. Fly the plane."

"Yes, ma'am." He couldn't stop grinning.

"You know what I wish?"

"What?"

"I wish I had a tall glass of sweet tea with lots of crushed ice." Charlee sighed. "I could suck down two gallons."

"I wish I had a cheeseburger and fries."

"No kidding? You?"

"It is my favorite food, remember?"

"It's Skeet's favorite food. Not yours."

"Fat and protein sound like heaven to me right now."

"I can do you one better. I'm so hungry I'd even eat some of those gross fish eggs you're so wild about."

"Better watch out, Charlee Champagne," he teased. "We're starting to rub off on each other."

"Egads!" She chuckled. "What is the world coming to?"

What indeed? In four short days everything in his life had changed. On the surface, it had changed for the worst. But why did he feel freer than he had ever felt in his life?

She cleared her throat a few minutes later. "You might want to consider not flying beside the road."

Mason looked down, saw the Malibu speeding along behind them and his grin disappeared. "They've got to be doing ninety to keep up with us."

"All this brouhaha for a rigged Oscar? I don't get it."

"Oscar wins are a big deal," he said, angling the plane north out across the desert. "Winning one can shoot an actor from unknown status to the exclusive twenty-million-dollars-a-picture club and it can mean billions of dollars for the studio involved."

"Do you suppose the accounting firm has been cooking the books on the awards ever since 1955?"

That was a chilling thought. Mason pressed his lips together. Since Cahill's revelation he'd been too busy dodging bullets and running for his life to fully consider the implications. But now, reality sank in.

His grandfather and his entire family's reputation hung in the balance. That's why Gramps had taken off alone. Somehow he'd found out about the bastardized accounting practices. That was why he had kept silent until he'd had a chance to investigate for himself. And that was probably why Nolan had taken the half-million dollars. He hadn't known ahead of time who he might have to bribe, hire, or hush up, so he'd taken enough money to cover any eventuality.

A spear of worry arrowed through him when he thought about Nolan and Maybelline. Where were they? If Cahill didn't have them, had Elwood recaptured them? And just where did Charlee's father factor in this whole Oscar scenario?

One thing was certain. They couldn't worry about Maybelline and Nolan. Not right now.

Top priority, they had to get to L.A. before the Academy Awards ceremony, audit the votes, and announce the real winner of the best supporting actor category. If he couldn't prevent Blade Bradford from getting the award, his entire family fortune would be destroyed.

But they had plenty of time. It wasn't even seven o'clock in the morning and L.A. was less than two hundred miles away. The Academy Awards didn't start until seven. That gave them a full twelve hours. No sweat. They would even have time for a meal, a shower, and a change of clothes.

And then the airplane sputtered ominously. Startled, his gaze shifted to the instrument panel.

The engine coughed. Once, twice, three times.

"Uh-oh," he said.

"What is it?"

"Look around. Quick. Help me find a good place to land."

"What's wrong?"

"We're out of gas."

Charlee ran a hand through her tangled hair and shook her head. She wanted to whine, but she was tougher than that. It seemed as if they'd been walking for weeks.

She was tired and hungry and thirsty. Her boots were rubbing blisters on her heels, her nose was sunburned, and she smelled of sweat and dirt and smoke and general run-of-the-mill funk. She wished for her cowboy hat and sunscreen and two dozen Band-Aids. She wished for toothpaste and a hairbrush and toilet paper.

But mostly, she wished for water. Cool, clear water.

So much for tough. Apparently, she was as soft as the next girl.

Mason had safely landed the plane, albeit in the middle of a cactus patch. Gingerly, they'd clambered out only to realize with despair they had no idea where they were.

It was long past noon, edging on toward one-thirty, she guessed.

"We've got to get to L.A. before the Oscars tonight," Mason said. They walked side by side, kicking up sand and dust behind them.

"So you told me. About a hundred times."

"I can't stress how important this is."

"I get it, I get it, but what can we do about it, Mason? We can't even find the friggin' highway and if we did, for all we know Sal and Petey are trolling it with orders from Cahill to shoot on sight."

"It's a big stretch of road between here and L.A. Sorry, but Petey and Sal just aren't that good."

"Hey, maybe even as we speak your grandfather is taking care of all this. Right now he and Maybelline could be at the accounting firm running roughshod on the number crunchers."

"We can hope."

"Boy, if that's your hopeful face don't let me see discouraged."

"Charlee," he said, "I'm on the verge of losing everything."

"That's gotta suck. Especially when you were on the verge of finding yourself."

He frowned at her. "What are you talking about?"

"When you were up in the air you were a completely

different person. Relaxed, calm, confident. Now the old Mason is back. Anxious, controlling, argumentative."

"I'm not argumentative."

"You're arguing right now."

"This isn't arguing."

"What is it?"

"Charlee, I still don't think you get it. If we don't stop Blade Bradford from winning and it comes out after the fact that our accounting firm cheated, the Gentry name will be destroyed. In a business like ours reputation is everything. Companies will pull their accounts. Our stock value will plummet. The scandal will affect not only my family, but also all the people who work for us, or do business with us. You saw what happened to the stock market after Enron and WorldCom and Tyco."

"Your family has that much influence on the U.S. economy?"

"That's what I've been trying to tell you."

"Oh." She paused a moment. She knew Mason was rich and powerful. She had no idea he was *that* rich and powerful. Her secret lingering hope that things could work out between them all but evaporated. "Well, then walk faster."

"I'm glad you appreciate the gravity of the situation."

"So," she said, a few minutes later, "what would happen if, say, Blade did win and you and your grandfather just kept your mouths shut?"

"You mean cover up the accounting discrepancy?"

She slanted a glance over at him. "It seems like the easy way out."

"You mean just let Cahill and Bradford get away with their scam?"

"It's what most people would do."

Mason shook his head. "Let's concentrate on getting to L.A. so I'm not faced with that temptation."

Two hours later they finally reached the highway. Mason was so wound up about the time slipping away from them that Charlee thought she was going to have to put Valium on the top of her "I want" list behind food, sweet tea, and a long cool shower. The Valium was for him, not for her.

They hurried to the edge of the road.

It was empty. Not a vehicle in sight.

"Shall we?" Charlee inclined her head toward L.A. and tried not to limp. Her heels felt as if her leather boots had flayed the flesh to the bone. The only consolation, she hadn't been wearing Violet's ankle strap stilettos for the trek.

"You're hobbling," he said.

"It's nothing."

"Guess those boots weren't made for walking."

"Ha, ha. Normally they are very comfortable. They're rubbing blisters because I don't have on any socks. Violet apparently doesn't believe in them."

He stopped walking, turned toward her, and motioned with his index finger. "Come here."

"What for?"

"I'm going to give you a piggyback ride."

"No, you're not."

"Don't be so damned stubborn, woman. You can barely walk."

"Mason, I'm no little thing. I weigh a hundred and thirty-five pounds."

"I don't care. Get over here."

"You say you don't care now . . ."

Before she could finish her sentence he stalked over and slung her unceremoniously over his shoulder.

"Hey, wait, stop it. Put me down."

"Only if you agree to let me give you a piggyback ride."

"Okay, all right, I'll do it."

They trudged along the shoulder of the road, Mason carrying Charlee on his back, her bare legs wrapped around his muscled waist, her skirt hem flapping as he walked. She felt guilty, but man-o-man did her feet ever feel better.

Minutes passed, then half an hour. No car. No truck. Not even a motorcycle.

"Why don't we take a break," she said, fretting about his back.

He stopped and let her slide gently to the ground. "Where is this godforsaken place?" he asked. "I didn't think anywhere in America was this deserted."

"It's just a bad time of day. The later it gets the more likely it is someone will come along."

"Charlee, we're still three hours outside of L.A."

"Okay, let's not get off on the time issue again." *Or I'll have to strangle you with my bare hands.*

"Listen."

They stopped walking and cocked their heads.

"Sounds like an engine."

"Quick, stick out your thumb."

"Better yet, I'll strike a pose," Charlee said and imitated Claudette Colbert from *It Happened One Night*. It helped that she had on a skirt so short Barbie could have used it for a hanky.

They peered into the distance, waiting. Heat waves shimmered up from the ground like gasoline fumes, wriggling and crinkling and blurring the edges of reality.

Finally, an aging flatbed truck chugged into view over the rise. Charlee wriggled her leg provocatively. Mason stuck out his thumb.

Please stop, please stop, please stop.

The truck putt-putted leisurely over the asphalt. A smiling dark-complexioned woman sat behind the wheel, three hound dogs lolled on the front seat beside her. She waved at them and pulled over.

Mason and Charlee raced to the truck.

The woman gave them a dazzling smile and said something in Spanish. They shrugged. She pointed to the back of the truck stacked high with crates of strawberries. Apparently she wasn't about to dethrone her dogs for hitchhikers.

Who cared? It was a ride.

"*Gracias, gracias,*" they repeated and hurried around the truck, ready to hop in the back among all those delicious-smelling strawberries.

Only to be stopped by an unexpected but totally wonderful surprise.

There, curled up in each other's arms, looking just as grime-ridden and road-weary and hungry as Mason and Charlee, sat their grandparents.

CHAPTER 20

*C*harlee flung herself into her grandmother's arms. "Maybelline! You're alive."

All four of them started hugging and laughing and talking at once with no one getting a word in edgewise. Charlee glanced over at Mason. He winked at her and gave the time-out gesture. "Okay, all right. One at a time. You start, Gramps. What happened?"

The attractive older man who shared a remarkable resemblance to Mason said, "Actually, the story starts with Maybelline. If she hadn't intervened, I might never have found out that Blade Bradford, his wife, and Spencer Cahill were rigging the Oscars."

Maybelline looked at Charlee with a happy glow in her eyes that she had never seen there before.

She's in love with Mason's grandfather. The thought hit Charlee out of the blue and when Nolan squeezed Maybelline's hand and smiled at her, she knew not only was it true, but that Nolan loved her grandmother in return.

Her stomach gave a funny little boot to her heart.

Charlee slid a sidelong glance at Mason and her stomach kicked harder. Were she and Maybelline going to end up with dual broken hearts after all this was over? The women from the wrong side of the tracks falling for the guys far out of their league?

"Have some strawberries." Maybelline passed around an open crate of the juicy ripe fruit like the perfect hostess. "Angelina told us to help ourselves."

Charlee grabbed a handful of strawberries, leaned back against a stack of crates, and nibbled them politely instead of wolfing them down the way she wanted. Mason was sitting on the opposite side of the truck with Maybelline and Nolan sandwiched between the two of them.

Silly as it seemed, Charlee missed sitting next to him. For the past four days they'd been side by side almost constantly.

"It all started forty-seven years ago," Maybelline began, "when I first came to Hollywood, met a charismatic actor, and thought I'd fallen in love."

Charlee shifted her gaze to Nolan. He shook his head, denying he was the actor in question.

"It was only later, after I got pregnant with your father, Charlee, that I discovered the man was already married."

"Blade Bradford," Mason guessed.

"Yes," Maybelline admitted.

"How come you never told me this before?" Charlee asked her grandmother.

"I was ashamed. Embarrassed that I'd been taken advantage of. I never told anyone. Not even Elwood."

"You had nothing to be ashamed of," Nolan said gruffly.

Maybelline smiled at Mason. "Your grandfather was wonderful. In fact, he stopped me from flinging myself off the HOLLYWOOD sign."

Her grandmother had once tried to kill herself? Charlee struggled to imagine her tough-minded granny as a young and vulnerable girl and finally gave up. The years had erased all traces of the naive innocent she had once been.

But then she caught Nolan looking at Maybelline. In his eyes, Charlee saw that young, troubled girl. How little she really knew about her own grandmother.

"Anyway, fast forward to the future," Maybelline said to Mason. "My son Elwood, who much to my unhappiness has always had trouble controlling his impulses, got in deep with gambling debts. He shoplifted cigarettes in order to get thrown in jail to avoid his creditors."

"I remember that," Charlee said. "I thought it seemed really weird at the time since he doesn't smoke, but he told me he'd planned on selling the cigarettes."

Maybelline sighed. "While he was in lock-up he met some guy who told him he could help him locate his biological father. Elwood got all excited. Not about the thought of meeting his father, but because it was another person he could put the bite on. I discovered all this after the fact of course."

"Let me guess," Charlee interjected. "Elwood blackmailed Blade Bradford."

The truck hit a bump and they all went sliding into each other. They righted themselves and Maybelline continued with her story.

"Elwood sent Blake a letter demanding five hundred thousand dollars or he threatened to go to the *National*

Enquirer with what happened forty-seven years ago. But Elwood got more than he bargained for. In the blackmail letter, he was talking about his illegitimate birth. But apparently Blade thought he was talking about how he and his wife and father-in-law had rigged the Oscar votes so he would beat out Nolan for best actor."

"And Elwood's threats couldn't have come at a worse time," Mason said. "Considering how Blade was up for another Oscar again this year."

"Exactly."

Mason ate a strawberry and glanced at Charlee over the top of her grandmother's head. He had to fight the urge to drag her into his arms, kiss those rich, berry-stained lips and make all sorts of wild promises to her that he feared he could not keep.

"And," Nolan added, "unfortunately enough, Spencer Cahill stumbled across the records from 1955 and he was putting the squeeze on Blade's wife to put in another fix."

"So," Maybelline told Charlee, "this was when Cahill got involved and sent hired guns after your father with the intention of rubbing him out."

"We're quite familiar with Sal and Petey and what they're capable of." Charlee shook her head.

"Elwood had no knowledge of the Oscar fix until he went to confront Blade in person and tell him to call off his goons. He found Blade in the process of shredding documents. He and Blade had a fight and Elwood stole some of the documents. He didn't really understand what he'd uncovered but the date was 1955, so he brought a copy to me."

"Your grandmother knew I'd purchased controlling

interest in the accounting firm for nostalgic reasons and she rightly supposed I had no idea I'd been cheated out of the Oscar in 1955. She called and asked me to come to Vegas and help her sort this out," Nolan told Charlee.

Then turning to Mason, he said, "I took the half mil from the company fund not only because I was going to pay Elwood's blackmail fee to keep him quiet about what had happened, but to get the family to send you after me." He grinned. "I knew they'd send you and not Hunter."

"You wanted me to come after you?"

"Of course. I needed help and I couldn't do this alone but I had to keep things quiet. Couldn't risk any of this leaking out."

"Why didn't you want them to send Hunter?"

Nolan laughed. "You've got to get over this second-son-in-the-Gentry-family syndrome, Mason. It held me back for too long. Kept me from my first love." He gazed tenderly at Maybelline. "Besides, Hunter couldn't find his ass in the dark with both hands."

Mason had to laugh too. "I can't take the credit for finding you. Charlee's the bloodhound."

"I'd say you make a pretty terrific team," Maybelline said.

This probably wasn't the time to burst their bubble and tell them that he and Charlee had found them purely by accident.

"Where's the money now?" Mason asked.

"I stashed it in a safe deposit box in Vegas," Nolan said.

"In the meantime," Maybelline said, "Elwood gets another visit from his creditors. He goes back to Blade, convinces him he's on his side, and offers to kidnap us and hold us hostage until after the Oscars are over."

Nolan continued the story, telling how Elwood had taken them to the vacant studio lot outside Tucson, how they'd escaped but been recaptured by Blade and Elwood working together after the camper broke down. He told them about being held prisoner in the abandoned mine shaft, how they'd found a false bottom in the floor, tunneled their way out, and hitched a ride to L.A. with Angelina.

Mason and Charlee then related everything they'd been through.

"What time is it?" Mason asked, after they'd finished their stories. "The Oscar ceremony starts at seven."

"But the Oscars drag on for hours," Charlee observed. "We can make it."

"Unfortunately, best supporting actor is one of the first nontechnical awards given out," Nolan said. "The sooner we get there the better."

"We have to get backstage," Mason continued. "Tell the presenters there's been a discrepancy. We can do major damage control if we can make it in time to stop the Oscar from being awarded to Blade." His eyes met his grandfather's.

"I know." Nolan nodded. "If we don't stop it beforehand, they'll think our family was in on the fix."

Maybelline consulted her watch. "It's five-thirty now and at the rate Angelina is driving, I'm afraid we're still a good two hours out of L.A."

They parted company with Angelina in Palm Springs and Mason's grandfather rented a Ford Explorer. Nolan drove hell-bent for leather, but the closer they got to

L.A. the thicker the traffic grew. By the time they arrived at the Academy Awards venue, it was twenty minutes after seven and the place was swarming with security and media.

"How the hell are we going to get in?" Nolan gloomily asked him.

Mason pulled the crumpled tickets Pam Harrington had given him from his back pocket. "I've got it covered. Once Charlee and I get in, we'll identify ourselves, explain what's going on, and send someone out after you two."

"Sound plan." Nolan nodded. "Go, go, go."

Mason and Charlee tumbled out of the Explorer and rushed the red carpet.

After running a gauntlet of security checkpoints where the guards simply couldn't believe these two dirty, bedraggled wayfarers held VIP invitations to the lavish event, they finally stepped inside the theater lobby at seven forty-five.

Don't let us be too late, Charlee prayed.

An usher came forward, nose curled in distaste at their clothing, to escort them to their seats.

"We're not going to be sitting down," Mason started to explain but then Charlee spotted a tuxedoed Elwood leaving the men's room. She grabbed Mason's arm and whispered, "There's my father."

Charlee glared at Elwood. He looked like a convict caught scaling the prison walls at midnight in his underwear.

"Dad, you freeze right there," she growled.

Elwood raised his palms in a defensive gesture. "Now, baby girl," he said, "don't go jumpin' to conclusions." A split second later he turned tail and raced toward the theater.

"I can't let him get away," Mason said and sprinted after her father.

In ten long-legged strides, Mason tackled Elwood in the archway.

"Sirs, sirs," the usher chided. "No roughhousing at the Oscars."

Elwood threw a punch but Mason blocked it.

Then her father tried to head-butt Mason. He simply grabbed Elwood in a headlock and the two men went down in a heap of windmilling arms and legs.

"Dad, stop it!" Charlee yelled. "It's over. You're busted."

"You really don't want to mess with me, buddy," Mason growled through clenched teeth. "I'd love to plow my fist into your kisser for the way you've treated Charlee alone, never mind blackmailing my grandfather."

"Stop fighting. Stop it right now or I'll get security," the usher cried.

Several elegantly dressed people seated near the entrance craned their necks to take a gander at the brawl, which was obviously more interesting than the thank-you speech of the guy who'd just accepted the Oscar for best theatrical lighting.

"And I want to thank my first grade teacher, Miss Dingleberry, and Phil, the guy who used to drive the Popsicle truck on my block, and my dentist, Dr. Purdy," the P.A. system resonated the award-winner's droning, endless speech.

Elwood flinched at Mason's cocked fist. "Don't hit

me, man. It wasn't anything personal against your grandfather. I had debts to pay."

"It was pretty damned personal to Charlee. Imagine, her father is a blackmailing scumbag who kidnapped his own mother for money."

Elwood slanted a shamefaced look toward Charlee. "I was in trouble. I owed the wrong guys money. They set my apartment on fire."

"You're always in trouble."

"I didn't mean to hurt anyone. Sorry, honey, but you understand, don'tcha?"

"I understand all right. I understand you never cared about anything except yourself and money." Uttering the words had a liberating effect on Charlee.

For years she'd made excuses for her father, unable to believe he simply was incapable of loving her the way she loved him. She'd hoped and prayed and wished for things to be different but they weren't. Once she let go of her childish expectations, she understood he no longer held the power to break her heart. Elwood was Elwood and she could never change him. So be it.

"Get up." Mason snatched Elwood by his lapels and lifted him to his feet.

"And next," the dulcet voice of a famous actress resonated throughout the theater, "the award for best supporting actor."

The announcement jolted Charlee's focus off her father. They were about to give away the award for best supporting actor. To hell with Elwood, they had to stop the award presentation before it was too late.

She jerked her head toward the stage and that's when she realized they were surrounded by cops.

"And the Oscar goes to . . . Blade Bradford."

Mason grimaced. The minute the words left the presenter's mouth, his life changed forever.

Music swelled. The audience applauded. Stunned, Mason watched as Blade Bradford got to his feet and made his way toward the stage.

"You are under arrest," said the cop who was snapping handcuffs around his wrists. "You have the right to remain silent."

Mason tuned out the rest of his Miranda rights, every bit of his attention concentrated on Blade Bradford at the podium waving his statue over his head in victory.

He'd been unable to stop Bradford from accepting his bogus Oscar. Mason had lost. He'd failed.

And now he faced the greatest moral dilemma of his life.

Save his family from scandal by covering up the accounting discrepancies and thereby compromising all his deeply held values, beliefs, and principles, or go public with the knowledge the Oscars had been falsified and accept the fact his family would be financially ruined.

As the cops hauled him from the theater along with Elwood, his gaze met Charlee's. The tears glistening in her eyes sucker-punched him square in the gut.

He realized then that if he took the easy way out, kept quiet and allowed Cahill and Bradford and their henchmen to get away with their crimes simply to salvage his money and reputation, he would be just like all the other men who had betrayed her. From her shiftless father to that creep of a senator who groped her in the pantry to Gregory Blankensonship who'd taken her virginity, treated her like she didn't matter and made her question her own worth.

He could not let her down.

In that moment Mason knew what he must do, the consequences be damned.

♥ ♥ ♥

CHAPTER
21

The next morning Charlee paced the hallway outside the meeting room of the Beverly Hills Grand Piazza where Mason had scheduled a press conference.

After the fiasco at the Academy Awards, Nolan had booked her and Maybelline a room at the hotel while he'd gone to retrieve Mason from the county holding cell. For the time being, she and Maybelline had decided against posting Elwood's bond. Let him stew in jail.

Charlee hadn't seen Mason since he'd been arrested and she was nervous. Going before the press, admitting his family's company had been involved in an accounting scandal so huge it threatened to rock Hollywood to the core, could not be easy. She also felt at loose ends with herself, not knowing what to say to him, uncertain of her role in the outcome of the unfolding events.

They'd left so many things unsaid. So many important issues not discussed.

What did he need from her?

What did she want from him?

Where did they go from here?

The place buzzed with news media speculating on the details of why they'd been assembled. Camera crews strung wires and cords throughout the conference rooms. A soundman checked the podium mike. Charlee forced herself not to chew her fingernails.

At five minutes before nine, a well-dressed middle-aged couple hurried down the corridor looking harried and concerned; beside them walked Mason's ex-fiancée-to-be, Daphne Maxwell. The man bore a striking resemblance to both Nolan and Mason.

And then she realized the couple must be Mason's parents.

Panic clutched her. Not wanting to be seen, Charlee glanced around for a place to hide, and spied the reprieve of a bronze metal modern art sculpture just a few feet from the open door of the conference room.

She flung herself on the other side of it and crouched down just in the nick of time. Her heart stabbed her chest. She heard the sound of footsteps on the terrazzo floor. Daphne and the Gentrys came to stand beside the sculpture. Daphne had her back to Charlee but she stood so close, Charlee could have reached out and wrapped her wrists around the woman's slender panty hose-clad ankle.

Oh, crap.

"Mason said he'd meet us here before he started the conference," Daphne murmured.

"I just hope we're not too late to talk some sense into our son," Mason's father said.

"I'm sure he'll listen to reason," his mother soothed. "If Mason absolutely insists on going public with this Oscar mess, then the least he can do is mend fences with

Daphne. After all, she's willing to forgive and forget, which is very generous of her, and he owes the family that much consideration."

"You're absolutely right," his father said. "Our stocks are going to take a terrible hit in the fallout. We can't lose Daphne as both our publicist and future daughter-in-law too. Our son has got to listen to reason."

"Mason just went a little crazy, dear, but I'm sure once we speak with him, he'll see the error of his ways," his mother went on.

"It's that woman," Daphne said darkly. "She's corrupted his values. Once he's back home in Houston, surrounded by friends and family, he'll forget all about his little road fling."

Charlee's throat constricted. Road fling. That's all she was and she knew it. She could never be good enough for Mason and his family. She was no sleek, chic, high-society woman.

More footsteps echoed and when she heard Mason's voice she came completely unraveled. Her knees shook and her hands turned cold and clammy.

"Mother, Father." A long pause ensued. "And Daphne. I want to thank you for staying on as our publicist and agreeing to represent Gentry Enterprises in this matter."

"Daphne isn't here just as our publicist, son."

"She's willing to give you a second chance and for the good of the family business your father and I feel you should listen to what she has to say."

Charlee wished she could see Mason's face. What was he thinking? How did he feel about the pressure his parents were putting on him? Would he eagerly embrace a return to his old life and leave her in his rearview mirror?

Before Mason could respond, she heard someone else approach.

"Mr. Gentry, Paul Stillson with KEMR news. Is the rumor true? Has your accounting firm been rigging the Oscar votes for almost fifty years?"

"Please," Mason said. "Have a seat in the conference room with the other reporters. I'm on my way in. Mother, Father. Daphne."

Everyone moved away.

Charlee let out her breath without even realizing she'd been holding it. She waited a couple of minutes, then crept from behind the sculpture and slipped into the conference room.

It was standing room only. She waited just inside the door, spotted Maybelline and Nolan sitting beside each other up front.

Mason and Daphne stood at the podium together. Mason was sharply put together in an elegant navy blue suit, white shirt, and red silk power tie. He looked as if he'd stepped straight from the pages of *Fortune* magazine. Daphne was equally snazzy in a dove gray suit with pearl buttons and a pink lace blouse. His dark hair contrasted with her pale blondness. They looked tailor-made for each other.

Charlee swallowed hard and glanced down at Violet's short skirt and the Hellraiser T-shirt she'd washed out by hand the night before. She hadn't had the chance to buy anything new this morning and last night all the stores had been closed.

'Nuff said.

No matter what secret romantic thoughts to the contrary had been swirling around in the back of her mind, she and Mason were never going to get together. They were too different. Their worlds diametrically opposed.

The rich boy and the girl from the wrong side of the tracks.

Mason cleared his throat and began to talk. A murmur of shock undulated around the room as he told the reporters what he had discovered about the Oscar ballot discrepancies.

Pride filled her chest. She was so damned impressed with him. He wasn't like the other rich, powerful men who'd disappointed her. He sacrificed his family's reputation for what was right.

Mason looked up from the paper in his hands and his eyes met hers across the room. Charlee gasped as his gaze branded her. She felt the heat straight to her bone.

She blinked, trying to break eye contact to regain her equilibrium, but it didn't work. They were connected, seared, linked by something much more powerful than mere chemistry.

A blast of air from the open window cut through her cotton T-shirt and in that awful moment Charlee realized how much she was going to miss him.

And then she knew.

She'd lost her cool. She'd fallen and she was never ever going to be able to get up.

No matter how hard she'd tried to avoid it, no matter how she'd fought against her feelings, no matter how she'd struggled not to let him under her skin and into her heart, she was in love with a man she could never claim as her own.

The second his eyes met Charlee's Mason's brain shut down. He forgot about the reporters in the audience, he forgot about his parents, he forgot about Daphne pressing her palm against his lower back.

He stopped speaking in midsentence, his stare focused on the lone woman standing at the back of the room. The reporters turned their heads to see what he was staring at. Daphne took the press release from his hand, stepped up to the microphone, and took over reading what he'd written last night while he'd been in jail.

At one time, Daphne was what he had thought he'd wanted. A woman to stand by his side as his business partner. A woman his family approved of. A woman with the right breeding, the right looks, the right contacts.

Mason realized that until he'd met Charlee, he'd had no idea what *he* really wanted.

To make amends for coming clean about the Oscar scandal and thereby causing deep financial losses to Gentry Enterprises, his parents were pressuring him to get back together with Daphne. But the old guilt trip no longer worked. For twenty-seven years he'd done what the Gentry name demanded, putting what was best for the family ahead of his own wants, needs, and desires.

What he wanted was Charlee Champagne.

But what did he have to offer her? Scandal. Shame. Dishonor. She deserved so much more than he could give.

These thoughts raced through his head in a matter of seconds. Daphne had finished reading the press report and the reporters were yelling questions at him but Mason didn't hear a thing they said. All he heard was the strumming of his pulse in his ears.

Charlee. Charlee. Charlee.

She was the woman he loved with all his heart. He'd

known it the night he'd made love to her and looked deeply into her emerald eyes. She had given him his freedom and she had taught him to let go and just live. She was the toughest, strongest, most independent woman he'd ever met and he loved her for it.

Because of her, he'd taken chances he would never have taken. He'd faced his fears and come out the victor. Because of Charlee he had learned to stop trying to live up to everyone's expectations and make the choices that were right for *him*. She'd taught him that a name didn't make the man but that the man made the name.

The realization sent his mind reeling. The liberty that a new belief in himself could bring opened up so many possibilities. He could be anything he wanted to be.

"Mr. Gentry," a reporter demanded. "Just how deep does this scandal go?"

Daphne nudged him in the ribs and Mason broke eye contact with Charlee to answer the man's questions. First he had to finish the press conference, but after this was over, he and Charlee were going to have a long, serious talk. He had to tell her how he felt. Question was, did she feel the same way?

He glanced at the back of the room again, hoping to find an answer in her eyes, but panic, much stronger even than what he'd felt the night before at the Oscars, knocked his world out from under his feet.

Charlee was gone.

Charlee's Band-Aid-covered blisters rubbed against the heels of her boots as she raced through the Grand Piazza, tears misting her eyes. Violet Hammersmitz's flouncy little skirt tail slapped the back of her thighs.

In the lobby, she stumbled through a crowd of curiosity seekers who'd gathered to hear the outcome of the press conference. People peered at her with prying eyes, escalating her sense of desperation. She had to get out of here. She saw Pam Harrington from Twilight Studios and Edith Beth McCreath among the milling throng. The women called out to her but Charlee ducked her head and just kept going.

Despair consumed her.

She lifted her thumb to her mouth to gnaw her fingernail but stopped with her hand halfway to her lips when she saw the flash of shiny red polish.

Be Still My Heart.

What on earth had compelled her to get emotionally close enough to a man that she would allow him to paint her fingernails?

Her crimson nails taunted her. She yearned to soak her hands in fingernail polish remover and eradicate all evidence that she had foolishly let down her guard when she'd known better.

From the minute she'd seen Mason Gentry in the parking lot outside her detective agency she'd known he carried the potential to break her heart. She hated this feeling. She wanted her cynicism back, her detached aloofness, her sharp-tongued defenses.

"Charlee!" It was Mason's voice and he was coming after her.

No. No. She couldn't bear to look into his eyes again. Couldn't stand knowing she must send him away.

"Charlee!" He was running to catch up with her.

She shouldered her way through the mob that was growing thicker by the moment and hit the revolving glass door that led to the sidewalk and freedom.

But she knew it was far too late for regrets. She'd already fallen in love with Mason and he was out of her league and out of her reach.

Let go.

A dissenting whisper started in the back of her brain, low and seductive, rousing a rabble of contradictory thoughts. Let go of what? The limitations of the past? Her love for Mason? Her regrets? What?

Let go.

But she didn't want to let go. Holding on kept her sane. Clinging to her beliefs about rich men provided a safety net. But Mason was different and she knew it. He didn't fit the mold. He wasn't a stereotype. He hadn't hurt her on purpose.

Let go of . . .

Her boots slapped against the cement as she hit the sidewalk. She cupped her hands over her ears to drown out the noise in her head but it was no use.

Let go of your . . .

She did not want to hear this. Could not deal with the consequences of the statement. If she let go, then wouldn't she fly apart into a million vulnerable pieces? She didn't want to let go. She just wanted to be free. Free of the dread now strangling her heart.

Let go of your fears, Charlee Champagne. Let go and accept the inevitable.

But she could not.

"Charlee, wait."

She ran but he ran faster. She chugged a good four blocks from the hotel before he caught her.

Mason grabbed her elbow and spun her around to face him. He was breathing as heavily as she. Charlee studied his broad chest and refused to look him in the eyes.

"Let go of me." She tried to pull away.

"I won't. We've got to talk."

"There's nothing to talk about."

"Why did you leave?"

"I don't belong."

"You do belong. You belong with me."

"Daphne belongs with you. You're two of a kind. You're perfect for each other. Your parents want you to be with her."

"I don't give a damn what my parents want."

"Since when?"

"Since I fell in love with you."

She sucked in her breath. Had she heard him right? Mason was in love with her?

He crooked a finger under her chin and forced her head up. "Look at me, Charlee."

Reluctantly, she looked into his eyes. Every emotion she'd struggled to deny knotted her stomach. Love and hope and longing and desire snarled together and grew bigger by the moment.

She caught her breath at what she saw swimming in the warm brown depths of Mason's eyes.

"I know we're night and day," he said. "I know we come from completely different worlds. I know we've been acquainted less than a week. I know at times we irritate the hell out of each other, but I also know I've never felt this way about anyone in my entire life."

"Not even Matilda?"

"Not even Matilda."

"Really?"

"Trust me, I never expected to feel this way but from the minute I walked into your office you turned my life upside down."

"Ha. You turned mine into a roller coaster."

"You made me hunger for a life I'd always shied away from. You made me feel wild and free. You made me stop and consider who I really was and what I really wanted. Always being in control can get old and you showed me how to let go and live in the moment."

"I did all that?"

"You know you did. But I don't have much to offer you now except chaos. My family's fortune is in jeopardy, my reputation is shot, I just quit my job as Gentry Enterprises' investment banker. For the first time in my life, I don't know what's going to happen next and I feel freer than I've ever felt before. There, I've laid it all out for you. So now I've got to know, Charlee, how do you feel about me?"

Her heart thumped. He loved her. "How do I feel about you?"

"That's the question." He swallowed hard and she knew it was mean to leave him hanging but dang if she couldn't help but savor the moment.

"Hmm. You're pretty compulsive." She frowned and stroked her chin with her thumb and index finger.

"Yeah." A nervous expression hovered on his face.

"And you worry too much about what other people think of you."

"Uh-huh."

"You have an irritating habit of always doing the right thing."

"Is that so bad?"

"You're overly cautious and a stickler for the rules and have this annoying tendency of looking ten times before you leap."

"Yes, yes." He tightened his grip on her arm.

Oh, she was a rat for keeping him on tenterhooks. Relenting, she cocked him a sideways grin and he rewarded her with his dimpled smile.

"You're messing with me."

"Lucky for you I'm none of those things."

"What are you saying, Charlee?"

"I'm saying you balance me, Mason. We're two halves of a whole. And I love chaos and I have never placed much importance on money so if you lose your entire fortune I could really care less and hey, you can always come work for me at the detective agency if you need a job."

He pulled her against him, lowered his head until his mouth was almost touching hers. "Say it, Charlee. Tell me what I need to hear."

Tears stung her eyes as the words leaped to her lips, words she feared she would never be able to say. "I love you, Mason Gentry, from the bottom of my heart, from the top of my soul, and everywhere in between."

♥ ♥ ♥

EPILOGUE

"Tell me your most confidential fantasy," Mason whispered to Charlee in the darkness of her newly renovated office. He'd snuffed all the lights, locked the front door, and drawn the curtains. His disembodied voice floated disconnected, heightening the mystery of their true confessions and sending her senses reeling. "I want to know every intimate detail."

"I am Princess Charming," Charlee said, loving the fact she was sharing her most private daydreams with him. Six months ago she would have rather had her tongue plucked out than reveal herself so openly to a man. But six months ago, she hadn't been married to Mason. She marveled at the changes in her, reveled in the thrill and closeness such sharing had brought into her life. "And you are Cinderfella. You must do everything I command."

"Yes, Princess."

"Take off your clothes." She heard his belt slither through the loops of his pants, the rasp of his zipper

going down, the whisper of denim. The sounds escalated her arousal.

"I'm naked."

"Come to me."

She heard his boots tread across the hardwood floor.
The neon blue boots that matched her own. Her breathing quickened as she imagined his nakedness, except for
those boots.

"I am here." His breath was hot on her neck.

She reached out with one long fingernail painted Be
Still My Heart red and slowly tracked her finger over
his bare skin, running down his shoulder to his chest and
beyond.

He hissed in his breath.

She chuckled.

"And now?" he asked. She could feel his heartbeat
thumping in rhythm with her own.

"Sweep my fireplace."

"What is that a euphemism for?"

"Guess."

He bit her ear. "Tell me or Cinderfella will have his
fairy godfather turn him into one very excited prince."

"Sit on the desk."

He obeyed. Princess Charming shucked her dress and
straddled him.

"No underwear?"

"A princess can never tell when she might need serv-
icing by her Cinderfella."

"Ah," he said and pulled her body on top of his, taking their intimacy to the deepest heights of all with love
and passion and secret whispers.

Later as they lay curled in each other's arms on the
couch near the window, Charlee couldn't help thinking

of all the things they'd overcome for their happy-ever-after ending.

The Oscar scandal had been front-page news. You couldn't turn on the television or pick up a newspaper or listen to the radio without hearing about the infamous accounting dishonor.

People had gossiped about it at the beauty salons, over the water-cooler at work, in soccer carpools and doctor's offices. On-line chat rooms had buzzed with rumors. Stand-up comedians had lampooned the Gentrys. The *National Enquirer* had a field day trying to guess which actors really had not deserved their Oscar for the past forty-seven years.

As Mason had predicted, the minute the news hit the Associated Press wire, the value of Gentry Enterprises plummeted. Actors had quaked in their boots wondering if their Oscar had been part of an illegal fix.

Cahill, Blade Bradford, and his wife were charged with conspiracy to commit fraud but their cases had yet to come to court. Nolan had been exonerated of all culpability in the accounting errors. Sal and Petey were currently serving ten-year sentences for kidnapping and attempted murder.

Maybelline had dropped the kidnapping charges against Elwood on the condition he go into treatment for his gambling addiction and surprisingly enough, while in treatment he'd found religion, become a preacher, and now officiated in his white Elvis jumpsuit at the Bells and Doves wedding chapel in Loflin.

It had taken several weeks but once the Oscar audits were completed and it was revealed the only cases of fraud happened in 1955 and then again this year, the stock of Gentry Enterprises began a steady rise.

The Gentry family forgave Mason for refusing to marry Daphne and for quitting the firm. Daphne and Hunter started dating. Nolan and Maybelline, Charlie and Mason had a huge double wedding in a fancy Houston church. Maybelline and Nolan were currently on a world tour honeymoon.

Mason was working on getting his pilot's license and he helped out at the detective agency. And every day Charlee thanked God for bringing him into her life.

"I love you, Mrs. Gentry," Mason whispered.

"I love Mr. Gentry," she murmured drowsily, and just before she fell asleep, Charlee realized that with her own rich, long-legged, brown-eyed, handsome, matinee-idol-smiling, beard-stubble-sporting man at her side, nothing but nothing scared her.

Especially, not love.

ABOUT THE AUTHOR

_L_ ori Wilde is the best-selling author of more than twenty books. A former RITA finalist, Lori's books have been recognized by Romantic Times Reviewers' Choice Award, the Holt Medallion, the Booksellers Best, the National Readers' Choice and numerous other honors. She lives in Weatherford, Texas with her husband and a wide assortment of pets. You may write to Lori at PO Box 31, Weatherford, TX 76086 or e-mail her via her homepage at www.loriwilde.com.

More

Lori Wilde!

♥

Please turn this page

for a preview of

CHARMED AND

DANGEROUS

available in

July 2004.

CHAPTER

1

*M*addie Cooper was twenty-two minutes into her Monday afternoon kickboxing class, her students' collective heart rates zeroed perfectly into their target zone, when she heard the incessant gallop of the *William Tell Overture* humming from inside her gym bag. She could just make out the digitalized noise above the thumping beat of Salt 'N' Pepa's *Let's Talk About Sex* blasting through the state-of-the-art surround sound system and she surmised her cell phone must have been ringing for quite some time.

Bad news.

Only two people ever called during her classes and both of them always wanted the same thing. It was either her mom asking her to go salvage her sister from her latest exploit or it was her identical twin Cassie begging Maddie to come haul her butt out of some pickle or the other.

The upshot was always the same. Good ol' Maddie to the rescue.

Like in college when she had to bail Cassie out of jail

for streaking through the Alamo during rush week on a dare from her sorority sisters. Or the unforgettable incident when her rambunctious twin called her for a ride at three A.M. after getting tossed out of a Hell's Angels Christmas party—which she'd audaciously crashed—for unruly conduct.

"Jab. Jab. Upper cut," she commanded into her headset and tried to pretend she was having an auditory hallucination.

A courageous shaft of February sunshine battled the gloomy clouds and slanted through the open blinds, momentarily illuminating the room with the hope of spring. Maddie studied her disciples in the floor-to-ceiling mirrors, monitoring them for correct form. She kept her own posture in rigid control. Shoulders straight and knees slightly bent, setting a good example.

"Nice work ladies," she called out. "Squeeze those abs. Keep your glutes clenched tight."

Phone? What phone? She didn't hear no stinking telephone.

"Bob. Weave. Roundhouse kick."

But no matter how hard she tried to deny it, beneath the sexy grind of hip-hop, there was no mistaking the bastardized version of classic Rossini. As much as she longed to ignore the summons for help, she simply could not. Her sister needed her.

Dammit.

"Water break," she instructed the class. "But keep moving."

Her more serious students frowned. They had been flying Zen and didn't want to stop, but her newer apprentices ran for their water bottles, gratitude for the unexpected reprieve shining on their sweaty faces.

Only slightly breathless, Maddie trotted across the room, wiping her slick palms against the thighs of her black cotton Lycra workout pants. She bent to scoop her gym bag off the floor.

William Tell was still giving it hell as she dug to the bottom of the bag and retrieved her 'track and field' themed Nokia. She jabbed the 'talk' button with a short, unpainted fingernail.

"'Lo."

"Maddie, it's Mom."

The connection came across faint, staticky, but then she didn't expect anything else. Costa Rica was a long way from Fort Worth, Texas. Her stepfather built bridges all over the world and Maddie was never sure where her mother would be living next, but she could be certain it was always some place interesting.

"I'm in the middle of class."

"I know sweetheart, I'm sorry to interrupt, but this is urgent."

Wasn't it always? Maddie suppressed a sigh and shook her head. A flop of streaky blond hair broke free from it's Scrunchie and fell across her nose. Irritated, she tucked the phone under her chin, stabbed back the errant lock with her fingers and rewrapped her ponytail.

"What's Cassie done now?"

"How do you know I'm calling about Cassie?"

"Because she is always our main topic of conversation."

"That's not true."

"So why *did* you call?"

Her mother paused. "Because I've been trying to reach your sister all weekend and she's not answering her phone and you know she calls me every Sunday."

Bingo! Maddie could have gloated, "See, see, see, you did call about Cassie." Instead a stab of worry winnowed through her.

She hadn't heard from her twin either. Usually, Cassie phoned her two or three times a day. She should have been suspicious over the unexpected silence. Instead, she'd selfishly enjoyed the peace and quiet. She should have known better than to relax her guard.

"When did you last see her?" Mom asked.

"I don't remember," Maddie hedged, not wanting to unduly upset her mother. "I'm certain it was sometime this weekend."

"You haven't seen her since Friday afternoon, have you?"

"All right. We had lunch on Friday and I haven't heard from her since."

"Hmm," her mother mused.

Maddie pinched the bridge of her nose between her thumb and forefinger. "Hmm what?"

"This is like that semester you and Cassie were living in Madrid and she was working at the Museo del Prado. Remember?"

How could she forget? That was the autumn after she had faltered at the Olympics in Atlanta and blown her chances for winning the gold. She had gone to Madrid both to lick her wounds and to keep an eye on Cassie who was on a work/study program for her degree in art history.

"And," her mother continued, "Cassie took off for a long weekend in Monaco with that Greek guy." She snapped her fingers. "What was his name?"

"Dominic Koumalakis."

"Oh yes. I'm hoping this is the same sort of thing.

That she's just off for a lark with this new boyfriend of hers."

"New boyfriend?"

Another long pause. "She didn't tell you about Peyton?"

"Uh, no."

"Oh dear." Her mother sighed. "I guess I wasn't supposed to say anything."

Pulling Cassie's impetuous fanny from various and sundry fires, had honed Maddie's protective instincts to a fine point and she was getting bad vibes. Her gut clutched and the hairs on her arms stiffened. Something was amiss.

The idea of her twin not bragging about a new boyfriend was like getting a box of Cracker Jack's without finding a prize inside. It rarely happened. If Cassie wasn't talking, that meant she *knew* Maddie wouldn't approve of the guy.

"Now, now," her mother said, uncannily reading her mind. "Don't go making snap judgments."

"So what's wrong with this guy?"

"Nothing's wrong with him. He's British and a few years older than she is, which I believe is a good thing. He does something in the art world, but I'm not sure what. Import, export maybe."

"Oh, that's just ducky. Mother, the guy sounds like a drug dealer."

"You're jumping to conclusions, drawing assumptions. He's not a drug dealer."

"How do you know?"

"Cassie uploaded his picture in my e-mail. He's quite the snappy dresser."

"And drug dealers don't wear nice threads?"

"Stop being so suspicious. I swear he looks just like Tony Curtis in *Sex and the Single Girl*."

"That's what you said about Dad and Trevor and Vinny and look how those relationships turned out."

"Can I help it if I used to be attracted to dashing irresponsible dark haired men? Besides, I'm with Stanley now and all's well that ends well, even if the poor darling is as bald as a cue ball and about as dashing as a pumpkin."

"But he loves you and he treats you right."

"Yes he does. I learned the hard way a sharp dressed man with a thick head of hair isn't everything. Give your sister time. Eventually, Cassie will come to the same conclusion I did."

"So how long has she been seeing this Peyton character?"

"About three weeks and she says he's a phat kisser."

"Mother!"

"What? Phat means pretty hot and tempting."

"I know what it means." Maddie didn't realize that she'd raised her voice until she spotted her students gaping at her. She turned her back to them, hunched her shoulders and whispered fiercely into the receiver. "Why does Cassie tell you these personal things?"

"I'm proud she lets me in on what's happening in her life. You, on the other hand, didn't even tell me when you first started your period. I wish you could be as open and honest with me as Cassie is."

"About my love life?"

"Do you have a love life, Maddie?"

"Jeez! That's kinda private don't you think?"

Her mother sighed. "Just as I suspected. No man in sight."

"Why is that so important?"

"I worry about you being alone. You're always sequestered in that gym. How are you going to meet anyone if you never get out, mix and mingle?"

"I'm not looking to meet anyone."

"Nonsense. You're pushing thirty, dear."

"And?"

"Tick-tock."

Maddie bit her tongue to keep from saying something she would regret. Apparently, Mom would prefer her to be like Cassie, with a new guy every few months, none of whom stuck around.

"You and your sister are night and day," her mother said. "If you two didn't look exactly alike I would have sworn someone switched one of you at birth."

"I feel like someone switched me at birth," Maddie muttered under her breath.

Hell, she frequently felt as if she was the only one in the family who had a firm grip on reality. Although in her mother and Cassie's book her steadfast practicality meant that she was dull as paste.

Okay, so maybe she wasn't a glam gal with a string of boyfriends lining up outside her door. Have curling iron, will travel was not her motto. But she paid her bills on time and she rarely forgot to take her vitamins and she never missed the opportunity to vote.

Omigod, she *was* boring.

Well, somebody had to be the responsible one, especially after Dad had bailed on them. She shuddered to think where they would all be if it weren't for her levelheadedness. She'd taught herself to cook when she was ten, learned to drive when she was thirteen. And when she was fourteen, in order to keep Mom from bouncing checks willy-nilly all over town, she'd taken over paying the household bills. She loved her mother with all her heart but if common sense were cupcakes her mother would starve to death. Thank heavens she'd finally found Stan.

"You overindulge Cassie," Maddie said. "You always have. She gets away with murder."

"We almost lost her."

"I know. I was there."

Maddie closed her eyes and a rubber band of memory snapped her back to the past.

Eighteen years disappeared and for one brief moment she was nine years old again and her sister lay in a coma in that stark antiseptic hospital room filled with ominous sounding machines. Their mother and father hovered over Cassie's bed, fear and worry lining their faces, the nurses moving silently on their rubber soled shoes.

Nobody noticed Maddie standing statue still in the corner feeling utterly responsible for the accident. Nobody understood the guilt and shame racing through her because she was supposed to have been looking after her sister. Nobody recognized the sheer terror weighting her stomach at the thought of losing her twin.

From that moment on, Maddie had sworn to God that if he let her sister come out of the coma she would never again give Cassie the opportunity to inadvertently do herself in.

"You weren't responsible," her mother said. She'd never blamed her for what happened, but Maddie had never forgiven herself. "One of these days you're going to have to let yourself off the hook."

Tension churned her stomach. She forced herself to take a long, slow cleansing breath and realized her students were milling around, clearing their throats, checking their watches. Salt 'N' Pepa had given way to Pink who was in the process of enthusiastically getting a party started.

"Listen, I've gotta go."

"So you'll track Cassie down?" her mother asked.

"You know I will."

"Call me when you find her."

"Yes, yes. Goodbye."

Maddie switched off the cell phone and turned to face the class. No way could she go back to work now. Not when she kept picturing her twin battered and bleeding and lying in a ditch somewhere.

Besides, she owned the gym. She could cancel the session with impunity, even if it did grate against her work ethic. She shooed the students toward the door with a wave of her hands.

"Class dismissed."

Thirty minutes before closing time, Cassie Cooper met her contact at the Ridgmar Mall food court, right across from *Spank Me*, her favorite edgy clothing boutique. In fact, at this very moment, she was wearing a *Spank Me* ensemble.

She had on a tight black sweater with a large diamond shaped cut out right at the level of her cleavage, revealing a nice display of tanned skin. The iridescent material of her short tangerine skirt caught the light as she stalked across the tile in her knee-high, tiger-striped leather stiletto boots. She wore a matching orange leather coat and carried a small silver handbag.

Many masculine heads turned in appreciation as she strutted by, but she pretended not to notice, even though she couldn't resist putting a breezy little wiggle into her walk. Cassie was a woman on a mission. Flirtation would have to wait.

For the first time in her life she was doing something important, something meaningful, something that would finally earn her Maddie's respect and by gosh she was proud of herself.

He was seated at a bistro table across from *Steak-on-a-Stick*, the man who two weeks earlier had offered her the opportunity of a lifetime and in the process turned her world topsy-turvy.

Cassie scooted her fanny onto the black wrought iron café chair across from him, folded her hands in her lap and offered her most seductive smile.

"Hello, handsome. We've got to stop meeting like this," she teased in a low sultry voice.

FBI special agent Reis Marshall *was* righteously handsome, in a rather rugged, unkempt sort of way. He was tall and muscular with a granite jaw and chiseled cheekbones that oddly enough, lent him a sensitive air. His nose was neither too big nor too small for his face, but it crooked slightly to the left at the bridge, as if he'd once used it to stop an irate fist.

He wore bland, nondescript clothing; often sported a five-o'clock shadow and he had this habit of jamming his hand through his short sandy-blond hair and mussing it up. Cassie had to resist the urge to smooth it down again. It seemed he didn't give a hoot about what he looked like. She got the distinct impression there was no Mrs. Marshall around to GQ him up.

And while he did possess a brooding magnetic quality that appealed to her, the guy simply wasn't her type. He was too intense, with his determined dark eyes that pinned you to the spot until you squirmed. Too By-the-Book-Straight-and-Narrow for her taste. Cassie liked her men sharply dressed with debonair smiles, easy-going personalities and a touch of wildness around the edges.

This uncompromising guy was much better suited for someone like her sister Maddie. A woman who enjoyed a good argument. Except Maddie was likely to fry this decisive man's last nerve with her incessant analyzing, deliberating and fretting. When would her twin learn that sometimes you had to fling caution to the wind, take a chance and live a little? Like she had by agreeing to spy on her new boyfriend for the FBI.

"Yes," Reis said grimly. Did the guy ever smile, she wondered. "We will stop meeting like this."

Cassie sobered. "What's up? You sound mad. Did I do something wrong?"

"I'm not mad and no, you didn't do anything wrong."

"What is it then?" She smelled fried corn dogs and chili cheese dip, popcorn and fajitas. The wide-open food court seemed to close around them like a kitchen pantry. Cassie held her breath and waited.

Reis steepled his fingertips. His bland expression was meant to calm, but if she looked closely she could see tension tightening the corner of his dark eyes. He wasn't fooling her a bit.

"I'm afraid we've got trouble," he said.

"Trouble?"

Her curiosity was piqued. Trouble usually spelled excitement and Cassie loved excitement. As long as it was good excitement, like driving a Corvette too fast on the freeway. And not the bad kind of excitement, like peering into the barrel of a gun. Not that she had ever been in trouble *that* bad.

"I'm pulling you off the case," Reis continued. "I was never for involving a private citizen in the first place, but we didn't have much of a choice. However, now that Peyton Shriver is consorting with the likes of Jocko Blanco, I refuse to allow your continued participation in this investigation. Blanco is a ruthless character and I won't endanger your life."

"No!" Cassie fisted her hands. This wasn't what she'd expected to hear. She'd expected praise for a job well done. She'd expected encouragement to keep up the good work. She'd expected a pat on the back not a boot to the butt.

"Yes," he said.

Reis couldn't be taking her off the case. Not now. Not yet. Not when she was so close to convincing Peyton she was madly in love with him and would do anything he asked. Like embracing his illegal lifestyle. Plus, she had a feeling he was falling for her just a little bit. Cassie had unerring instincts about that sort of thing. If she played her cards right, she would soon have Peyton surrendering his ace of hearts.

She envisioned herself on the cover of *Art World Today* magazine with the grabby headlines, *Museum Employee Nabs International Art Thief, Proving to Her Naysaying Sister She's Not Such An Airhead After All.*

A thrill ran through her at the thought. Try that on for size Maddie. Me, on the front page of a magazine, for capturing a renowned art thief.

Of course there was the teeny issue that Peyton *had* snookered her into believing he was an overseas art dealer completely smitten with her beauty. She would have been just another hapless victim, if Reis hadn't shown up and recruited her to help take down Shriver. He'd told her Peyton's M.O. was to cozy up to female museum employees, gain their confidence, use their security clearance to make off with priceless works of art and then leave the women to take the rap.

"Haven't I been doing a good job?" Cassie asked. His words had punched squarely in the solar plexus and she was finding breathing evenly a chore.

"You've done an excellent job. It's not you."

"What is it then?"

"The situation has changed. You're no longer safe."

"But Shriver is about to make his move." Cassie struggled hard not to sound desperate. *Please, please, please let me help you nail him.* "I can feel it."

"Cassie." Reis reached across the table and laid his big hand over her small one. "Don't worry. We will get him. I promise you that."

She shuddered at the resolute set of his jaw, the determined lust for justice in his eyes. She'd hate to be in Peyton's shoes right now. Reis Marshall was as indomitable as a badger in urgent need of an attitude adjustment.

"Yeah," she murmured. "But I wanted to be there when you arrested him. I wanted to see the look on his face when he realized that scatterbrained Cassie Cooper was the one responsible for bringing him down."

Reis shook his head brusquely. "I'm afraid that's no longer an option."

"Listen, I'm tougher than you think. I can take care of myself. And I do know how to make use of my feminine wiles." She winked and toed his shin under the table with the tip of her boot.

He gave her the once over, assessing her outfit, her make-up and her soft, curvy physique with an amused quirk of an eyebrow.

"Sweetheart," he said, and she grinned. Cassie liked being sweet-talked. "Forgive me for saying so, but while you're as appealing as all get out, you're no match for Jocko Blanco."

Anger ripped through her. Oh hell. He was no better than Maddie. Treating her like a kid. Acting as if she were some helpless southern belle who needed his big bad male protection in order to survive. She'd spent her life being babied and coddled by her mother and her sister and she was sick of it. She could stand on her own two feet, dammit. And working with the FBI was supposed to be her chance to finally prove how strong she was.

Drats. Everything was slipping through her fingers.

She was about to try again to persuade Reis to give her another chance, when he raised a palm and cut her off in exactly the same high-handed manner Maddie might have used. Cassie grit her teeth.

"We want you to take a vacation. Get out of town on the taxpayers' dime. How about Padre Island? We'll arrange with the museum for you to take time off from work and we'll send an agent with you. What do you say?" he coaxed. "Sun, surf, a little R&R. You've earned it."

"You're telling me that I might be in real danger?" Cassie gulped and splayed her fingers over the base of her neck. Momentary panic squeezed her heart.

Okay, she wanted to prove she was as tough as Maddie; she just didn't want to have to die for it. She was an adrenaline junkie, no doubt, but she was not a fool.

"It's simply a precaution. In case Shiver figures out

you've been helping us and he decides to send Blanco after you."

"Oh."

At the thought of being hunted down by Peyton's creepy scar-faced, tattooed pal, Cassie began having second thoughts. Maybe being a wussy wasn't such a bad thing after all. Maybe being smothered in the cocoon of your overly protective sister's love wasn't such a horrible way to go.

"We want you to know that we appreciate all the information you've passed along to us. You've been a valuable asset to this team." Reis was still giving her his 'so-long-sucker' speech. It was the most she'd ever heard him speak. Normally he was rather taciturn.

Cassie nodded, but she wasn't hearing him any longer. Something across the length of the food court caught her gaze. Something tall and blond and furious. Something that could strike terror even into the heart of someone as cold-blooded as Jocko Blanco.

Her bossy twin sister Maddie on a rampage.

THE EDITOR'S DIARY

Dear Reader,

Why is it that the most irresistible men are always the ones we can't—or shouldn't—have? But Charlee Champagne and Joy Hudson are about to face their demons, sexy smiles and all, in our Warner Forever titles this December.

Romantic Times said that **Lori Wilde's** previous book "has it all," but wait until they get a load of her latest, **LICENSE TO THRILL**. Nothing, but nothing, scares wisecracking Las Vegas P.I. Charlee Champagne, except for black widow spiders and gorgeous, dark haired men. Both fears arise from experiences best forgotten and Charlee has vowed to avoid them at all costs . . . until Mason Gentry steps into her office. Mason's beloved grandfather has run off to Vegas, taking half-a-million dollars in company funds with him, and Mason is desperate to find him. But he only has one clue—Charlee's grandmother's name. With bullets whizzing past their heads and goons on their tail, Charlee and Mason take off on a road trip to find their grandparents and clear the Gentry name. And Charlee will discover just how delicious facing your deepest fears can be . . .

Moving from the flash and the heat of Vegas to the warmth and the charm of Kentucky, we'd like to introduce **Edie Claire's** first romance, **LONG TIME COMING**. Joy Hudson swore she would never return to her hometown of Wharton, Kentucky. After the tragic death of her best friend, Jenny, when they were only seventeen, Joy's every memory is stained with loss. But when her father becomes ill and needs her help, Joy moves home to make a fresh start. She certainly never expected to run into Jeff Bradford, the man she holds responsible for Jenny's death. Gone is the awkward teenager and in his place is the handsome doctor who is caring for her father. But can Joy find the courage to let go of the past and find love with the one man she's blamed for all these years?

To find out more about Warner Forever, these December titles, and the authors, visit us at www.warnerforever.com.

With warmest wishes,

Karen Kosztolnyik

Karen Kosztolnyik, Senior Editor

P.S. The holidays are over and it's time to relax. So curl up and check out these two Warner Forever titles guaranteed to set the room ablaze on even the coldest winter night. **Pamela Britton** pens a wickedly funny Regency tale about a man looking for a nurse to tame his willful daughter and finds the perfect candidate in a beautiful and outspoken woman with less than pure motives in **TEMPTED**; and **Susan Crandall** delivers another poignant story of a woman who returns to her hometown to face her past and encounters the man who broke her heart years ago and the passion between them that hasn't waned in **THE ROAD HOME**.